BRANDED GRAVES

DARK RANGE
BOOK TWO

RANDI SAMUELSON-BROWN

WOLFPACK
PUBLISHING
— EST 2013 —

Branded Graves
Paperback Edition
Copyright © 2022 Randi Samuelson-Brown

Wolfpack Publishing
9850 S. Maryland Parkway, Suite A-5 #323
Las Vegas, Nevada 89183

wolfpackpublishing.com

Paperback ISBN 978-1-63977-793-8
eBook ISBN 978-1-63977-792-1
LCCN 2022947671

BRANDED GRAVES

PART I

CARRION

THE STEER'S HEAD SWAYED IN THE BREEZE EVER SO slightly. Suspended from the ranch entrance crossbeams and dangling from an old, modified headstall, it got their point across, loud and clear.

It might not have been so menacing had the skull been weather-bleached like a Georgia O'Keefe painting, or even if it had been treated as a decorative emblem of the Wild West. But this skull hadn't been boiled clean or left out in the elements over time. No, the skull hanging from the sign *LOST DAUGHTER RANCH Established 1888* held another purpose entirely, and it sure as hell wasn't decoration. The skull's purpose wasn't to attract buyers into the valley. No, the steer cranium swung in the breeze replete with rotting meat and withering eyeballs.

Well, the remains of the eyeballs that the birds hadn't yet pecked out.

The remnants of the eyes had dried and withered, folding back into the depths of the sockets. Hide remained attached in pieces and strips, but the brains were since devoured or dried up—the elongated jaw stretched into a gruesome and cadaverous grin.

No, that skull didn't carry any welcome, but rather a stark warning of gore and carnage.

The steer skull offered a declaration of how the West used to be, and the message was simple.

Keep out or be prepared to go down swinging.

The inhabitants further along that ranch road weren't backing down. In fact, they *never* backed down. Never had in over 125 years of hard-fought history. Never would, while they controlled and held that singular patch of hard-won ground.

EMORY CROSS HAD COME HOME. Reluctantly, perhaps. But there was no doubt she was home, no matter her misgivings on the subject.

She pulled to a stop right before the Lost Daughter Ranch sign, killed the engine, and climbed out of her truck. She stood in front of the crossbeam, hands on hips, staring at the skull swaying in the wind traveling down from the high country.

Yep, definitely home.

Upon closer inspection, a single bullet hole pierced the frontal bone dead center, and the remnants of the eyes—what hadn't been pecked away—had shrunken down and shriveled. The nasal cavity declined inward and most of the surrounding hide had fallen away or weathered. The underlying flesh, although exposed for little more than a month's time, had succumbed to the birds and the elements. The meat no longer remained fresh or red, but rather brown and rotting. Taken all together, the display remained hideous. Ominous. A declaration in no uncertain terms.

Emory found it a wonder that complaints hadn't risen to a level that demanded the exhibition's removal from public view.

If such demands had been ventured, she knew how her father would have responded. And so, the skull remained hanging from the ranch gate for all the world to see.

More importantly, to heed.

She stuck her hands into her back pockets and scrutinized the cranium a while longer, turning notions over. If she were of a mind to be truthful, she would admit that there was something about that steer head hanging which felt about *right*. Justified, even. When she tired of considering the carnage, she tore her gaze away and focused upon the beauty of the valley in the winter.

It was nine o'clock on Saturday morning in the shallows of January. The tops of the rimrocks blanketed in snow stood guard, their sheer cliffs and drop-offs boasting their original colors proud and distinctive. Long, thin reeds of grass poked through the depressions where the snow whittled out, low. Great drifts stood tall, caught against the wooden fence posts, rendering the strung barbed wire invisible beneath the snow crests and waves.

The overpowering azure blue soared as far as the imagination could carry, and another hundred miles beyond even that. Not a cloud marred the surface of all that brilliant, frigid blue. Below, the snow blanketed the land, flattening out the swells and drop-offs and glittering. Glittering like a scattering of a million mica flakes cast to the wind and glistening where they landed. The snow blew in wisps hugging the ground, bearing the imprint of the wind's currents and patterns. And the day shone blue and the sun blazed bright in that frigid January morning and set the snow to dazzling. The valley sprawled out wide and clear and grand, the same as it ever had. Like back in the day when Hank Cross, her great-great-grandfather, first crossed the valley, sized up the landscape, and filed his legal claim.

And few more claims besides.

The old homestead evolved over time, earlier houses and listing structures surrounded by years of debris. No other ranch matched the Lost Daughter, when it came right down to it. The rest of the valley probably took that knowledge for granted and sighed with an apprehensive relief.

What the hell, she thought to herself taking one lingering look at the skull.

She'd come home.

At the sound of her truck pulling up out front of the ranch house, the door opened, and Emory's father came out onto the porch.

"Have any trouble finding the place?" he called out over the distance. Didn't bother to come down the three steps it would have required to stand at eye level. "It took you long enough, and we've got work to do."

"Nice to know you missed me, too. Kai and I've been on the road since a bit before six. Gotten any complaints about that skull?"

Her father's eyes twinkled, and he cocked a grin. "Nah. Why would anyone want to complain about a thing like that?"

Emory shook her head. "Let me get Kai out of the trailer and settled. What's the plan for this morning?"

"You forgot how this place works already? We gotta ride the fence lines, before the weather comes in. No need to settle Kai, he's gotta work and so do you." He stuck his hands halfway into his pockets as he scanned the Never Summer Range before turning his attention back to her. "If you're really going to put in all them hours at the stock show, you might want to consider leaving Kai here."

Flat-out, she hadn't considered that possibility. "Might be a good idea. That's one less arrangement to manage. I've heard that the hours are long and while it might be hopping, it's going to be tiring for sure."

"You've got good timing in taking those vacation days," her father said in his slow twang. "I've got plenty of chores for you to get caught up on."

Again, she shook her head. There was always a lot of head shaking where her father was concerned. She didn't break her stride, but moved around behind the trailer, unlatching the door. "I should have opted for Hawaii," she muttered.

Her father caught her words and laughed away the notion. "Didn't know you had that option," he teased.

AFTER A DAY of fence-line riding and making sure that water troughs weren't frozen solid, the two reunited Crosses wound down as the evening hours took hold. Emory cleared the dinner dishes as her father folded himself down into his chair and pressed the TV remote in one fluid, practiced movement.

"Anything you want to watch?" he called out in the direction of the kitchen.

Emory remained by the sink, drying dishes and giving the place a once-over. For an old bachelor, her father wasn't doing bad, but cleanliness and organization were slipping.

"No. I don't care what you put on," she called back. "I've spent enough nights in front of the TV in Greeley that it's all the same to me by now. When's the last time you cleaned out some of these cabinets?"

A grunt would have to suffice as the answer; a grunt that could mean any number of things. But the evidence stared straight at her. Glasses were shoved onto the shelf any which way, and the plates below weren't arranged according to size, but stacked haphazard, and the cereal bowls listed at an angle. Running her finger along the shelf edges, dust collected there and in the corners. The best plan would be to take all the contents out, wipe down the shelves, rearrange everything, and to start over.

As she poked around, she also found a chipped cup with random nails and metal parts, rusting and orphaned.

"The dish cabinet isn't for hardware, you know."

"Don't bother me none," came his reply.

The faucet still dripped into the same brown rust stain, which had taken on a permanency that never should have been allowed in the first place. She could always try to bleach it later.

That was part of the problem. Routine chores didn't always get done, and it showed. It showed every and anywhere a person cared to look.

Flipping off the light switch, Emory absorbed the darkened view outside the window—the mountains settling into their velvet sleep while the stars glinted as cold as ice fragments in the clear winter sky. Shades of the darkest midnight blue contrasted with the brightness of the moon blazing high overhead—the snow a pale bluish gray, the skies spangled with stars and the shadows drawn out long and deep. A view she'd grown up with, but a view that still held the power to beguile. The old outbuildings listed and the stoic, castellated rimrocks guarded the ranch's perimeters the same as they had always done, ghosts illuminated in the moonlight. The scene beyond the kitchen window promised a quiet and peaceful night on the ranch.

The silence perfect, except for the television din which marred the sense of perfection.

If she said as much, her father would have just stared.

"I'm going to go check on Kai and Draco before I get too settled in," she announced, pulling on her coat that hung by the front door.

"The barn latch needs some work," her father said, slumped in his chair. "It's been hitching."

Emory stepped out into the crisp, cold air, feeling the dark embrace of the ranch at night. She lingered on the porch for a long moment, inhaling the scent of the land and tasting the approaching snow drifting in the air.

She stepped off the porch and took a few paces into the yard before stopping. The yard light should have flicked on, but it didn't.

Just another thing to fix.

The moon provided enough light to navigate, although she could have reached the barn blind—the route ingrained upon her like the lines on her palms. Upon reaching the barn door, she struggled a bit with the latch that indeed needed tightening and a squirt of WD-40, but it came free after the brief tussle. The door cracked and protested as it swung open wide. Inside, she switched on the fluorescent overhead lights, blinking for a moment as her eyes adjusted. Those banks of lights gave off a harsh greenish glare that sure didn't leave much room for poetic leanings.

Those same lights did their job, enabling her to catch the glimpse of a mouse tail as it scurried back into a hiding place near the hay.

Unconcerned about either lights or mice, Kai dozed in his stall and Draco stood equally at ease and settled in his. Emory checked their water to verify both were full and clean.

"Good boys," she crooned, and Kai's ears flicked but he didn't open his eyes.

Leaving the stalls, her attention snagged on the tack. Over to the side a saddle she hadn't seen before waited. Not that there wasn't plenty of room to go around. The Lost Daughter used to host at least five hands plus the family. Now it boiled down to her and her father—and whoever the mystery rider might be.

Pretty ordinary and plain, it carried the appearance of a saddle that hadn't been used for a very long time. But recently conditioned, it offered the hint of an intention to come back to life.

She'd be certain to ask her father about that castoff—convinced that she already had an answer that she wasn't quite ready for.

One thing about many that she knew of her father, he didn't collect or trade saddles for the hell of it.

Switching off the light, she shut the barn door and fumbled with the latch. She'd get to that in the morning. She headed back toward the house and across the dark yard, still pondering that saddle. But that musing broke off, right quick.

In the distance, headlights aimed toward the ranch house. Her jaw set out of reflex and eyes narrowed as she watched the headlights aim in her direction...then they went dark. Switched off, in fact. It took a moment to register what she witnessed. She maintained the firm sense that the truck still approached and would have sworn she caught a dark glimmer of the moon reflecting off metal.

No lights reappeared.

She waited unmoving for a few more moments, just to make sure.

Puzzling, but nothing came closer that she could detect. No sound of a motor reached her. Tired, her eyes must have been playing tricks after a long, hard day. But she didn't usually see lights.

Likely it was nothing more than an optical illusion from a bend in the road.

Back inside the ranch house, she wasn't the only one who felt tired. Her father's eyes closed at half-mast.

One thing stood out as a given—they needed to hire another ranch hand and soon. *Cade's replacement.*

She ruffled her father's close-cut hair, just the way he liked to do to hers when he could.

"The yard light's not working," she said.

"Yeah," he replied, voice gruff, waking up a bit and smoothing down his hair. "I'll take a look at it tomorrow morning."

Just another thing to do on a long list of many.

All she had was a pointed question in response, and one she didn't bother to soften or conceal. "Has it been that way long?"

A slight flinch, and a shift in his chair. "Don't think so. Or if it has, it's been nothing more than a day or two."

Emory raised her eyebrows. Yard lights were of paramount importance, and it wasn't like him not to notice something like that. "I've noticed a couple of other things as well. First that we need to get another hand hired. Second—"

Her father raised up his index finger in the air. The code to stop speaking.

She cut off midsentence.

They both listened past the noise of the TV. Emory indicated the TV in a pointed question, but her father shook his head to leave it alone.

With silent, practiced movements, he got up from his chair, spry from necessity. Decisive and muscles taut, he moved against an out wall waiting for the next move.

Emory strained to see through the windows without approaching the glass which would give her interior location away, and her father did the same. Listening. Gauging.

The TV flickered and droned on, the same as always. As if the inhabitants within were occupied and off guard.

He long-legged it toward the kitchen. His steps crossed the linoleum to the back office where the gun cabinet stood. Decisive and unhesitant.

The sound of road ice crunching and snapping under tires carried. Still, no headlights.

She didn't need to be asked, but stealthed behind, equally silent and intent.

"Who is it?" she asked in a whisper.

"Don't know," came her father's whisper as the truck crunched to a stop.

"Lance Cross?" a man shouted outside, words ricocheting off the rimrocks and bouncing back.

The Crosses exchanged dark glances. Her father pulled his rifle out from the gun cabinet.

"Who's asking?" he shouted in return.

One of the porch boards protested underfoot.

Lance Cross glanced at Emory, who pulled out a Winchester 1873 Sporter from that same gun cabinet, checking that it was loaded.

Her father primed his weapon and approached the front door, passing through the kitchen and into the living room. Careful to stand to the side of the unlocked door.

Crouching, Emory ran toward the staircase right as a spray of bullets hit the side of the house. Shots which came from a completely different direction than the truck.

An automatic.

"Don't shoot!" the man hollered from the direction where the snow-crunching tires passed.

Her father pointed for her to go to the second floor.

As quiet as she could, she bolted up the stairs, taking her position alongside the bathroom window and out of the direct line of fire.

Another shot reverberated. Single this time.

A crouching shadow in the distance ran toward one of the outbuildings for cover. She opened the bottom window and took her aim, but she held her fire.

A voice shouted from the porch.

"Holy cow, Lance! It's Iver Holstead from the Highland!"

Lance Cross's eyes narrowed. "What are you driving around without your lights on for?"

"I was afraid you'd start shooting!"

"I ain't firing!"

The slightest of pauses. "Who is then?"

"Don't know but you'd better get your ass in here."

The crack of another shot, and the thud of a body falling.

"Iver?" Lance called out.

No answer.

He called again. "Iver!"

A groan.

"Someone's taking cover behind the outbuildings!" Emory warned.

"What's the direction of the fire?" Her father's voice cut across the distance in return, measured and cool. Dead calm, in fact.

"Hard to say," Emory didn't feel near as calm. "Sounded like two directions to me, but I only see the one taking cover in the west and trained on the door. Their angle must be off, wide. Whatever you do, don't go out there."

The glint of a gun pointed from around a building... the shadow of a shoulder coming into view.

Although not holding her rifle tight enough, Emory squeezed the trigger, the recoil walloped against her shoulder and a body fell, partially visible from her vantage.

"Damn," she cursed. She'd have a bruise.

"You miss?" her father grilled.

"No, I winged him," came her reply. "Don't think killing anybody is a good idea."

But she might have, all the same.

True enough, that figure picked himself up and darted behind either the old two-story house or one of the sheds nearby, clutching his shoulder and likely bleeding.

"He ain't alone," her father cautioned, rapid steps moving back toward the mudroom's door.

Again, Emory scanned the outbuildings. No more movement. She changed her position as well, moving over to her father's bedroom window.

Nothing stirred in that direction.

Instinct drove her back to the bathroom window.

Against the backdrop of snow, a single man ran behind the old corral, toward an awaiting truck. He didn't hold his shoulder. A different man. Man number two.

The crack of a single shot came from the bottom part of the house and the second figure fell. Then he struggled to his feet and hobble-loped to the truck. He pulled himself inside and drove off.

"Should we let him go?" he shouted up to Emory.

"I guess," she replied, finding her target. Aiming for the truck, and not the driver, she took one final shot to mark the tailgate with a bullet hole. "I've lost the man I winged," she called as she rushed downstairs, leery about leaving her vantage point. Her father had already slipped out the front door to check on the neighbor.

"Call an ambulance," he barked. "Iver's alive. Then get some towels or bandages. We need to stop the bleeding."

She checked her cell, half dreading the state of it. Relief at finding it charged.

She dialed as she searched the linen closet.

"911, what is your emergency?"

"We need an ambulance at the Lost Daughter Ranch outside of Stampede. There's been a shooting..."

2

THE COVER OF DARKNESS

IVER HOLSTEAD LAY ON THE PORCH BLEEDING FROM HIS midsection and in bad shape.

Lance Cross knelt beside the man, worry and confusion etched on his face and liking absolutely none of it.

"That weren't no bolt-action rifle," Lance muttered like the make of the weapon mattered.

Emory crouched down alongside of the two men and thrust out the pile of towels she held in her hands. "Here. The ambulance is on its way."

"Did you get them?" The words cost the bleeding man.

"You bet," her father replied.

Emory lifted her eyebrows at the lie.

"Good," the man gasped.

The rancher grabbed the towels from Emory and dropped them down on the porch, selecting one to hold against the wound in a near futile attempt to stanch the bleeding.

The wound appeared serious—too serious to take the chance of dragging him into the house.

A half scream forced through Iver's clenched teeth as her father applied pressure.

"Hang on now," Lance Cross said. "You can make it through this. It's just like getting gored a bit." The man had a gunshot wound to the stomach. Never a good thing.

Her father's chosen words were the understatement of the century.

Iver faded in and out of consciousness. When his eyes fluttered open, he tried to tell the Crosses something. Something important. But his words strangled, hard to come by.

Her father blustered on ahead, oblivious and intent upon fixing the immediate problem. "Iver, when I get you patched up, you're going to have to explain all of this to me."

"Money…" the man gasped.

"Keep your strength," Lance's voice came out kinder than most bleeding men at the Lost Daughter would ever hear.

The sound of sirens threaded their way through the valley.

"They're coming." Emory glanced at the neighbor's shirt, everything dark, but the fabric yet darker still with his blood. Blood which appeared to be slowing, and maybe that wasn't a good thing either.

The Crosses exchanged glances as the sirens strengthened upon approach. Emory said in a low voice, "We don't know where the first man went."

Her father quirked his head.

"Think I should call his wife?" Emory asked, crouched down and still holding on to her rifle. Cautious.

"Don't know," Lance replied, patting Iver's shoulder. "Wouldn't be a good conversation to have right now."

Emory pulled out her cell and snapped a couple of pictures of her father and Iver, but mainly Iver and Iver's blood.

"What'cha doing that for?" Her father squinted at her.

"Evidence. Direction. Showing assistance." She pressed her lips together. "You know what some of the deputies out on the plains have started calling me? Calamity Jane. That's what. Geez. Kind of hard to argue at this point."

The sirens drew nearer. Emory crossed the porch and hurried down the three sagging steps—she flattened against the side of the house to watch them come in. Her caution felt overstated, but then again, she didn't understand the plot.

Two sets of headlights dipping and weaving along the contours of the rutted ranch road approached. The sheriff's car arrived first, with the ambulance following behind by about a quarter of a mile.

"Em, get them to turn off them sirens. They'll scare the horses."

The horses would have already been plenty spooked by the gunfight. With a stab of guilt, until that moment, Emory had clean forgot about them.

She'd check on the horses when she could, but at the moment, Iver's life hung in the balance.

The sheriff's car skidded to a stop. Sheriff Bob Preston killed the lights and the sound without having to be asked.

"What in the hell happened out here now?" He threw the question over at Emory as he jogged by in a bullet-proof vest, aiming toward the two men on the porch.

"We're not exactly sure," Emory responded to his

back with SHERIFF stenciled on it, decisive, clear, and somewhat unnecessary.

The sheriff leaned over Iver but scanned the horizon with a hunter's eye before returning his attention to the unconscious man, and more pointedly to the ranch's owner.

"One's gone now for certain," Lance offered in a low voice. "But there was at least two of them. Maybe three."

"When the call came in, I figured you'd had some sort of accident," Sheriff Preston chided.

"In a bulletproof vest?" Lance Cross mused still applying pressure. "And as for your rotten record, this ain't no damned accident neither."

IN WHAT SEEMED A LONG TIME, but in reality, the gap between arrivals lasted three minutes at most before more help arrived. The regional ambulance sped down the ranch road and under the hanging skull—the medics likely never even noticing the talisman in their rush.

Under the stress of the immediate situation, neither would they have cared one way or another.

Lights flashing and sirens blared into the dark landscape that swallowed them up whole as if they were of little consequence in the vastness of the night.

"Have them turn off the sirens, please." Although she couched it with a *please*, Emory's words came out as an instruction, and the sheriff's expression registered them as such.

"Cut the sound," Sheriff Preston yelled, then turned his attention back to the scene right in front of him.

The first EMT ran over with a jump pack, standing up straight and tall.

"Get down!" the sheriff barked. "There may still be shooters."

The paramedic ducked—a young man who's face struck Emory as vaguely familiar.

"Nobody said anything about an active shooter," the medic muttered.

The second paramedic joined them, carrying a scoop stretcher and making himself small, although his eyes came across as plenty large and worried. He went by the name of Jimmy something or other. Emory knew him in passing from the local rodeos.

Both knelt alongside Iver, Jimmy kneeling along the edges of the dark pool.

"He's lost a lot of blood." The first EMT pointed a pen light at the wound before looking into Iver's mouth, checking his airway. "It's clear." With that pronouncement, he placed an oxygen mask over the fallen rancher's nose and mouth and looped the elastic around the back of his head.

"We're preparing to transport an emergency patient to the hospital," Jimmy said into his radio. "Gunshot wound to the stomach. We're stabilizing now. Active shooter possible."

A voice crackled through the radio. "Ten four. Do you know the location of the shooter?"

"No. Putting a pressure bandage on the wound and cervical collar on."

The first paramedic looked over at Jimmy. "I'll insert the two large bore IVs into him in the ambulance. Considering the situation, that's the best bet."

Jimmy spoke back into the radio. "We'll IV him inside of the ambulance. Then we're getting the hell out of here."

In nothing flat, they scooped Iver up onto the

stretcher and hunkered down, running and loading him into the ambulance. Kind of like they would in combat, which although not unwarranted, still struck as a bit extreme.

But no further gunfire came.

The ambulance drove out of the ranch yard and down the dirt road, rapid but silent, although the lights flashed. The sirens flipped on once they reached the highway, meeting another siren approaching from the opposite direction, the sounds competing and reverberating off the rimrock walls made quite the racket. Every moment—every movement, one way or another—had to do with what transpired on the Lost Daughter Ranch.

"Cut the sirens," Preston barked into his radio, gruff and displeased.

He should have mentioned the possibility of active shooters earlier and knew it. "Note, suspects may still be in the vicinity, armed and dangerous."

That, her father would say, came down to the sheriff's problem. He'd forgotten how things never truly changed in their part of Colorado.

The deputy, a newcomer waylaid somewhere, would likely bear the brunt of the sheriff's failing. But once the tall young man arrived, he wasn't wasting any time, alighting and already wearing a bulletproof vest as he joined the sheriff's side.

All four of them crouched down on the porch, exchanging anxious glances and expressions between each other and straining to see out into the roiling darkness.

"What exactly is going on out here?" Sheriff Preston's strained tone bore no malice, only uncertainty.

Emory spoke clear. "Like I said, we don't know. Iver came up to the house, driving without his lights on. He called out to us as bullets started flying and he took a hit. The shots came from somewhere behind those outbuildings."

She made a point of looking at the blood, trying to determine the trajectory. Like a bird dog, straight-armed she indicated a northwest compass point.

"What's back there?" The sheriff wore that hunter's look again as he stared into the darkness.

"A bunch of debris and castoffs among the old buildings, pens, and corrals. You should find blood from the two that got winged." Emory glanced at her father, kept her voice low. "We don't know if the second one is still back there or not, not to mention a possible third."

The sheriff trained his attention square at the rancher. "And who'd you shoot, Lance?"

"Not Holstead!" The protest came out a bit loud. "It was one of them other guys. The ones who drove off."

"Can I have your rifle, then?" Sheriff Preston held out his hand.

"I'm losing my touch," her father muttered, nevertheless he passed the rifle over. "Whoever that intruder might be, should be laying out there in a heap, but I sure don't think he is."

The sheriff sniffed the rifle barrel. Observed Lance closer. "It's been fired."

"I just told you that," Lance replied, a razor's edge flashing in his tone. "Wasn't you *listening*?"

The sheriff and the rancher locked eyes, but Sheriff Preston broke the standoff first, handing Lance back his rifle. Pointedly, he turned his attention to Emory. "Sounds like we've got some outbuildings to check. What else am I looking for?"

Emory peered out into the deep-blue night that

turned tragically silent. Silent like nothing at all out of the ordinary had transpired.

"Another set of tracks. There were definitely two men. I only saw the one get into the truck. Dad?"

"Yeah," the rancher replied. "That's about the size of it. Still, we'd best be careful. It's doubtful anyone's still out there, but who's to say there wasn't a third."

"If there was, I don't think he fired," Emory ventured.

"That makes him smart," her father snapped.

The new deputy, still squatting down, scanned the horizon and blinked a bit at Lance Cross's words.

In profile, Emory couldn't help but notice the deputy's nice features and a square jaw. *A heck of a thing to contemplate when all hell broke loose.*

Distracted, Emory realized in passing that the sheriff hadn't bothered to ask for, or check, her rifle.

"Either one of you have a problem acting as back up?" The sheriff's question came out dry and unnecessary.

"Nope, no problem." Lance cracked his rifle open, fished around in his shirt pocket and loaded one single bullet into the chamber. He closed the rifle, and it locked back into place with a reassuring click.

"In that case, you are both temporarily deputized."

"Shit," Lance replied, as if that pronouncement amounted to the most outlandish thing he ever heard. "Don't go getting any ideas."

"Believe me, I won't," Preston hissed. "Now, Emory's already got a badge. If you want to stay put and be undeputized, be my guest."

That rubbed the rancher the wrong way.

"Like hell I will. I ain't going to send my daughter out to do what I won't."

The sheriff didn't even bother to react to the bluster, he desperately needed Lance's special brand of Cross expertise and knew it. "If you were one of the shooters, where would you hide out?"

Lance Cross snorted. "I'd be hunkered down in the outbuildings if they are still out there. All we have to do is keep our heads down and follow the tracks in the snow."

"For the record," Emory announced, "I fired two shots." She showed the sheriff her chamber.

"Understood," Sheriff Preston replied.

"La-di-da," Lance countered. In a lowered voice he added, "No need to go announcing our intentions at any rate."

Emory inhaled and underspoke her reply. "I haven't been near the outbuildings, since before I left, have you?"

"Not since it snowed," her father shook his head. "And Iver came around the side of the house. His truck's still there."

Emory stuck out the rifle barrel, using it as a pointer. "Behind the old homestead cabin is where I winged the first guy."

She turned to the sheriff. "Then I shot the truck as it drove off to mark it."

"Show off," her father muttered.

"Lance, how do you want to handle this?" Sheriff Preston didn't come across any too pleased to be asking for advice. Especially not from the rancher.

"Don't you lot have lawman rules?" Lance's question caught both officers short.

The lawman frowned. "In this case, I'm willing to try it your way."

Her father surveyed the yard, and raised his eyes to the moon, then resumed scanning the blue, shadowed world below. "I think we should split up into two groups. While I doubt anyone is there, there's no need to go getting careless. One group goes left, the other right, and we meet up behind those buildings and press on in."

The sheriff pulled out his gun and nodded for his deputy to do the same.

"Em," her father directed, "you go with Bob, and I'll take Junior here. Go wider than you think. That way if someone happens to be out there, they'll be trapped between us. Try to stay out of the open."

The deputy, acting jumpy, clearly didn't like being referred to as *Junior*. Lance Cross could have cared less. He frowned and gestured with his rifle for the man to get moving. Sheriff Preston set out in the southern direction, signaling for Emory to follow. Lance Cross strode on ahead taking the northern track, leaving the young deputy to follow along or hang back. He didn't need his help.

Lance Cross's actions made that point clear.

The crested snow crunched underfoot, steps coming across as loud in the relative silence. Too loud.

Emory couldn't place her finger on it, but the atmosphere felt different. *Charged and changed.* She watched as her father took cover alongside one of the old sheds and pulled the deputy beside him. The events and peril felt so distant...like a dream playing out.

That sense of detachment often cost lives.

There was no mistaking the signal the rancher made —a fist held at cheekbone height. He wanted them to stop moving.

"Psst," she exhaled to pause the sheriff.

He glanced at her, and she pointed to the side of another building. The sheriff cut over in that direction, hit a snowdrift bank covering a decline, and went down. A muffled curse. It took a moment for him to struggle back to his feet and resume pressing onward.

No tracks encountered…yet.

Breathing heavily, both Emory and the sheriff made it to the nearest building and took cover against the weathered wall.

Once each of them settled, Lance signaled to stay put.

He pointed his rifle in the air and fired one single shot that rang off the stone cliffs.

The night closed back down around them, silent and swallowing that piercing sound whole.

Rule number 1: Don't assume your enemy is stupid.

Her father pointed at her.

She purposely took aim at the edge of one of the outbuildings and squeezed.

The twang of the bullet hitting the old lumber rang out, just like in the movies. The old wood splintered. Again, no returning shot.

That lack of return fire could mean one of two things.

Either all of the men had escaped, or one or more of them remained behind. And if any of the intruders had stayed behind, the Crosses' fire wasn't drawing them out. That lack of response meant that the intruders were practiced and canny.

Or dead. *Preferably dead.*

3

HUNTING BY NIGHT

THE TWO FACTIONS RESUMED PRESSING FORWARD IN formation—just like a noose tightening around a cattle thief's neck.

The moon overhead backlit the clouds rolling in from the west, creating a complicated, shadowed affair of changing landscapes. The once-glistening snow faded and dimmed down, only to brighten again. Shadows faded and then reappeared, causing the steadiest of minds to play tricks when the images didn't register quickly enough. Nevertheless, they stalked the shadows.

Desperate in a surreal landscape with nothing as it seemed.

All their minds raced as they searched for tracks, bodies, or blood.

Who acted the part of the prey and who the hunter, remained another one of those "fine points" left up for debate. Later debate, when everything ended with tallies taken.

Another dense wave cloud covered the moon as Emory and Sheriff Preston veered left, while Lance

Cross and the deputy pursued the righthand cut. Generations of castoff remnants provided plenty of cover for a trespasser to hide behind.

Emory had never once considered the hazards those old buildings, sheds, corrals, and cabins presented. The two-story house the family outgrew somewhere around the turn of the last century stood sound enough, able to provide plenty of shelter and good vantage points for shooting. Shooting at *them*—the rightful owners of the land.

A flitting notion passed and left her wondering whether her father had ever considered padlocking the old doors but doubted it.

The Crosses would play the hand of cards that they were dealt at that precise moment, the same as they'd always done throughout their storied history.

Regrets, in their minds, were nothing more than wasted currency.

Debris—scattered fence posts, coils of rusted barbed wire, fencing, and accumulated random detritus—protruded from the snow at intervals. Plenty of other hazards lay buried beneath the surface, waiting to entangle.

"I'd better lead," Emory whispered, choosing her path and scanning for footprints, signs, or anything else that stood out of place.

More importantly, she watched for movements that didn't belong.

The night ran blue and cold and deep. The wind picked up, keening and rushing down from the high mountain ranges. Wood creaked and settled in the abandoned buildings, breathing a sense of half-life into the decrepit structures. A stronger gust rushed down, slamming a rusty-hinged door shut with one hell of a crack.

They all spooked.

Guns drawn and at the ready, nevertheless, no one squeezed a trigger by mistake. They strained to listen past the wind but found nothing. Caught nothing. Nothing more than the wind whistling through the wire.

With hearts thudding, Emory and the sheriff edged toward one of the rough and rickety shacks, wood already well-splintered from years of harsh weather.

Those preservation people wouldn't be too happy about any of this, but what the hell.

The Lost Daughter wasn't the preservation people's ranch. It was theirs, and they were the ones fighting for it.

The sheriff, uneasy, took a darting glance around the wooden corner and signaled for her to follow. They kept pressing on.

A few yards further in, Emory pointed out dark stains on the snow. Blood.

The sheriff drew a wide, sweeping circle with his hand, indicating tracks in the distance.

The shooters hadn't come from a southward direction after all.

Chances were, in that case, they came in from the northwest.

The sheriff flicked on his flashlight to illuminate the stain. Bright crimson red against stark white. Running or staggering footprints led back toward the direction where Lance Cross and the deputy waded through the drifts.

"I don't think anyone else is out here," the sheriff said in a low voice.

Agreeing, Emory looked to her father, signaling by holding her rifle up above her head with one hand.

Her father, about to lift his rifle in response, halted. A

bullet whizzed by, lodging in the wood of one of the nearby buildings. Splinters flew.

They all sprang for cover or flattened in the snow.

Waiting for another shot or movement, that never came.

After a long, silent moment of uncertainty, the hum of a snowmobile reached them, trailing up from the direction of the BLM land. *Right in the approximate location where they had caught Cade with his bag of drugs and her father had shot him in the foot.*

That wasn't good. Not good at all.

Emory raised herself to kneeling in the snow, then to squatting as she brushed herself off. She waited, turning different scenarios over in her mind as the motor's hum grew faint in the distance.

That final shot meant at least three trespassers had come in. *Trespassers* being a kind word for their part in an attempted murder. Who in the hell were they, and what did they want with the Lost Daughter or Iver?

When the sound of the snowmobile could no longer be heard, the law enforcement and the Crosses regrouped.

"Should we go to the back gate?" Lance eyed the trackless ridge to the west.

Sheriff Preston weighed the options in his mind. "There'd be tracks coming up through the BLM land. It wouldn't hurt to try to find shell casings, but I guess we could tackle that at first light. Right now, we might ruin whatever evidence might exist. You keep that back gate locked?"

"Never have," her father admitted. "It's one of them foregone conclusions that'll be changing from here on out. In the old days, anyone who snuck onto the ranch without good cause took his life in his own hands. Of course, we used to be a lot rougher in them days, but we can bring that back if needed."

The deputy swallowed, eyes large and glittering green.

Sheriff Preston, knowing them well enough, wasn't rattled by Lance's words, but neither did he entirely dismiss the threat that the rancher offered.

"While I take your meaning and the sentiment behind it, don't say things like that in front of me," he remained calm. "I'm the law in this valley, you know."

"That's what you keep tellin' me," her father chided. "Ain't you ever heard of the 'make my day' law? They come back here, and I'm going to change that to the 'make my century' law, because they'll still be talking about it one hundred years from now."

"Easy now, Lance. Those are the type of things I'm referring to."

"I'll do as I damn well choose on this land."

The subject plummeted dead at their feet like a frozen raven falling from a tree. A carcass just as cold and unyielding as the surrounding terrain. Rimrocks that stood witness to the Cross family's struggles and tribulations over the last century now more simply absorbed the struggle below.

Rimrocks, crevasses, and boulders were features of the ranch that could work for them, as well as against them. *Any of them.* Family or foe.

Sheriff Preston rubbed the back of his neck, an uneasy feeling stealing over him. As well it should. The ghosts of the dead Crosses most likely grew restless, disturbed by the offending events, and summonsed by the spilling of blood.

That remained one of those *things* about the Lost Daughter that outsiders didn't understand. *Couldn't* understand. Any one of the Crosses might appear, on the surface, isolated at the ranch. But they were never alone, not really. The past lingered around them all—thin, ghost-like fingers tendrilled around the Cross descendants.

Those earlier Crosses in their graves, well, they didn't rest. They lay in their shrouds and coffins, biding their time and waiting for the occasion that would cause them to rise.

And rise they would.

STILL SENSING the uneasy turmoil and restless spirits, the sheriff pressed on forward while her father and the deputy doubled back toward the direction where the intruders parked their truck. The trail of blood started out in a splattered burst when the person had first been hit. Then, apparently clutching the wound and moving fast, the blood marked the snow, trailing and falling in wider intervals.

Locating a bled-out corpse could never be considered the most pleasant of options. But bled-out corpses no longer presented much of a threat.

Nevertheless, either "dead or alive" brought its own set of difficulties.

Just another fragment of history to have to live down.

"I don't like this," the sheriff muttered.

"And I do?" Lance shot across.

"Dad," Emory snapped. "He said nothing of the sort."

Adrenaline still coursed, and that old survival instinct raised its head and waited.

The sheriff kept his voice level. "Let's try to figure out how many men were in this area."

"Who's to say they were men?" Emory got strained looks in response to her questioning of basic assumptions. "Women can shoot, too. Anyhow, there's only one set of tracks that I can see."

Judging the evidence in the snow and scanning the dark buildings, a picture started to emerge. "The blood is pretty red, and the drops are small. Wherever they got hit, I guess he or she could cover the wound with their hand and get the hell out of Dodge. I still think we should look through all the buildings. Someone might be unconscious or even dead inside one of them."

"Yup," her father said, tone dry. "Probably wouldn't be the first time, neither."

Emory set her jaw at his words, which would likely do more harm than good.

Sheriff Preston twitched, unamused. "Like I said. We're talking ancient history here, aren't we? I will need you to confirm that."

Her father cocked a half smile. "Confirmed," he replied, then sobered. "I'd feel better on hearing how Iver's doing."

The sheriff half struggled and pressed his radio's transmitter button after scanning the terrain and seeing no sign of movement. "This is Sheriff Preston. Any word on Iver Holstead's condition? Over."

Static.

The sheriff's mouth compressed downward into a line as the disembodied voice returned. "He's in the operating room. No further news. Over."

"Thanks. Keep me posted. Over."

An uneasy silence fell between them, unspoken accusations swirled.

The sheriff shook his head. "Why'd he come out here in the first place?"

"Iver? Beats the hell out of me," Lance Cross responded. "It's not exactly like we saw eye to eye on almost anything. Besides. He's the type that lets people run over him."

If that were even true, Emory reckoned, at least Iver proved smart enough to ask for help. But help with what?

There was nothing further to be done beyond turning their attention to the shadowed tire tracks in the snow, intent on gleaming any possible clues. Strong flashlights picked up where the moonlight and cold stars left off. They all followed the drops and trails of blood, and their phones snapping pictures that probably wouldn't amount to anything much at all. Just tracks in the snow. Tracks that could have belonged to almost anyone.

"Measure that footprint and take a picture, will you?" the sheriff instructed the deputy in no uncertain terms.

"Measure with what?"

They had tape measures in the barn, but her father didn't offer.

"The sheriff pulled out his wallet and took out a bill. 'It's better than nothing."

Her father held his rifle, ramrod straight and observing. Jaw set and clenched. She could see that jaw in the shadows. He was still plenty pissed off that, as Crosses, they'd been caught flat-footed.

In days of old, that wouldn't have happened, or so the theory held.

So much for their rumored inbred ability to catch people stealing up on them.

Emory marked the footprints in the snow—bloodless tracks that came down from the old two-story house. Twenty yards away, the door stood ajar four inches, beckoning. Rifle locked and loaded, and without saying anything to the sheriff, she headed in that direction.

The tracks in the snow hesitated and doubled back, uncertain.

Her father saw her step away and went one step further to provide cover. "Say, Bob and deputy...what did you call yourself?"

"Walter Gering."

"Walter, it is. Say, looking over here, don't you think..."

Emory stopped paying attention to their words at that point, constantly scanning the dark windows for any sign of movement within. Reaching the doorframe's shelter, she nudged the door's opening wider with her boot toe.

When nothing moved in the empty, hanging silence, she pushed the door open wider with her rifle barrel.

Another moment passed. She stepped into the inky interior. In the shadows, the outline of an old table claimed the corner while stacks of old boards were propped against the walls at intervals.

The old wood creaked as the night wind rose, groaning through the breaches in walls and roof.

Heaven only knew the last time someone from the family entered the house. For that matter, it didn't *feel* as if an intruder had ventured inside. Moonlight streamed in through open gaps, revealing the thick dust that blanketed the wide plank floor and anything horizontal.

Glancing over her shoulder, she saw nothing but the tracks of her own boots crossing the floor.

She could have sworn that she heard the whisperings of long-gone ancestors and sensed an unexpected pull of heartbreak.

She understood none of the emotions swirling, except that she felt them in her marrow.

"Emory!"

It wasn't her father's voice, but the sheriff's.

"Coming," she shouted back, leaving the old house to its secrets and longings.

But she would be back. The house knew she would return.

She jogged over to the men, gathered in a stand a few yards off from where she had left them.

"We found two additional trails of blood," Sheriff Preston explained, shining the light on the snow and traveling to the pickup stashed between two old sheds. "This one leading to the driver's seat, and this one to the back of the truck. Guess that's how the second one got away—by jumping into the truck bed."

She and her father locked eyes but neither said a word.

Sheriff Preston spoke into his radio. "Be on the lookout for people seeking medical attention from gunshot wounds. Alert the hospital and the local doctors. Over."

The local medical center, the pride of the district, acted the part of a regional hospital, and the only medical facility for at least forty miles in all directions. The town doctors all practiced out of the building, although two operated their own offices in town. Getting the word out about people suffering from gunshot wounds wouldn't take long. While such notifications could either benefit the law or go against it, the very need for those warnings pointed out one glaring aspect of the events unfolding that night.

In the Old West, matters such as right or wrong concerning gunshot wounds weren't always immediately clear. Like the Old West, neither were they clear-cut in rural Colorado.

As most of the longtime inhabitants knew, making determinations between who acted the part of the good or bad in a gunfight depended an awful lot on perspective.

And perspectives, as history often proved, remained susceptible to change.

4

THE TIMES, THEY ARE A-CHANGING

TOGETHER, THE FOUR OF THEM CONVERGED UPON IVER'S truck. Not single file as truly they ought but fanned out like a football team and mucking up the playing field in the process. The sheriff aimed his flashlight first at the vehicle, then at the tracks.

The driver's door gapped open wide in a hurried, vehicular scream.

Cowboy boot tracks led toward the house; the snip toe gouging deep into the snow, the heel sank deep enough, but within the footprints a distinct motion held, along with a rising sense of panic. Anyone able to interpret tracks even superficially would make no mistake—Iver for sure hadn't wasted any time getting onto the Crosses' porch.

Her father analyzed the remnants of the panicked scene. "Shit," he hissed, before spitting.

The sheriff's eyes shifted over to the rancher, appraising and none too friendly while he was at it. "You mentioned something about hard feelings?"

The question came out light enough, but it held a

barb at the end.

Her father didn't rush to answer. Instead, he scanned the distance covered by the old ranch, putting his hand upon the side of the house, stiff-armed and bandy-legged from all the years of riding horses. "Oh, nothing important that needs airing."

The tension between the two men palpitated.

"I'd say it does." The sheriff's voice traveled across the silence, low and serious.

Lance responded with a half-cocked grin, that meant he either found the sheriff's insistence amusing or beneath contempt. It was a warning sign, all right, but the sheriff didn't seem to care.

"Iver Holstead ain't too good at fighting," Lance remarked. "Only he once thought he was, before we got that part straightened out."

The sheriff nodded that her father had best continue and get on with the explanation, quick.

But Lance refused to be goaded and took his time. She shot him a warning glance.

"That dustup must have been about twenty years ago. Emory stood only about yea high." He marked the space mid-thigh. "Put plainly, Iver didn't like the fact that he sold me a horse he thought couldn't be rode, and I rode him, alright. One of the best horses I ever owned, in fact. Bought him cheap. That meant Iver sold too low."

"That's the sum of it?"

"Yeah. As far as I know. Pride can be a terrible thing," he smirked, relishing the memory.

But then he stopped fooling around.

"Which is why," her father continued, with emphasis upon the *why* and dead serious, "I don't understand what he was doing here in the first place, driving up with his headlights off and hollering my name like hell's a-poppin'.'"

The sheriff looked over at Emory, who tilted her head in agreement with her father's rather limited account.

Plain and simple, Lance's description covered as much as either of the Crosses knew.

Stern and frowning with a doubt-laced expression, the sheriff motioned for the deputy to get on with snapping pictures for evidence.

A gesture the deputy completely missed.

Emory caught him giving her the eye instead. As did Sheriff Preston, who cleared his throat to get the young man's attention back onto the work matters at hand.

Caught, he glanced away out of guilt, and started clicking.

Yeah, Emory thought. *That's usually how it went. And he had no idea about her or the Lost Daughter's reputation, although he should have. Unless he was another newcomer. She could even scare the hell out of him if she wanted to. But now didn't seem like the time to yank his chain.*

Her heart just wouldn't be in it.

The problems of that moment boiled down to fundamental matters. It stood more important to figure out the reason for the gun battle, than to go flirting or scaring inexperienced deputies just because she could.

And for that reason, the Crosses didn't have much else to say as the sheriff and the deputy finally loaded up and drove off.

Father and daughter stood shoulder to shoulder in the darkness as they watched "the law" depart.

"That old snakebite sure enters my veins when bullets start flying." Her father's comment, although dry, struck a chord.

Knowing that same feeling herself, she long eyed him. Coursing adrenaline amounted to a type of poison or drug in her experience. She thought back to the biker she killed in self-defense. "Yeah. It's probably nothing to go around bragging about."

Her father somehow picked up on the chord in her voice and softened a notch as he understood her meaning. "It's a survival thing, Em." That was more than enough softness for him, and he rallied. "Hell, prior to 1950, you wouldn't have had to think twice about it."

She turned toward him to check if he was kidding. He wasn't.

"What is all this shit really about? And don't tell me that you don't know."

Holding the rifle in his right hand, he spread his left-hand fingers wide. "That's just it, Em. I don't know. I don't know a damned thing about it. Cross family honor."

They never used that oath other than for serious life or death matters.

She backed down. "If you insist. But why does this shit always have to happen to us?"

"Because of who we are, Em. Because of who we are."

She already knew that. But how long would that reputation last, and how long would it take to live down?

If word about her killing a man got out and made the rounds, that was one more generation who would have to live it down—her children's. If she ever managed to have any children in the first place.

"The yard light really needs fixing." A pause. "You've never killed anyone, have you?"

"I've still got time," he replied, clamping a large hand on her shoulder and giving it a squeeze.

Her eyes teared up and she turned away, but not in time.

"Now," he claimed, breaking the mood and never knowing how to handle a woman's tears. "What we need is another steer's skull for the back gate. I'll bet those bastards came in through the BLM land to scout out the lay of the ranch."

Emory dabbed at her eyes, pretending. Always pretending that *nothing was wrong*.

"Regardless, I doubt skulls would have scared them off," Emory countered, discomfort passing and defiance returning.

That gang member would have killed her. As fortune had it, she proved a better shot. Life or death. She lived, he died. He started it.

Her father sensed the shift of mood. "You don't know that a'tall. Them skulls could be like a talisman. *Our* talisman."

"Either way, but I do know there's an extra saddle in the barn," Emory tossed out that accusation, almost casual enough that it would pass for a mere exchange of information.

She was rewarded with her father's infamous squaring of his jaw. "You noticed, did you?"

"I wouldn't be mentioning it otherwise."

"That Paulson woman wanted to go riding, and I said she could leave her saddle here. Just in case the notion strikes again."

With a chuckle, her father moved off into the house leaving Emory to follow, as she chose or not.

"Doesn't look like it's been used in a good, long time," she called out, aiming square between his shoulder blades and mean-spirited to boot. "It's awfully brittle."

"Who cares about the saddle?" He flung back over his

shoulder, back to his old ways. "That's not the only thing that hasn't been used for a while, but brittle don't enter into it."

The innuendo stabbed, sharp and deep.

Flat-out, Emory didn't want to know about her father's sex life, and by extension, the lack of her own. She decided to knock the rhetoric down a notch, but something inside of her wouldn't let it die completely out. "Does that mean you're actually *listening* to those preservation people?"

He paused on the porch. Right about where Iver's blood must have stained. "At least one of them."

Splendid.

"Wonders never cease. I hope you've finally got her name right," Emory taunted in a singsong way. "Those tax grants would go a fair ways on repairs. Anyhow, I'm going to go check on the horses."

Damned near intolerable was her first thought on the matter, but there would be nothing for it.

She stopped thinking about shootings, Iver, or whelp deputies. She wasn't even thinking about how the Lost Daughter had been breached.

Un-fricking-believable. It had been just the two of them, for such a very long time.

INSIDE THE BARN, the horses stamped and strained sensing the tension in her, and in the air.

Not to mention the gunfire that left them unsettled.

She propped her rifle alongside the barn door, and she checked on their hay and water.

"Kai," she said rubbing his face, "I sure wouldn't have brought you along if I knew what we were getting into."

Kai—a blood bay quarter horse—snorted in response, tossing back his head, bothered.

She patted him a bit more and glared at Draco, her father's dark horse, although that wasn't fair.

Moving over to the Percheron cross horse, she fussed over him for a bit. "Try to keep my dad in line, would you?"

Of course, that would prove next to an impossible task.

She returned to Kai for one last pat, glaring at the intrusive saddle as she left. *The one that didn't belong. It wasn't a serious saddle, anyhow.*

Emory returned out into the night, alone except for her rifle.

She paused out in the yard, standing in the middle of their domain and listened to the wind moan overhead. Considering the lights on in the house, she cast a glance toward the barn shadowed in gray for one last look. Checking, always checking. But the barn doors were fastened tight.

Yeah. It was one hell of a homecoming, all right.

Drawn toward the blood on the porch, contemplating its existence rather than the changes afoot felt preferable. Somehow safer. But maybe it all amounted to one and the same, tangled into a mess. Dark, the neighbor's blood dulled, but still glistened by moonlight—thicker than water and all of that shit. Emory stepped over the pool as she made her way into the house.

She felt it keenly, how times were a-changing.

She hoped she proved equal to whatever task they were up against.

THE FOLLOWING morning broke bright and cold, ominous in its false simplicity. Regardless, the horses and livestock required tending before anything else. They *always* came first, come hell or high water. That fundamental belief remained one of the very few rules on a spread that didn't hold much store in convention. But the horse and livestock rule held and held firm. *Livestock first, people second.* Never the other way around.

One hasty cup of coffee allowed before heading off to the barn to get chores started.

Emory stood staring out the kitchen window, coffee in hand when her father came down, dressed and ready to work.

"I'm going to scrub off that blood," she said.

"Leave it."

She intentionally gave him the sideways glance that he had always hated. The one that said she doubted his judgment.

He did the Dad puff up—the prelude to a one-way lecture. "Never pretend everything is alright when it ain't. Not unless there is something to be gained from it. You see anything we've got to gain here this time around?"

"Not off the top of my head, but that Paulson woman might not like it."

He wasn't exactly staring her down, but calculated a notion deeper in. Something curled up beneath his words. "You sure you want to be needling me already? That didn't take you long."

Emory smirked, blowing on her coffee. "Just statin' a fact. Pools of blood tend to put house guests off."

He couldn't be serious about her, could he?

Lance bolted the contents of his mug down and

pulled on his denim fleece-lined jacket. "You here to work, or just jaw?"

Emory set her cup down and moved over to her jacket hanging on its hook. "This has been one hell of a homecoming."

Her father frowned, knitting his brows together. "You ain't Queen Elizabeth, you know."

But he made no move. Instead, he paused with the door closed. Uncustomary in his delay.

A slight shake of his head, he strode past her toward the back of the house.

"Rifle or .45?"

That question snapped foreboding along her spine. They didn't walk around armed in the broad daylight to do their chores by habit. "Rifle. That is, if you really think it's needed."

"I do," his voice came from the back of the house.

He emerged, Winchester in hand and a strapped on hip-holster carrying the .45. "And not a bolt action neither. Keep this with you, at least for the next few days until we know what we're looking at."

"Man, this really is now turning out like a chapter from the Wild West," she muttered, taking the rifle and checking the sight.

"That's the spirit," he chuckled, then turned serious. "And don't you forget it neither, 'cause the others will. Mark my words, that's how we'll end up claiming the advantage. While the year might change, the fundamental facts of life sure as hell don't. Not out here and not until we're good and ready."

Armed and equipped with deadly weapons, Emory followed her father out to the barn, rifle in hand as she stepped over the blood much like a common puddle in the road. She glanced at the stain, all right, but she kept any comments to herself as she surveyed the evidence of carnage.

She paused, a few paces past Iver's blood.

The morning light cast the scene in a worse picture than the darkness. Iver's blood streaked like war paint where the stretcher or the rancher himself dragged through the then-spreading red pool.

Glancing away from the gore, the snow sparkled pristine in the morning light, the sky an azure blue—the same as it had yesterday's morning.

Yesterday's morning before all hell broke loose.

"You know, I thought about what you said," Emory spoke to her father's back as she followed him along to the barn. "About you wanting another skull for the back gate."

He never broke his stride. "So?"

"I read a book where a pioneer woman's family was killed by the Blackfeet in Montana Territory. Anyhow, they traveled in a single wagon alone with the family onboard. The Blackfeet attacked. They all tried to fight them off but were outnumbered. The husband might have killed one or two warriors before he died. In the story, she had three children, and they were all killed one way or another in the attack. Then the warriors came after her, but she managed to kill a couple straight-out with an ax. Guess she lost her mind afterwards, all alone on the mountainside surrounded by the corpses of her family. Do you want to know what she did?"

Wary, he gave a sharp nod for her to get on with it.

"She chopped the heads off the Blackfeet with that same ax and stuck them on wooden pikes along the perimeters and sat in the middle of it. Some trapper came along and built her a cabin. No one, white or Indian, ever bothered her after that."

Her father squinted. "Was she a redhead?"

"What kind of question is that? I'm telling you about a story…"

"A crazy redhead might scare a lot of people off," he teased. "Your great-great-grandmother, Idella, had red hair, come to think of it. *I-del-la*. Bet you didn't know you was named after a crazy redheaded woman."

"Middle name," Emory corrected. And no, she hadn't heard about Idella being a redhead or much anything else. Certainly nothing about her being crazy. However Idella acted, she'd possessed enough sense not to go getting herself drowned like the Hapless Susan.

Her father likely just pulled her leg.

"Why do you say she was crazy?" Emory eyed him close.

"She possessed a definite temperament that wasn't exactly social, but she could ride like the wind." Admiration laced his words. He didn't think she was crazy, not deep down. "Legend has it that she couldn't bake break worth a damn."

"The steer skull out front didn't keep people out as you figured," she countered on Idella's behalf.

"What's chapping your hide?"

"Nothing," she lied.

It always amounted to the same damned thing. Men counted, woman…not so much. Unless they were the last line of defense standing.

Then their estimated value increased tenfold.

The crow's feet around her father's eyes deepened as he waited her out.

She didn't want to get into an argument for the hell of it. Not just then. "Maybe you're right. Who's to say it hurt? Next beast that dies by natural causes or gets butchered, I suppose you could stick its head down there."

"Why, thank you for your permission," he halfway bowed. "I guess your hair does have some red to it, after all."

"Only when the sun hits it right." She fiddled with the latch that needed tending, and managed to get it to release. "Speaking of the back gate, you haven't seen Cade limping around town, have you?"

A slow wag of his head and nothing more.

"That's a 'no' then."

"That's a I-don't-want-to-talk-about-it-right-now because I don't give a damn about Cade. Now, you turn out them horses, load hay in the feeders, and muck out the stalls. I'll go check on the water tanks to make sure they ain't frozen solid. We'll both haul the hay, and then it'll be our turn to have breakfast. Sound like a plan?"

"Sure I can't clean up that blood this morning?"

Another slow wag of his head, eyes glinting blue and cold. "Best to leave it for the time being. Anyhow, it don't bother me much."

"Yes, it does," Emory countered.

Her father met her eyes. "Mebbe so. Should bother you as well."

She turned away and closed her eyes as she faced into the breeze as the wind picked up singing a mournful, rushing water song.

Despite the musical quality, the song that blew in wrapped around her with warnings.

"And you're sure that nothing strange has happened out here while I've been gone." She made it a statement for the simple reason that her father didn't approve of questioning aimed in his direction.

"Nothing comes to mind," he replied, defenses lowered. Searching his memory and sounding as close to bewildered as she had ever heard him. "That's why I'm going to go see Iver about whatever that money comment meant."

"And if they won't let you in to see him? He might not be ready for visitors yet."

"Not today. Tomorrow. I'll give him a few more hours to pull his shit together."

Perfect and back to normal. Her father now intended to give ultimatums to a man lying in a hospital bed. But then again, Iver brought his trouble to the Lost Daughter Ranch himself.

And the wind from the peaks kept on singing their faint warning song.

5

THE OLD HOMESTEAD

"WE AIN'T DONE," HER FATHER TOLD HER, DUMPING THE last pitchfork full of hay into the feeders.

"Never said we were," Emory replied.

She had already turned out the horses into the snow-covered pasture, the pair of them roughhousing in the morning rising blue and brilliant. Their hooves thundering as they loped the length of the enclosure, manes blowing and streaming like ribbons.

Both stopped to watch them for a moment.

"They don't seem too bothered," he remarked.

"They're animals," Emory's words did an injustice to the horses, and she knew it. But that morning wasn't the time to go all poetic about the merits of Kai and Draco.

Not when blood streaked the house and the snow.

"Guess we're searching for something missed in the darkness," Emory stated. "You got anything particular in mind?"

"No. Just anything that stands out." Her father's eyes scanned the ranchland where he had lived his entire life.

Father and daughter didn't need words as they aimed

toward the abandoned pens with the two old homestead houses standing like aging matriarchs among the castoffs. The older one, built with more skill and care, withstood the ravages of time a fair amount better.

As they approached the perimeter of the trespass, the disturbed snow didn't come as a surprise, but it got their hackles up all the same. Of course, there were the tracks made by the law and themselves, not to mention the intruders.

Hard to say which would prove worse, as far as standard Lost Daughter operations worked. A badge-carrying member of the law herself, Emory knew she straddled a very fine family line.

But unwanted visitors were unwanted visitors, and no two ways about it.

To drive that point home, more tracks circled the two-story building.

Funny, as in unforgiveable, how none of them had seen those trespasser's tracks during their nighttime search.

Half in the sun, and half in the shade, Emory pointed with her rifle, again in silence. Words in such cases provided little more than something to trip over and fight about.

As clear as anything, those tracks headed around to the back of the first house, instead of to the front.

The two Crosses approached, staring at the footprints.

Tennis shoes.

Now *that* only added insult to injury.

"Who in the hell would come out here wearing those?" Her father's brow wrinkled at the sheer stupidity.

Judging by the placement of the tracks, at one point

the intruder stood against the wall, leaning back and likely coming up with a plan.

"People not from around here," she replied, although his question was more of the rhetorical variety.

The hair on the nape of Emory's neck rose. She glanced over her shoulder and figured out trajectories. From that very specific vantage point, the shooter had enjoyed a fine, unobstructed view of the current ranch house.

"That's what I was afraid of," she said, using her full arm to indicate a straight line of fire. "Last night I assumed someone had gone into the old house, but when I went in, there wasn't a trace, and the dust remained thick and undisturbed."

Her father chewed on that scrap, still scanning the tracks of the vanished man like he could actually command him to appear.

"Dad," Emory ventured, for reasons beyond the immediate concern. "Who lived in this house?"

He blinked a couple of times as his mind switched gears. Pushing back his hat, he straightened up and shrugged. "Guess I never gave it much thought. The oldest cabin became the ranch office. Why?"

"Curiosity."

He eyed her, sensing an undercurrent he didn't quite understand. "This doesn't have anything to do about your mother, does it?"

"Nope," she replied with as much emphasis as a one syllable word could carry.

He wasn't falling for it, but he played along. "The old cabin's where Hank Cross started out, bunkin' with the boys. Figure when the family came out, he built them something better, maybe the skinnier two-story." He pointed to another two-story house, narrow and weather-worn like everything else.

Of course, her father acted more concerned with Hank. After all, Hank was a *man* and the founder.

But she searched for something different. The trace of the women who were every bit as important, even if no one ever said as much.

Lance Cross seemed to sense another losing battle, so tried to be a bit more accommodating.

"I think they built this other one here about 1900 or 1910. Don't exactly know. Likely Idella lived in one of them at some point—maybe both. Hard to say. Everything got passed down until it wore out, I reckon. Then it turned into storage. Our house dates from about 1930. Is that what you're lookin' for?"

"Maybe."

Her father turned exasperated in the deep waters. "Planning on movin' into one of these, is that it?"

"It'd be a lot of work. Just interested, that's all."

He curdled, a bit sullen. "That time in Greeley turned you strange."

"Maybe just independent. Now, do you think we should put locks on the doors? I never once stopped to think how people could hide out here among all these old, abandoned buildings and whatnot."

"Yeah," he said, feeling on safer ground. He spat. "Shit. People ain't supposed to come out here at all."

Maybe not, but they had come. More blood soaked into the snow—drops nowhere near as alarming as Iver's gushing—but their mere existence proved an event that should never have occurred.

"That's gotta be the shoulder wound," Lance snarled. "Not that much blood hit the ground because he clamped his damned hand over it, I'm figuring."

Emory eyed the snow-covered hill and the drifts that crested along the two-track road. "Do you still want to go out to the back gate?"

"Nah. The sheriff's either found the casing from the one and only shot fired from that direction, or he hasn't. Either way, it's his problem, not ours."

"Guess we better tell the sheriff about the tennis shoes." Mentioned as a veiled aside, she figured it a critical piece of evidence.

Her father knew that as well but didn't want to come out and admit as much. "Maybe," he replied.

Yeah. Sometimes the less said, the better.

TRACKING DONE and somewhat accounted for, Emory jumped into her grandfather's pickup truck. She flipped down the visor and consulted the mirror on the underside.

"What are you going to do about any of it?" she asked her reflection, noting her eyes flecked with gold came across as greener than usual. The bridge of her nose remained flat where it had busted and her hair proved a wind-tossed mess, but that's how it went out in the middle of nowhere.

Turning over the ignition and stamping on the gas, she drove out to the outer perimeter. It stood to reason the intruders had knocked down a segment or two of fence during all their maneuverings. *Just more work to be done that hadn't needed doing just the day before.*

The rimrocks ringed the valley, as impassive and impressive as ever. They stood sentinel, all right, but they sure weren't giving up any secrets.

Bouncing along the frozen, rutted ranch road, she passed under the skull and gave it the finger.

It hadn't done them one ounce of good, as far as she could tell.

She slowed her speed upon reaching the ranch boundaries right up against the road. She turned to follow the northern perimeter along the county road, the crossbeams fading from sight and mind as she traveled along the 92, following the fence and wire.

Going slow.

A red sports car of some sort sped right up on the truck's tail. True, she drove under the speed limit, but that didn't justify pure tailgating. Glancing into the rearview mirror, Emory ignored the fence line for the moment, and watched as the car tried to pull around her, only to be driven back by oncoming traffic. Another attempt, and another swerve back. Intentionally, she slowed down further.

The car flashed its lights and blasted its horn.

In time, the oncoming traffic opened up, and the car sped around her. This time, she received the ever-pervasive third finger as he drove off.

Colorado plates.

Just marvelous.

She felt the spirit of the Lost Daughter Ranch laughing at her expense due to her blatant lack of respect.

The ranch would take its due.

And likely there would be a bend in the road with that asshole's name upon it.

Just another yuppie from Denver in a rush to reach the "true" mountain experience he would never understand. Not in one hundred years.

Then she saw it. A section of wire clipped.

Pulling over to the roadside, she jumped out of the truck to stand near the cut barbwire—a hole that yawned open wide.

She considered the tire prints as if they could speak— noting how they veered to the west and down a slight ravine to where the old wagon road traced through. No one who wasn't local knew about that faint whisper of a road, especially not when covered by snow. The road once connected the Lost Daughter to an area further out near the Parsons' place a long time ago, but no one used it anymore.

Emory snapped a few pictures—if phone pictures were good enough for the sheriff, they were good enough for her. She picked up a fence post and pounded it back into the hole it started from. She removed a pair of pliers from the truck box, tightening and wrapping the barbed wire to hold as best she could. Jerry-rigged for the moment, she climbed back into her truck, following the crested and windblown tracks.

Hair rising on her neck, she stopped the truck, looked around with caution, and retrieved the rifle from the storage box in the truck bed.

There was no excuse for making the same damned mistake twice, thank you very much.

And she scanned the rimrocks and the landscape, uncertain.

THE SHOOTER'S vehicle was likely a four-wheel drive equipped with snow tires. Just the same as seventy-five percent of the vehicles in the county, if not more.

Rifle loaded and carried under her arm like she meant business, internally she debated the sense of a bolt-action rifle. The ranch code established three shots in succession meant trouble, and automatics in such instances were easier and quicker than bolt actions. A single shot...well, those happened all the time.

Emory followed the traces in the snow, melting with the sun and the rising temperatures. The snow stood about five inches high on that barren part of the ranch, scoured stiff by the wind. The tire prints led down to the ravine where the old wagon trail threaded through the outbuildings and neared the house. If there was anything to find, it would lurk along those bottoms. Crunching through the quarter mile of snow to reach the suspected hiding place, she kept scanning the brush, uneasy.

All the while, the jagged-edged frozen river babbled on the same as any other time—the trout slumbered in the depths, sluggish in the winter cold.

The water offered a safety for the fish that she didn't have.

The intruder's tracks followed down the existing ruts pretty near one hundred percent on target.

Whoever the intruders were, they knew the lay of the ranch well. Too well.

The name of Cade Timmons sprang to mind.

EMORY HALF SLID, half climbed down the embankment, skirting the clear flowing river. Fringed with ice and frost covered branches, the beauty would sparkle but briefly in the sunlight before melting off and disappearing.

Like those tire tracks were bound to do.

The driver took the bend toward the outbuildings just fine. They continued straight on, and the brush remained the same as ever. She scrambled back up the bank, her rifle resting on her shoulder as she scanned the horizon, looking for trouble.

A glancing realization caught her by surprise—the Colorado plains ought to have been a straightforward proposition, but that wasn't how they played out either.

In fact, she could have been killed.

THE NEXT SECTION of downed fence listed a half mile further—an old wooden branch uprooted and suspended, hanging from three barbed wire strands. Strung up like that, the next two segments completely downed and run over, it all came off as feeble at best. Another line of defense that didn't do all that great in hindsight.

Shit.

The tracks turned and wheeled, now erratic no longer following any established roads or depressions. Freewheeling, this read as a trail of a panicked person who did not know the lay of the land, or if he did, sure didn't recognize it.

Maybe the ink of darkness threw him off kilter.

Or, more likely, it was the loss of blood.

Running full-on and into barbed wire fences should have caused noticeable damage to the truck's grill and front end. Still, the wire hadn't been maintained as taut as it should have been. Another failing on their parts.

She chewed on that thought as she snapped a few more pictures for proof. Of course, she could start checking the trucks in town for damage, but people tended to get funny about their personal property, and trucks were personal.

Emory stared at the tracks and the patched fence a bit longer, turning events over in her mind. She walked alongside those tracks, marking the swerves and where the vehicle collided into brush, crooked turns reversing and turned in on itself and backing around only to run into more unyielding brush.

That crookedness spoke of injury.

The driver must have fought hard for consciousness at that point, or if not that, his shoulder and arm were rendered useless for steering. The most erratic driving aimed toward the highway to get the hell out.

Wounded, and hopefully scared, getting the hell off Cross land had been their goal.

They wouldn't have been the first to flee the Lost Daughter. But all of that happened before her time in the 1890s. Still, she glanced once more at the propped up fence segments, grateful no cattle roamed in that section.

HER FATHER LINGERED, uncharacteristically, in proximity to the house instead of riding the range. Happily, or so it seemed from the distance, he stood on a ladder, tinkering with the yard light that needed fixing.

At least that was one thing tended to.

"What time are you going to see Iver tomorrow?" Emory called out, climbing out of the truck and staring at him perched up there.

"About that," he said, eyes fixed on the wire he twisted.

She waited. He paused.

When finished, he climbed back down. "Just don't feel good about leaving you here alone," he replied.

Emory tilted her head, but Lance didn't stand around

for talking and marched back to the house, leaving her to follow or not. However she saw fit or chose.

The long afternoon shadows drew in; the mountains blocking the setting sun with its accompanying warmth dwindled and died. Those hollow, late afternoon hours were the ones she always half dreaded especially in those years right after her mother left. Her mother's betrayal allowed the melancholy to seep into her bones and settle.

Those cold hours were upon them now.

Across the way, she considered the two old houses hunkering down dark against the blue-shadowed white. She wanted to go back to them, but for reasons other than intrusion and gunfights. Emory, tearing her eyes away, trotted into the house after her father.

He flicked on the yard light, nodding when it worked.

"One down, twenty to go," she said.

"Killjoy," he replied.

"Back to Iver then."

He scuffed his boots on an old latch hooked rug, plenty faded, and colors bled out at least twenty years back.

"Dad, I'm just as good with a gun as you."

"That may be," he replied, "but you ain't mean enough. Besides, you got a badge. No…thinking about it, it would be best if you go on in tomorrow and give visiting Iver a try."

"Chicken," Emory replied.

"Why, you got something better to do?"

She had. *Those old houses*. "No, that's fine. I'll try. Besides, it sounds like his wife might not like you much."

He chuckled at that. "Smarty-pants."

"Say, you think we should get locks for those outbuildings? Especially that house. Something about it makes me uneasy."

"You want a padlock?"

"Sure, why not."

Her father shrugged. "Those preservation people, for one."

"I sure didn't see any of them around when the bullets were flying."

"Yeah, you do have a point on that one." He chuckled at the notion. Or maybe he thought of the Paulson woman, but he wasn't about to share.

"We've got stuff laying around here that should do the trick. I want to think about things before we go drilling holes."

His hesitance definitely concerned that Paulson woman and her notions.

That struck Emory wrong. *Just splendid,* she thought.

THE NEXT MORNING'S silvery light found Emory climbing in her old truck and scanning the snow for more tracks the entire length of the ranch road. She found nothing at all. The specter of the steer head came into view, hanging down from the crossbeams. Slowing, she peered up through the windshield as she drove beneath the skull in all its gory glory.

She knew better than to give it the finger this time around.

Likewise, she knew that they got lucky when the knocked down segments of fence happened where no cattle fed. Barren with only long dry grass and sagebrush piercing through the snow, that pasture remained seldom used in the winter months. But had it been otherwise, cattle might have wandered onto the highway unsupervised, and nothing good could ever come of that.

Cattle escaping happened to them all, now and again.

In fact, people still moved their herds on that very same road to change pastures if their holdings were segmented.

Another tangible holdout from older times. Cars be damned and the cattle drive held sway.

When those drives happened, tourists would be clicking away, locals would simply turn around, and assholes would get all frustrated and mad, and not a damned thing that they could do about it.

That last part was fun.

6

VISITATIONS COME IN DIFFERENT FORMS

ASIDE FROM TENDING THE LIVESTOCK, THE MORNING drive into town took precedent over most anything else and her father would perform the brunt of the morning chores, giving Emory a clear shot to visit Iver early.

As figured, not many trucks or cars were on the road into town. The turnoff from Main Street to the hospital passed through a spartan neighborhood in the throes of waking. Oblivious to the turmoil at the Lost Daughter Ranch, no doubt toasters toasted, coffeepots filled, and the Denver news blared.

And people would watch the news askance at the crime unfolding in the large city one hundred miles away.

Emory's stomach knotted.

She eyed the empty parking lot and figured her truck would stand out like a sore thumb. Once again murmurs and unkind musings would circulate—one of the hazards of small-town living.

One of the hazards of history.

She claimed a spot on the side street, in front of the old birthing house.

A battered, white clapboard building, it didn't come across as sterile white as the snow. Its original purpose served the ranching women coming into town to give birth and recover without a myriad of chores pressing. No doubt the hospital still owned the property, but Emory didn't know what purpose it currently held. Nor did she care enough to spare more than a passing thought for it on that morning—other than to acknowledge in passing that like her father and grandmother before him, she'd been born in there, too.

Her grandfather, on the other hand, had entered the world during a snowy winter on a day in a year when it hadn't been possible to safely travel into town.

His mother died giving birth.

Things like that happened, too.

History aside, she hopped out onto the pathway edging between the parking lot and the hospital building. At that point, while her truck might have been inconspicuous, she sure wasn't as she walked right through the large sliding double doors at the entrance.

There weren't all that many people stirring enough to watch the comings and goings to the hospital, anyway.

Low down to the ground, the hospital had started out life as a one-story building. However, in yet another sign of the changing times, the building received a several-million-dollar makeover, and now boasted a soaring glass atrium-like addition. A far cry from the old, 1950s building she grew up with.

While the soaring atrium sure might have impressed, in reality it amounted to nothing more than high-priced window dressing.

Crashing back down to earth, she recognized a girl

she knew from high school. *Mandy Evans.* All grown-up and still disapproving and seated behind the reception desk.

"Where is Iver Holstead, please?" Emory made her voice as clear as a bell and pretended that she didn't recognize the young woman.

Never seen her before, in fact.

Mandy didn't buy any of it. "Heard he got shot up at your place, and don't you pretend that you don't recognize me, because I recognize you plenty well. Everyone does. Some things never change—at least not where your lot is concerned. Say, Cade Timmons came in with a gunshot crease to his foot a while back. What do you suppose happened to him?"

Warning bells jangling.

Emory shrugged, cold edging in around her stomach. "No idea. Didn't he say?"

"Didn't want to talk about it then, and still doesn't. But he felt good enough to ask me out," she smirked, watching for Emory's reaction, closely. Too close. "We are now an *official* item."

Relief at Cade's reticence quickly died down as icy cold fingers clenched around her heart. She stared at the receptionist as disinterested as she could make it.

"Uh-huh," she uttered, as if she didn't believe a thing in Mandy's words.

Deep down, Emory wanted to say something about the shooting—to explain how none of it had anything to do with them, as far as she understood. But caution always served well. The less said, the better.

Of course, her nature made it damned near impossible not to fire a parting shot. "Guess he did always like peroxide blondes, come to think of it. Just point me in Iver's direction, will you?"

"No visitors," Mandy snapped.

The hospital retained the same approximate footprint as ever, and Emory moved around the desk and headed down the hallway, the overhead fluorescent lights reflecting off the pale tiled floor.

She gave Mandy a look that dared her to chase her down.

Of course, she didn't.

Sure enough, as Emory turned the corner however, she heard Mandy's raised voice, tones urgent and pressing the situation upon the hospital security guard in no uncertain terms. Straight ahead, however, there stood a woman of greater interest—tired and dressed in work-worn jeans and a Western shirt. The woman leaned against the wall outside of a patient's room, eyes closed.

"Mrs. Holstead?" Emory asked, voice gentle and low.

Commotion behind her rising.

The woman's eyes opened. "Emory Cross, is that you?" She then peered down the hallway as Mandy and the security guard rushed around the corner.

"There she is!" Mandy pointed straight at Emory, the index finger and long arm accusing.

Mrs. Holstead frowned as Emory stiffened.

"I invited her here," Mrs. Holstead leaned toward Mandy, tone clipped and taking no guff. "Don't you have anything better to do with your time than chasing down visitors?"

"It's too early for visitors."

"We're ranch people," Mrs. Holstead snapped.

The security guard gave the receptionist the stink eye. "I thought you said she barged into a patient's room that couldn't have visitors." Wagging his head, he turned back to the two women.

"My apologies, ladies." He half bowed, before turning on his heel and disappearing back down the hallway. Muttering. Clearly muttering.

"You still here?" Mrs. Holstead asked Mandy, who acted like she had swallowed a lit can of Sterno.

And like a can of Sterno, the girl spluttered some more as the lid clamped down, and she threw up her hands.

"Never did like her," Mrs. Holstead noted, eyeing her backside as she scuttled away. "No one with an ounce of sense ever would." Then, the rancher brightened. "Look at you! All grown-up and pretty to boot. I heard you're making something of yourself. What is it again?"

"I'm a brand inspector," Emory smiled, standing a bit taller and straighter. "Over in Greeley. I came home taking a few vacation days before the stock show, and all of this happened..." Emory gestured, hands expressing the futility of finding adequate words for a situation none of them understood. "How is Mr. Holstead doing?"

A shadow passed over the woman's expression and her words were laced with worry. "He's weak but he'll pull through. He's tougher than he looks."

"Of course, he is. He had us more than just a little concerned. Mrs. Holstead, we don't know why your husband came to the Lost Daughter or what any of the shooting involved. I swear to you," she put her hand on her heart without thinking, "it wasn't us."

Emory dropped her hand when she noticed the gesture. That old distrust seeped between them, each having embedded knowledge of how history ran hard and divisive.

"I believe you, Emory." Her sharp eyes locked with Em's. "I hardly know what to think myself."

"How long do they figure he's going to be laid up?"

"Oh, knowing Iver and knowing the way hospital bills run, I'd say he'll be out sooner than later. We don't have insurance, and he can rest up at home."

Emory nodded. Precious few people held insurance in Stampede. Even if they did, chances were high that they didn't like loafing around, and that's how they viewed hospital stays. Unless they were serious. Plenty serious. Iver likely fell into that category, but wouldn't admit as much unless push came to shove.

"He mentioned something about money." Money tainted everything, at least in Emory's mind.

"Yes. Money," his wife said, deflating. "You seen the prices land is going for these days?"

"Sure have. Sky-high and then some."

Mrs. Holstead inclined her head in agreement. "That's what he wanted to see your father about. I don't know the details because he wouldn't tell me. It's not like him, keeping secrets."

The Holsteads were distant neighbors and Emory didn't know a thing about their marriage, either of them keeping secrets, or anything else personal to them for that matter. She only knew about the horse that sold cheap.

"He wanted to see my father about land prices? That's not something we could do anything about."

Mrs. Holstead brushed a strand of hair out of her eyes. "He wouldn't expect that."

Emory tired of the lack of information. "You don't suppose I could flat-out ask him, do you? You see, we are plenty bothered about the fact that Iver, I mean Mr. Holstead, got shot on our porch. I winged one guy and my father hit the other, but they both got away. Apparently, a third shooter waited on a snowmobile on the BLM land. We didn't understand what the fight was about, or why we were even fighting. Still don't, in fact."

Cocking her head, the older woman appeared a bit livelier at the mention of shooting the intruders.

"Iver wanted help," his wife said. "I'm glad you managed to hit them since they tried to kill my husband. Almost succeeded, too."

Emory shrugged again, eyes narrowing. "But why us? My father would have come down today himself, except for the fight about a horse or some such twenty years ago. Dad figured he might get tossed out, like what almost happened to me." Emory smirked to make light of what she could.

"Everyone likes you, Em."

"Mandy back there doesn't."

Mrs. Holstead pursed a smile. "That's just because she's jealous of you."

Those kind words hit a sore spot, and Em's voice lowered. "I don't know what she would have to be jealous about."

Cade went out with Mandy Evans.

Mrs. Holstead caught the tone but stayed kind enough not to pry. "Iver doesn't look so good, but sure. We can go in and ask him. Since he almost got killed over it, he might have changed his mind about keeping secrets. At least he's breathing on his own now. Come on."

Arm outstretched, Mrs. Holstead pushed the door open wide, and led the way into the hospital room. In truth, Iver, hooked up to various machines, didn't look all that great. His washed-out skin tone came across as a gray-tinged pallor—a pallor that had more than the fluorescent hospital light to blame.

"Look who's here, Iver. Emory Cross. She's come to see how you are doing."

"Hi, Mr. Holstead," Emory offered.

The man in the bed raised a hand, and let it fall back down, limp.

"You had us scared," Emory added, troubled by how weak the man appeared.

He moved his hand over to where he'd been shot, cut open, and then bandaged up again. Not as good as new. "Did you get 'em like Lance said?"

Her mind cast about, deciding whether she should offer the lie he obviously wanted, or to tell the truth.

"Not exactly. We winged the two near the house, but there was a third person on a snowmobile waiting out by the back gate. He came up through the BLM land." *Where Cade took off after her father winged him in the boot.*

Iver grunted.

"You know, we don't understand any of it," Emory prompted.

"I didn't mean to lead them to you, for that to happen."

"No. Of course not. Dad is puzzled why you came, however."

"Money laundering," he wheezed.

"You think we're doing that?" Emory didn't even try to keep the astonishment from her voice.

"Not you. I wanted to tell Lance what I found out."

Doubt must have shown in her eyes.

"Your father's a bastard, but he's our bastard," the old rancher wheezed. "Let the outsiders try locking horns with *him* and see how they come off."

At that moment, a nurse entered the room and judging by her decisive bearing, it appeared that Mandy had gotten to her and given her an earful. "I think that's enough visiting for one day," the nurse announced.

Her stiff posture indicated that she expected Emory to leave, and to leave immediately.

"But who are they?" Emory pressed Iver, ignoring the woman.

The nurse inserted herself between Emory and the man in the bed, herding her toward the door with the skill and determination of a good cattle dog.

Emory shot Mrs. Holstead a pleading glance, and received a slight, understanding nod in return.

Half escorted, half pushed out, Emory found herself in the hallway, looking in. Mrs. Holstead claimed the visitor's chair where she sat on the edge of the seat and clasped her husband's limp hand.

The door shut in Emory's face, stranding her out in the hallway.

She stood there for a second, staring at the wooden door's laminated surface.

"This is stupid," she muttered under her breath, but whether she referred to herself or the situation, she did not know.

Having little choice in the matter, Emory walked back out of Iver's hospital wing, down the hallway, bracing herself as she prepared to pass the reception desk. No doubt Mandy would have some snark-ass comment to share.

But as luck would have it, Mandy's peroxide blonde head bent over paperwork, displaying her natural dark roots for all the world to see. Occupied with signing a patient in, her immediate task didn't preclude her from glaring daggers over at Emory. If people hadn't been present, an argument could easily have sparked.

As it so happened, Emory took those long-legged

strides right out of the hospital, left Mandy to her woes, climbed into her grandfather's truck, and drove back in the direction of the ranch. The basic problem still remained. Emory did not know a hell of a lot more than she had when she first ventured out that same morning.

Ignorance couldn't be considered a blessing. Not when guns were fired, and blood spilled.

Not when the fight landed on the Lost Daughter Ranch, and none of them had the slightest idea why.

It always helped to have a reason, and a good one, when fighting a war.

7

STAMPEDE'S BAR FLIES

THE ACE HIGH.

The watering hole of choice presented an entire topic based on its merit (or lack thereof). The only bar in town, the other choice was to drive thirty miles to drink in the liquor store's parking spaces. No matter personal preferences or opinions, everyone pretty much agreed that the Ace housed a world unto itself.

Probably the less said the better but it remained standing and an institution of a sort in Stampede. A well-traveled and sagging false front on the Main Street whether people liked it or not. Some figured the entire town might die away if the singular bar of note uprooted or died, but Emory had her doubts on that score. Some other place would open up, if it wasn't in the process already.

Fancy people ought to like fancy places, but that didn't always stop them from slumming around.

Regardless of the pros and cons, the Ace High served a valid purpose, and she planned on availing herself of that purpose that very same evening. The thought of travelling into the Ace High always set her nerves to jangling with anticipation. Anticipation of what, precisely, remained elusive, but possibilities abounded. Odds were, she'd know more when she left that establishment than she would have upon entering.

Of course, the information might come across garbled.

The problem would boil down to *discernment*. Another one of those fancy words that people didn't often use in the ranching district.

Steering into the ranch yard and avoiding a few potholes, she parked and killed the engine just as her father emerged from the barn, lugging a hay bale with two hay hooks.

"Saw Iver," she called across.

Her father set the bale down and detached the hooks, decisive. "And?"

"Looks like he's going to make it. Told me he's worried about money laundering, of all things. Guess outsiders are scaring the locals, and 'they' want you to deal with them."

Lance Cross took off his leather work gloves, lined the tips of the fingers up before folding them over and sticking them into his back pocket. He quirked his mouth, shook his head, and didn't say a damned thing for a long moment. A very long moment.

"What outsiders?" His tone was caught somewhere between curiosity and disgust.

"Not sure," she replied, feeling a bit sheepish. She ought to have asked but hadn't thought to. "Any and all strangers are suspect, I'd guess. Especially the ones with money."

Her father snorted. "Figures. And I don't even need to ask who 'they' are."

She half shrugged. "Iver said something along the lines that you're considered a bastard, but 'their' bastard, for what it's worth."

"I don't know a damn thing about money laundering, and I ain't sure I want to find out."

More silence. The code of the West remained alive and well and living in Rimrock County.

Emory, being his daughter, knew how to jostle him into a response. "Maybe I forgot to tell you that someone knows the lay of this ranch. They came in along the old wagon track, but you could've seen that yourself."

"I have," he replied.

Accusations weren't a thing to toss about for the hell of it, but silence didn't always get the point across, no matter how accustomed everyone might be to unspoken gestures. "Now who do we know that would know about that wagon track?"

"I already thought about Cade," her father said with a disgusted, dry laugh. "But that's an accusation that would need backing up. Anyhow, I knew I should've kneecapped him when I had the chance. On principle, if nothing else."

"*Dad*."

"Emory."

They locked eyes.

Something in his expression said that he knew how it was with her—how she still harbored a tender spot for the errant ranch hand.

Not that he approved of Cade Timmons one whit. "Seems to me a whole lot of problems could have been avoided if I gave him a serious thrashing."

"You shot him in the *foot*," she eyed him. "Which Mandy Evans knows about, for your reference. She works at the reception desk in the hospital."

That piece of barbed information grabbed his attention, all right, yet he stayed silent.

Emory toed the mud underfoot. "Cade never told her how it happened, and I guess he's remaining close-lipped because she doesn't know despite her boasting of their romantic entanglement. Anyhow, I'm going into town tonight to see what I can learn. Maybe *you* should go try to see Iver tomorrow."

"That's the plan. Maybe I should—and get a few things straight while I'm at it. Want to go get that fence put back up the right way?"

"Might as well," she replied. "But like I said, I'm off at five. Six at the latest."

"For what?"

"Like I just told you. To hear what's being said in town."

A grunt from Lance said he wasn't quite buying what she was selling, but he let it go.

Cade's contraband, however, remained an open issue in Emory's mind at least. "What did you do with the drugs Cade tried to toss away?"

Her father didn't answer. Just stared into her eyes with his as cold as the mountain granite.

"The reason I'm asking," Emory sighed and continued, "is it's best to know whether you turned them in, destroyed them, or kept them."

"Don't want you to be an accessory, Em. That's the type of shit you could lose your job over."

Although he was likely right, her being an accessory didn't change the situation all that much. She knew her father well enough to be nigh on certain that he kept the drugs. Turning them over to the law would have been a bit too close to act the part of an informant or snitch for his comfort.

But having drugs in their possession wasn't good.

On the other hand, that illicit baggy might come in use for blackmail, if nothing else. That said, reasons for threatening Cade needed to remain strategic.

Then again, she could rile him up for the sheer hell of it.

———

THAT EVENING, wires pulled, and fences shored up, Emory's arms ached and her back felt the strain. Setting fences proved a different type of physical labor from regular ranching altogether.

Nevertheless, and plan in place, she wasn't about to let aching muscles change her decision one whit.

"Want a ham sandwich?" she called from the kitchen as her father lowered himself down into his recliner.

"Whatever happened to staying home to make your old man a dinner?"

"Wrong daughter," she called back. "Now, do you want a sandwich or not?"

"I'll take it," he replied. "Don't go getting drunk at the Ace."

"Didn't plan on it, Dad."

"Always drink bottled beer. That way no one can slip anything into your drink."

"You've been watching too many true crime shows," she countered. "This is Stampede."

It sure as hell was. And the look he gave her told her what she already knew—*Stampede was changing*.

She choked down her hasty sandwich, leaning against the doorframe watching the flickering TV as the evening news blared. Her father listened to the discourse as he chewed in an absent way.

The Lost Daughter might not look much better than it did one year ago, but things had turned around. Her father ran the operations with an interest, now that he no longer drank like the saloon might run dry.

Emory ruffled his hair as she passed. Too tired to protest, he patted his hair back into place.

Through the living room, and up the narrow stairs, she stopped first in the bathroom to get ready. Checking her reflection in the mirror—her hazel eyes sparking at the prospect of going out...no matter that the evening contained the clear potential to turn south. She'd be ready if words—or more—broke out.

But *girl stuff* first.

On went the blush, then eyeliner, mascara, and a final coat of lip gloss. She sprang into her bedroom and pulled on a figure-hugging black shirt, and knew she looked good. The mirror didn't lie, but good lighting never went amiss either.

She grinned. That good lighting definitely included flashing neon bar signs.

As she bounced down the stairs, her father glanced over in her direction with a cocked eyebrow.

"You go to all that trouble for Cade?"

"Nope. You never know who you might meet..."

"In the Ace High."

"In the Ace High. Now, I shouldn't be gone long... think everything will be OK here?"

"That I do," her father stretched out a bit. "Whatever you do, if and when you see Cade, don't fall for any of his bullshit. And don't, *don't* apologize for him getting shot. He had it coming."

He clicked on the remote, and the TV changed channels to reruns of pro bull riding. "Is your phone charged?"

"Yes, Dad. It is." She crinkled her nose.

"Your rifle loaded?"

"Of course, but it's in the truck. And so's my .45. It'll be in the glove compartment just in case."

"Good girl," he replied, "but stick it in your handbag instead."

"Hell, why don't I just strap on a holster instead?"

"That's a fine idea," he drawled. Knowing full damn well no tourist would approach a woman wearing a weapon. The locals, on the other hand, were a bit more of an iffy proposition and she grinned.

Either way, *good* girls didn't go around armed in bars, did they?

SHE DROVE in silence away from the ranch, noting the stars in the deep-blue night sky, creating a blue-hued world below. The cold winter night felt quiet and chillingly beautiful, but darkness could hide terror. Nights, while beautiful, concealed threats.

Emory kept the radio silent as she drove through the deepest of shadows. The rugged landscape could hide danger without a second thought and she scanned the darkened land more so than her usual custom, searching for anything out of place or that might be construed as a warning. In truth, the night fell the same as countless others as she passed beneath the skull, the bone glowing faintly in the light of the clear full moon.

That dang steer skull came across more menacing at night than in the light of day, which must have all been a part of her father's original plan all along.

A stab of pride accompanied that thought.

However, it would take more than a steer skull to scare this newest lot away.

Her father almost certainly knew that part as well.

STAMPEDE'S SIDEWALKS were all but rolled up when she rumbled into the town of scant streetlights. The stores had closed for the night. Their windows' dark, empty eyes overseeing the lack of traffic on the street—seeing precious little of note. And just like every other two-track town, the neon lights switched on when the sun declined, and Stampede proved a card-carrying member of that club. The highway morphed into Main Street once the buildings started populating, and the Ace High's sign beckoned at the end of the line like hell itself. Boasting gaudy neon tubes of lime green and flamingo pink, it got its point across.

The evening hours were when the whiskey really started flowing and the music cranked up.

She parked the truck, hopped out, and headed in like the other stragglers and layabouts. Slipping inside of the door, the interior smelled about the same as she recalled —a stench of stale cigarettes and beer spills despite the all-encompassing Colorado smoking ban. Underfoot a demoralized reddish shag lay beaten down and dirty. She doubted the carpet ever had a true cleaning, and she sure as hell didn't want to dwell too long upon that notion.

Like the Lost Daughter had a whole lot to talk about.

An older man she did not know worked behind the bar.

"Coors Light, please."

"Can I see your ID?"

Unaccustomed to carrying a purse, her movements

were clumsy and unpracticed as she removed the strap from her shoulder, set the bag on the counter, and struggled with the zipper.

Emory moved aside the gun to get to her wallet.

She glanced up at the man and saw where his glance landed. He saw the gun alright, although he pretended that he didn't. Maybe he also caught sight of her brand inspector's badge in there also, but she wasn't about to ask if he'd got a good enough glimpse.

For his part, he turned away ever so slightly, and pretended like he saw nothing out of the ordinary. Nothing at all.

Her brand inspector's badge wouldn't offer all that much protection if she shot someone inside of a bar, but there was no need to go advertising the fact.

She pulled out her wallet and handed the driver's license over.

"You from the Lost Daughter?" the man asked, calm as he read the details.

"Yep. I'm one of *those* Crosses."

She waited to see what he would say next—a comment offered about the gun, her badge, or anything else carried in her purse or bloodline. Her rifling through her purse would provide an easy opening for him to make a crack had word traveled about the ambush and the shooting.

"Draft or bottle?"

"Bottle, please."

He slid open one of the cooler doors and selected out a beer.

"That's four dollars," he said. "Want a glass?"

She shook her head 'no' as she pulled out a five. "Keep the change."

"Why, thank you," he replied, making change and

putting the dollar into the tip jar. "That's a pretty old spread your people have."

"Do you know my father, Lance Cross?"

"Of him, by reputation," the man replied—a steady glance pointedly offered nothing further.

"What happened to Jeff?"

"My nephew? He succumbed to the bright lights of Denver of all things. Seeing as how he ain't the brightest bulb even in this patch, the big city'll chew him up and spit him out in no time, I reckon. But that's his problem, and not mine."

Emory flashed a smile she didn't feel and took the beer by the neck and found herself an empty table where she could sit and wait. She nodded brief acknowledgments at the few people she knew in passing, but the crowd that hung around bars weren't her type of people for the most part, and never had been either.

With no one to talk to, she watched the door like an old gunslinger who thought retribution neared. Drinking her *bottled* beer and listening to the music and the pool balls clacking at the rear of the building, she wondered how on earth it was possible that, in a town that size, she could feel so very much alone.

An outsider, even.

The clock on the wall read 8:25 p.m.

At 8:43 p.m., the front door opened, and three men arrived in a gust, entering in as a pack of wide shoulders and cowboy hats. Joking and jostling for attention and roughhousing for fun, they breathed a sense of life and possibility into the bar. Like a magnet, Emory found Cade with no trouble at all. Too damned good-looking, and every inch the bad boy. He hadn't seen her at all, but she sure as hell saw him. There he shone in his full glory, standing among a passel of rowdy young men ordering drinks—beers chased by shots of whatever to get down to business and to kick-start the night that much faster.

Drink orders in, the men started sizing up their prospects. One of the three that she didn't recognize let his gaze fall upon her. He smiled wide—an even, white-toothed grin—and turned his back to the bar to face her square. Cade followed his eyes to see what held his attention, or more precisely who he had in his sights. His gaze landed square upon her.

"Oh shit," he said.

"What?" the other *cowboy* asked.

Cade didn't even bother to answer, but stomped over to her table, beer in hand and limping slightly.

"You're back, I see," he said, kicking out the chair like in an old Western movie, and sitting down without invitation.

"How's your foot?" she asked.

"It hurts when the weather's cold," he snarked.

"That was your own damned fault."

Cade laughed without mirth. "You lot are lucky I didn't press charges."

"Doubtful," she countered, warming to the task. "You pressing charges would have meant that you'd have been forced to explain what you were doing out on our property in the first place."

"So?"

"We turned those drugs of yours in to the sheriff."

Cade went bug-eyed at the notion and spluttered. "He never talked to me about it…"

Emory shrugged as unconcerned as she could make it. She did, however, allow herself a crocodile smile. "I guess that means you owe us a favor."

The music swelled, growing louder at that point, as the conversation between them dried up and shriveled.

Cade stretched out acting unconcerned, but it all amounted to just that. An act. Nothing could be further from the truth.

Emory would have waited him out, but she wasn't in the mood. "Who are those fellows you came in with?"

Cade glanced back over his shoulder at them. The flirting one cut his losses and cast around for another target but the pickings, so far, proved slim.

He didn't answer.

"They don't look right," she added, jerking her chin in their direction.

"Not right?" Cade echoed, but he knew what she meant.

"Not right." She eyed him. "Who are they?"

"Want their social security numbers? Guys from the ranch. Guests. What's it to you, anyhow? If you liked the one, all you had to do was smile. Sheesh."

"I'm curious what they want in here. The Ace High is kind of down-market for them, isn't it?"

Cade sneered. "It serves its purpose—if what they want is to get laid."

Emory leaned back in her chair and folded her arms and looked down from the great height of moral superiority.

"Your foot's giving you some trouble you said?"

He acted as if he found the question funny, but he retained enough sense to be troubled deeper down. "A chunk's missing, if that's what you're asking."

"You do know that he intended to shoot further up, don't you? I stopped him from doing that."

Cade blanched a bit around the edges. Shifted in his seat and sat forward, fingers laced and wrapped around his beer bottle.

"Forget the dudes," he hissed. "Why are you in here?"

"Town?"

"Or the Ace High. This ain't no casual social call."

"No," she admitted. "No, it ain't. You hear of the trouble at our place?"

Cade stiffened, wary about the eyes. "I heard that Iver's laid up. You know as well as anyone that word travels. What happened?"

Emory shrugged, prepared to stand up. "He got shot, that's what happened. I also heard that you're seeing Mandy Evans. She told me herself."

"What of it, Em? It ain't nothing serious."

"According to you."

He sniffed. "Iver got shot at your place. Seems to come with the territory, doesn't it? Still, you know I would never do anything to hurt you, don't you Em?"

Again, that damnable tug although his words were nothing more than lies.

Still, she wanted to believe him all the same.

"Maybe," she conceded, right before she decided to pour salt in an open wound. "How's Dirge?"

Cade flinched. Almost imperceptible, but the mention of his cousin bothered him. "Last I heard, he's fine."

Halfway toward flattered, she decided to rub it in. "Now there's a man that can shoot," she praised. "Apparently none of the happenings the other night concerns you then. And keep it that way, Cade."

She pretended an afterthought. "Say, what *is* this latest influx of newcomers anyhow?"

For that, Cade checked over his shoulder. "Don't know the particulars, but they've got a lot of money to throw around."

"You met any of them personally?"

"Seen a few and heard some mutterings. Nothing

concrete. Real estate from what I hear." Cade slapped the Formica tabletop, all false hearty as he stood. Voice carrying in case anyone cared to listen. "Nice to see you, Em, and it's been good catching up. I'm going to rejoin my buddies at the bar."

He turned and walked away, leaving her sitting there. Alone under a buzzing neon Coors sign making it hard for a dignified exit.

The good news, as she saw it, was that she *almost* no longer cared. Time away had cured her of that much.

Appearances, surface and deeper in, were often deceptive. At the moment, it appeared as if she lacked friends of her own while Cade boasted a full posse. And sometimes the truth hurt. She truly didn't have many friends of her own.

Well, hell.

Let them eat dirt, and let Cade go first.

8

GHOSTS THAT RATTLE

THE MORNING LIGHT STOLE GENTLY ACROSS HER BARE windowpane after a restless night. As always, the case on working ranches, plenty of chores awaited.

Out of habit, she seldom pulled down the shade at night, preferring to gaze at the stars above. Those uncovered windows allowed the morning light to stream in—a natural alarm clock in the best sense. However, winter mornings started in darkness, and their workdays ended in darkness as well. Considering the shooting, only idiots would leave their windows uncovered, making easy targets of themselves.

As a precaution, she and her father drew the blinds and didn't pass in front of backlit windows.

That dark, winter morning Emory sat up, stretched, and planted her feet square on the floor. Without turning on a light, she opened her curtains, standing to the side. The cliffs were shadowed outlines beyond. Come rising light, she knew the contrast between the glorious snow-covered view and the dingy interior of their house couldn't be more pronounced. When warmer weather rolled around, she might attend to the grimed walls that needed a lick of paint and more than a few prayers. But that morning, as the subtle hues of a rosy dawn rested like a low reef against the horizon, she knew the promised sun would rise, and the morning's denim darkness would brighten into a searing blue.

All it took were the passing hours to progress and the sun to soar.

Accustomed to the layout—for nothing ever changed—Emory didn't flick on the hall light before venturing down the narrow hallway, the discolored and naked walls softened in the early morning darkness—a darkness almost comforting as a mere shade or two lighter than the interior gloom. The window on the eastern end of the hallway boasted no coverings, but that didn't pose a real problem. She glanced at the darkened glass in need of a garden hose washing to dislodge the lingering spiderwebs spun in the corners.

Bare feet on a bare wooden floor, Emory counted on luck to dodge splinters in the thin slatted yellow pine. The bathroom waited at the western end of the hall and needed renovation. Maybe she would have time to replace the rust-colored linoleum while she "vacationed" at home—this time she would make sure that the purchase covered the entirety of the floor's surface. Whoever laid the last round of flooring sure had done a piss-poor job of it, probably using remnants that cost next to nothing, picked up somewhere along the line.

Those gap-tooth edges along walls bothered her, as they would any normal person with two eyes in their head. Just another half-assed attempt at the Lost Daughter Ranch. Well, times were a-changing.

Wetting her face and grabbing the hand soap in the pedestal sink's depression, the weight of the ranch hung over her. Bringing a new ranch hand into a range war brewing felt like a tall order. An unfair order. Still, it remained a demand that needed answering.

She met her eyes in the mirror.

Thicker in build than was fashionable, she might as well wish for a boyfriend while she stood there longing for any number of things.

If wishes were horses, she'd have a whole herd...

THE COFFEEPOT WAITED NEAR enough to full when she walked into the kitchen, her father already with a cup in hand.

"I thought about waiting up for you last night, but your young-person's hours are killing me," he deadpanned.

She shook her head, pouring. "You used to stay up plenty late."

"That was then, this is now." He eyed her, shrewd. "You got somethin' you want to say?"

Emory blew on the liquid, stalling. Gathering. "As expected, Cade turned up. I told him he owed us a favor for not ratting him out about the drugs he tried to ditch."

A nerve throbbed in her father's jaw, but he said nothing.

It wasn't the time to play coy. "Anyhow, I asked him about the new crop of strangers in town. He said he's heard that they have money. Sounded like more of the same to me, but this time with an undertone. I don't rightly know. Anyhow, he didn't act like he knew what happened out here, but I still don't think we should trust him."

A brief shrug. "Are you OK to get things started out here on your own this morning?"

"Sure. Going to try to see Iver?"

He nodded.

"Visiting hours don't start until nine o'clock."

"Yep. That's why I'm fixing to go early. To at least try to get him alone before people butt in."

Emory's mind struck out elsewhere. "Dad, remember how you said that you found a biker messing around with Cade's truck and you scared him off a while back?"

"Yeah."

"You don't suppose that had anything to do with this, do you?"

Her father clicked like she was a horse he wanted to get moving. "Hadn't thought of that one."

"Maybe it's all tied together, and we just don't know."

Her father's concerned eyes still twinkled back at her. "I always said you was a smart girl, Em. Guess I don't tell you often enough that I'm proud of you."

"That's because you're a crusty old bastard," she replied, giving him the rare hug.

He found that funny. "Maybe so," he said into her hair.

He wrapped his arms around her and gave her a quick squeeze. They both stared at the ranch beyond the kitchen window.

"Whatever this is," Emory said, "we have to win."

"Goes without saying," Lance Cross replied.

If ever an opportunity presented to get both of them with one shot, that was the moment. Inwardly flinching, Emory still didn't move away.

HER FATHER DROVE off through the muck and the mud, leaving her to consider the retreating tailgate of the truck before turning back to the tasks at hand.

Rushing more than usual.

She strapped on a holster and a .45. thinking how she preferred a rifle, and how a rifle would be the better choice for shooting at a distance. The problem with them were that their length got in the way of her chores.

In the end, practicality won out and she settled for the .45.

But if she watched her father drive off, so could others. Others who waited for such an event to occur.

That knowledge didn't spook her, but it did demand a certain measure of caution. That caution played against what she wanted to do. She wanted to take advantage of being alone to explore the outbuildings and to visit the family cemetery. The whispers from the past provided a rising and incessant pull. While that pull might be a flight of fancy on her part, there was no guarantee that was the case. Every Cross retained a healthy regard for those Crosses who came before. It felt prudent, given their history.

Still, she harbored a mild embarrassment about such notions. Her father would know what she was doing if he caught her at it. Mooning about, he would call it. But since he was away in town, his absence offered a clear chance to investigate the Lost Daughter as she saw fit… and consult with any whispering ghosts she felt along the way.

Emory rushed to complete the most immediate of tasks, and skipping over some, promised herself that she would return when time allowed.

Kai whinnied across the pasture, watching her as she lugged the hose over to the water tank to fill.

He ambled up near her to supervise.

"Hi, Kai-Kai. I'll ride you later, once I get everything done."

He stared at her and she patted his nose, as he flared his nostrils and blew.

Clouds blew up from behind the mountains, hundreds and hundreds of feet high in a cold front rising, building. The sky grayed as the wind strengthened and pressed down while the outbuildings groaned and rattled. Despite the cold wind, Emory decided the first point of business meant visiting the ranch's old burial ground. Located atop a swell beyond sight from the current ranch house, the plots offered final resting places overlooking the western facing segment of the spread below. The Cross family graveyard had never been an easy walk for more reasons than one, but especially not in the snow. The path climbed, steep and treacherous, and Emory slipped uphill as she walked, but she kept on. Family lore held that in the beginning, those first corpses were carried draped across a horse's back.

The harsh image alluded to outlaw funerals. Maybe all of them would always be considered outlaws, of one variety or another.

In later years, if caskets were used (a notable *if*), the deceased would travel to their final resting place via wagon. The consideration of who merited coffins and who did not would never be solved…unless those historic preservation people had their way and dug up the lot of them.

An archaeological dig, they would call it, but it all amounted to the same thing.

Everyone, it seemed, wanted to know who was buried on the Lost Daughter, but the ranch never did give up its secrets easily. Not even to her.

She navigated the snowy ruts to the plot of land that held what remnants, whole or partial, could be gathered of their deceased. Undoubtedly, not all of those graves held complete corpses. *Appendages* would be missing. With a wry smile at the notion, appendages was just another one of *those words* harkening back to her school days. School days when she didn't fit in, tall and lanky and carrying a family history that always produced raised eyebrows. She spent most of her free time in the library opposed to out in the school yard.

Either whole or partial corpses, the graveyard claimed the same plot of land her father intentionally mortgaged to cover the underreported cattle fines.

As she rounded the forlorn rise, seeing the white snow pierced by dried grasses poking through drove a home truth into her marrow.

Each and every grave marked a person who had died defending the ranch in one way or another. Even if those graves held the bodies of those who succumbed to old age, they had fought plenty of fights in their lifetimes, one way or another.

She and her father were nothing more than modern links continuing along a lengthy, ongoing struggle. To *quit* meant to lose the ranch. To *die* usually meant that the ranch might live. One known trademark of the Crosses held that they never shied away from a fight.

Normally, they picked the fights, as a matter of fact. But this time, the fight had been brought to them and it didn't sit well. Emory wondered how many in those graves might say the exact same thing and felt pretty sure of the answer.

All of them. Every last one.

To cover any eventuality, one empty grave was dug

each fall, right before the winter when the ground would freeze. It waited, wide open.

She glanced at it, knowing the reasons. As she knew the reasons for the firepit rings with large stones.

"You called to me and I'm here," she said to the graves or to the ranch. It didn't much matter as long as her words got across.

Every burial plot faced west toward the proverbial setting sun. Deep down, the course of the sun made no difference to those interred, one way or another but they overlooked the valley and ranch, spreading to the mountains beyond. Older wooden boards from the 1880s stood shoulder to shoulder alongside faded marble from the turn of the last century. The early years transitioned into markers hewn from solid granite, marking the most recent departures. Of course, like the Crosses themselves, there were peculiarities from the onset. The earliest graves, the wooden boards that listed and weathered from years of exposure to the elements, held vague imprints of names and dates, fading from sight and returning to the earth.

The most important graves were considered those of Hank Cross and that of his first wife, Polly. Those wooden markers were once branded by Lost Daughter branding irons. Every so often those marks would be rebranded into the fading wood. That sign of ownership grew faint, which meant there hadn't been any deaths in a good long while. Not since her grandmother passed on.

The next time someone died, the old brands would get rebranded.

That would be either her or her father.

The long reach of history pressed down.

Hank's second wife, Idella, fared a bit better as far as

monuments were concerned. Her final resting place boasted a small marble headstone, and this time the Lost Daughter brand faced an improvement, chiseled into the soft stone.

The weather deteriorated it just the same.

A scattering of large rocks here and there marked infants who perished, and ranch hands who spent their lives alongside the family.

The Hapless Susan, the Lost Daughter's namesake, well, she had no grave at all.

The modern graves retained legible information, like that of her grandmother, Verna, the sage of the refrigerator advice. Her husband, Charles Cross, a son of a bitch by all accounts, read crystal clear and menacing.

And they all carried the brand in one form or another.

Drawn to Idella's grave, Emory stood in front of it for a long while trying to catch the sense of the woman.

"You know my middle name is after you," she said aloud, but the wind caught her words and blew them away before swallowing them whole.

She addressed the entire graveyard, raising her voice so that it would carry. "Where are the other bodies buried out there? Who were they and why?"

At this question, while the wind circled and blew, her words caught and lingered. Invisible but heard. Definitely heard.

Those bodies in the ground knew where the skeletons were buried. Each and every last one. *And why. They had to know the whys.*

She returned back over to Idella's marker. "I thought a man used your house for cover, shooting against us. Your own flesh and blood."

Emory's blood quickened, and she felt the shift. The

shift that brought electric-like current into the air and made the hair on her arms rise.

"I thought all of you ought to know," she finished, heading back to the path as she caught the sound of her father's truck approaching.

She cast a glance back at the graves. "I'll see you later," she said.

But no answer came. They were thinking about it. She'd bet her last dollar on that one.

HER FATHER WHISTLED THAT CLEAR, air-splitting call. She offered her own cutting whistle in return—the signal that she heard and was in the process of heading back to the ranch house without problem.

She rounded the bend and skidded in the snow. Her father wore a bemused expression at her approach.

"Where were you?"

"Up at the cemetery," Emory felt a tightening around her stomach.

A short, clipped laugh. "Did they say anything?"

"No," she answered with a measured caution, "they did not."

Her father lightened up a degree. "The dead don't have to do a damned thing, you know, but I go up there sometimes, too. Now, I did manage to get in to see Iver briefly. He sure don't look good."

"What did he say?"

Her father pulled off his cowboy hat, ran fingers through his silver-streaked dark hair, before clamping his hat back down. He gave a brief shrug, bothered. Silent.

Emory knew better than to interrupt the spinning in his brain.

Lance Cross inhaled.

"He thinks that fight has come to town. A fight between the old guard and those coming in with pockets full of cash. He claims that some of these expensive properties are being paid for with dirty money."

Emory frowned and shook her head at the madness of it all. "The same as I told you. Why should we care? Seems to me that we've never questioned too closely in this valley where a person's money came *from*, exactly."

"Couldn't agree more, and Iver's always been a bit of a stickler that way. But they brought the fight to us. We didn't bring it to them. Just as he got to the good part, the part that was going to sell me on whatever notion he's holding, his wife walked in. I mean, what is the point of having visiting hours if they don't get enforced?"

"Dad..."

"I mean, I *snuck* in damned near like a rustler. Waiting outside, pretending to be waiting for *someone*, until that front desk stood unattended. Then I stole right on in, walking as quiet as I could. Them lot keeps banker's hours."

"They save lives," Emory countered.

"That may be, but they sure don't watch real well."

Her father had missed an opportunity and he didn't see it. But she did. She saw it clear.

"You know, you could have spoken in front of Mrs. Holstead."

Her father shrugged the notion away. "I got the notion Iver wasn't too keen on that idea."

Emory scanned the horizon, then turned back her father to make her point. "I don't know why that would be. They've been married a good long while. How many secrets could they have?"

Her father snorted. "That shows what you know."

The wind blew down, and she had no intention of pursuing that line of conversation that would get them nowhere useful.

"What do you know about the scattered buried bodies?"

That caught him, and that old caution crept in along the edges. "What do you mean?"

"You know, the burials out on the range. The unmarked, shallow ones."

Quirking his mouth, she could see that he wondered why she asked.

"Hard to say," he said at length. "They're out there. I think I know where a couple are, but I don't think I could locate them under the snow. Why?"

"Just thinking. Wondering."

Lance stuck his hands in his back pockets, willing to go along although uncertain as to the meaning of the conversation. "Story has it they branded the corpses before they got shoved in. I guess with the earliest ones, they just left them to rot in the weather. Those ones they most certainly branded."

She'd never heard any of that before. "Why bother to brand them—what could have been the point?"

"Marking territory, I guess. Those would be the strangers or the bandits. The ones that *lost*. Family and hands are all up in our plot."

"The one you mortgaged."

"One and the same." His eyes sparked laughter, crow's feet pronounced as he squinted in the bright light and snow. "I think I'm going to go talk to Evan Wright."

"Who?"

"The banker."

That gave reason for concern, right there. "You *have* been making those payments, haven't you?"

Another smirk. "I have indeed. The money from those two calves you branded. Just because you didn't want the proceeds, don't mean it can't be put to good use. Besides, I don't particularly feel like getting haunted by them lot. I wanna hear what he knows about all these sales. What he's got to say."

"I thought we didn't talk about those calves."

"Oh, lighten up. It ain't nothing that hasn't been done before."

Still, Emory stiffened. Ever since she turned brand inspector, it rubbed against her grain.

"And what is it that you think the banker is going to tell you?"

"The general outlook on borrowing against the land," he crooned. "If he's not forthcoming, I might just sit down and make myself at home across that fancy desk of his."

Enough said.

"Before you go parking your butt in someone's office, why don't you call Sheriff Preston to see if he's figured anything out?"

The wheels in Lance's mind turned. "You mean act like a concerned citizen?"

"Precisely," Emory replied. "Why don't you—right now."

"Pushy," he chided. Still, he withdrew his phone and scrolled through his saved contacts. Curious, right there.

He lifted the cell to his ear and waited.

"This is Lance Cross. Have you learned anything about the shooting that took place here?"

Silence as Lance listened.

"Well, we've done some checking ourselves."

More silence. Judging from her father's expression, he held onto the receiving end of a lecture.

"No." The single word came out short. "Listen. Do you know who these people are that are buying the high-priced ranches?"

More listening.

"I'm aware." He drew Emory into the near one-way conversation. "They're all high-priced," Lance Cross insisted. "I'm just saying that you might want to check out who's buying them. Rumor has it their money ain't clean, but shootouts bring it to a whole new level."

Or maybe an Old West level.

Emory shifted her stance. Some questions provoked old wounds and memories. Her father knew that as well as she did. Maybe even better.

History could be a hard thing to outrun, especially when all was said and done.

9

SEXY SENIOR CITIZENS

THE STOCK SHOW LOOMED LARGE, AND IN THREE DAYS' time Emory would be required to report to work, shooting or no shooting. Her father hightailed it back into town to torment the banker as threatened, and she readily took advantage of his absence.

More than anything else, she wanted to listen to the voices of the past. Of course, those ghosts and voices just might not cooperate. The Cross family had always been peculiar in that way, no matter whether living or dead.

Let 'em figure it out for themselves.

Unless the ranch itself was at stake.

One thing for certain on that mild winter morning, she took an enigmatic type of historical inventory however she, or anyone else, cared to frame the task. The graves, already visited and viewed, still urged and pressed in the back of her mind. The notion gripped that an accurate accounting of the buildings rose to the top of importance as she surveyed the past—what purposes they fulfilled, and how old they were. It remained unclear why that specific task demanded completion, although chances pointed in the direction that it concerned learning lessons from their past. The unspoken urgency could not, in good conscience, be ignored—not when the ranch tried to tell her something of note.

She needed time and space to listen to the undercurrent.

Knocking down old buildings for fear of someone using them for cover didn't exactly strike as a good option.

Fighting, on the other hand, did.

But the ghosts stayed silent on the how, why, and where of it all, as she suspected they might. Those whispers and voices would wait, biding their time. Until she proved herself to them.

When their messages formed enough to be interpreted with a degree of success.

Regardless, there were measures she and her father could take right now, first and foremost, she needed to get the patriarch to concentrate upon general upkeep. Together they could make needed determinations, but certainly they could do away with items such as old, rusted box springs and coils of barbed wire too far gone to ever be of use again.

Emory wondered what that Paulson woman would have to say about any cleanup and figured that she wouldn't like it. Not if it wasn't her own idea.

But that was too damned bad. Their heritage and their trash belonged to them to do with as they chose. Not to the Paulson woman, nor to any of the others.

Pointedly aware that she'd lost her job as chief cattle accountant on the Lost Daughter, she could act the part of the family building inspector instead.

She would use her own reckoning, thank you very

much, instead of relying upon that Paulson woman and her band of roving historical preservationists. Being a Cross, she knew better than most that there were two versions of history and two sets of accounting. One for themselves and the other for outsiders.

This time around, she figured she'd do the insider type of tallying.

Crunching through the snow, wearing a beat-up sweater and an open vest, the sun felt warm on her face, and her blood coursed strong as she began her strangely obscure undertaking. Rifle in hand, Emory stood in the center of the ranch yard and surveyed the outcroppings of land and buildings. Corrals and loading chutes aplenty, all sagged in varying states of disrepair and decomposition. The round holding pen near the house held together solid and usable, as did the working corral over by the barn. Hank Cross's primitive cabin hunkered down as a rough relic of the early days. Located in close proximity to their "modern" house, which wasn't all that modern when push came to shove, it served as the ranch office for years.

The sound of two pitched keerings of hawks gliding overhead drew her attention upwards, into the wide-open sky.

A hunting pair of redtails; she tried to recall what her book about Native American beliefs said about the raptors. Strong energy, the raptors saw everything on the ground below, including her admiring their graceful flight.

Hawks signaled otherworldly vision and the ability to see far into the distance.

Or maybe into the past, as she attempted to do that day.

One thing for certain, their appearance likely meant

something. But she didn't know how to interpret their arrival, watching them glide upon the thermals, searching for prey.

Like the hawks, the Crosses could tear off the heads of any snakes that crossed their paths as well. Human or reptilian. To a person, they were built strong and powerful, harboring the inbred ability to kill.

Perhaps even the Hapless Susan, namesake of the Lost Daughter Ranch, had that killing ability running inside of her. The pity of her plight amounted to the simple unfortunate fact that she couldn't swim. That, or didn't have enough sense to stay with her team.

ACCOMPANIED by the watchful eyes of the hunting pair, on that fortuitous omen, Emory left the yard and entered the hollow on the other side of the road. She walked right past Hank's old bunkhouse, far more interested in the houses beyond. She made it about five yards past the rear log wall before the hairs on her neck rose.

The sensation made her stop dead in her tracks.

Slowly, she turned around.

The round logs used in construction tended toward a bleached out, pale silver-gray caused by the unrelenting high-altitude sun. Over the years, and battered by the elements, splits formed in the dried wood. The saddle-notched joints held strong and unyielding at the corners, but much of the chinking and daubing fell out over time, leaving gap-toothed walls that allowed the wind and elements to pass.

She yielded to the call from the past as the hawks circled overhead, watching her movements.

For her part, she stared at the rough-hewn door built

from the last century's mill waste. That door boasted handwrought iron hinges that were forged to outlast them all.

Those hinges groaned open, protesting. Peering into the interior and the hard-packed dirt floor, an abundance of stored old crap lodged in there over the years, but she pressed her way inside.

Plenty of dust, corrosion, and rodent droppings to go around.

Cardboard boxes stood stacked and rotting, threatening to give way if moved. She sniffed in the century of disuse, the logs giving off that old, heated wood smell as the outer walls warmed and dried in the sun. The Formica kitchen table from the 1960s waited alongside floor lamps and yet more boxes, piles of newspapers, and whatever other crap got thrown in there for good measure. As she turned, something in the corner drew her eye.

Against the far back wall and shoved into the recesses, an old trunk corner protruded.

Clearing a path by moving anything stacked in her way by shove or by kick, she wrangled the trunk free and into a better position where she could get at the contents.

Flinging back the lid she found yet more boxes—smaller boxes. She opened one, to find a collection of papers written in old-time pen and ink. Setting them aside, she dug further in, interest growing and building.

Her fingers touched cowhide.

She removed more boxes, and at the very bottom of the trunk an antique, brittle cowhide rested.

Was it what she thought it was?

She removed the hide from the trunk and held it out to inspect. Age-stiffened, she gingerly unfolded it, noting the Lost Daughter brand with a large dose of suspicion.

Unfurling the relic, Em turned the hide over and discovered the original brand which had, predictably, been altered. People called such activities "venting."

The rumors held true.

"Well, well, well," she said aloud, and felt the ghosts laugh at her expense.

A vented hide at the Lost Daughter.

The sound of a strange motor approaching cut the ghostly laugher off short.

Emory strained to listen as the vehicle drew closer, glancing at the rifle propped up next to the open door.

Glancing at the hide held in her two hands, she tossed the incriminating evidence back into the trunk and slammed the lid shut. As she kicked the trunk away, her actions struck her as verging on ridiculous, worrying about secreting a hundred-and-fifty-year-old hide. But there she stood, and that's what she did.

Some secrets were undoubtedly worth keeping.

She grabbed her rifle propped up beside the doorframe, and kicked the door shut further, leaving an inch and a half gap to fire through, if needed. A green Jeep Wrangler threaded the road downhill, aiming for the ranch house. Having no idea who caused that intrusion, she somehow doubted that the shooters would just come up in broad daylight.

Another old range rule popped into her head.

It don't matter the horse they rode in on or the time they arrived, their guns fired just the same.

Her mouth twitched. *Yes, provided they knew how to load them.*

Measuring up her Jeep-driving opponent, she waited in the old bunkhouse and sized up the arrival from her vantage point. When a well-upholstered woman sporting a stylish haircut emerged from the driver's seat, Em knew who and what she spied upon—*that Paulson woman* and she'd been to the beauty parlor since she'd last seen her.

No doubt, the woman sought her father.

On a beef body score, Emory rated her an eight.

Rifle in hand—yes, she considered leaving it behind but decided that wouldn't serve her purposes nearly as well—she emerged from the old bunkhouse and closed the door behind her.

The woman watched her approach, and she certainly took in the rifle Emory carried.

For her part, Em carried it in as nonthreatening a manner as possible. Not for the benefit of the Paulson woman, but to save herself from her father's outright wrath—a different type of preservation.

"Can I help you?" Emory called out within earshot of the woman and her Jeep.

"Emory? I'm Linda Paulson, we've already met."

Hand outstretched, the woman took a half step forward but thought better of it when she took into account the rifle.

"Oh yes," Emory replied, caught somewhere between guilt, politeness, and get-the-hell-away-from-my-father. "I remember."

"What's the rifle for?" the woman asked.

"To shoot people," Emory replied, point-blank.

Mrs. Paulson blanched at that answer, and Emory did her best not to chuckle, because that would have ruined the effect.

"We've had a bit of trouble," she offered, grudgingly.

She blinked, uncomprehending. *Her father hadn't spoken to the woman lately.*

"What kind of trouble?" the blonde woman asked.

"Nothing that needs airing," Emory replied, although she made sure her voice wasn't rough when she said it. "What can I do for you?"

Color rose in the woman's cheeks. "I was hoping to see your father."

"He's gone into town."

"I see." The woman's blue eyes didn't really see, but a definite impression built and gathered behind all that blinking.

"Did my father fill out all the paperwork he needed?"

Back on to safer ground.

"He did the preliminary application," she nodded. "I helped him do that to get it all straight. He took me on a ride around the property to get a better impression. It's some place that you have."

"Which horse did he put you on?"

"Heavens," the woman flapped her hands around a bit. "I don't remember his name."

That was one point against her right there. "We've only got five these days: Draco, Kai, Red, Aspen, and Alfredo."

The woman blinked. Emory held her ground, unwilling to move the conversation ahead until the woman chose a horse.

"Draco, I think."

That wasn't good. *Her father's horse.* The Paulson woman might have gotten it wrong, but if she didn't...

Emory just nodded, like it didn't matter in the least.

"Your father rode one that seemed hard to handle."

Alfredo.

"Probably so. Draco and Kai are the ones that get ridden the most. Anyhow, I suppose you didn't come here to talk about horses."

The woman hesitated, uncertain what to confide.

"I haven't heard from your father as of late and was passing by. Is he alright?"

"Dad? Sure, he's fine." She wanted to leave it there, cutting off any more details. But that wasn't exactly playing fair. "I'm home for a few days, which probably threw off his routine. Do you want me to tell him that you stopped by?"

Emory's posture relaxed a bit, taking the tension down a notch.

"What's the gun for? *Really*."

"Like I said, to shoot people. There's been some trouble, and we aren't playing around. Question for you, if we put locks on those outbuildings, does that hurt our chances for getting those grants?"

The woman's eyes darted to the buildings then back to Emory. She turned her head to a slight profile, having caught a whiff of something not quite right.

"Did something *in particular* happen?"

Emory located a half-truth in the recesses of her mind. Just enough rope to hang herself by. "Sure did. Some trespassers came in through the BLM land to take a look at the buildings."

Again, the widening of the eyes and the blinking. "I don't think you should be gun toting and scaring off tourists, do you?"

"It's private property," Emory countered. "We aren't part of the chamber of commerce."

"Lance wouldn't even let me go into the buildings," she spluttered.

Score one for Dad. "They're unsafe."

"That's what he said, but I just wanted to look inside," Linda Paulson all but whined. "It's my profession and I'm trying to help you both. It certainly would have made for a more persuasive application."

"That's why we need the locks. Someone could fall through a floor, and then we'd get sued."

Judging from the woman's expression, she already knew Emory's version wasn't the entire story but exercised enough good judgment to drop it.

"Do you know when Lance will be back?" Emory felt as if she purposely did not refer to him as her father.

"No. I guess that depends how things go at the bank."

"Bank?" the woman echoed.

Nothing scared a woman off faster than the notion of taking on hefty ranch debt.

Yet another one of those inconveniences that the flatlanders didn't understand. Running a ranch never did come cheap.

THE BACK END of the Jeep sure made a hasty retreat out along the ranch road. In fact, the woman acted like she couldn't wait to get off the Lost Daughter.

Emory smirked, but she'd likely be hearing about this one from her father.

If he and that woman were a true item.

Then again, he sure didn't let just anyone ride Draco.

One problem temporarily handled—and while she never did get an answer about the locks—she could use the time unsupervised.

Turning back to her immediate task of surveying the buildings, her cell rang just as she placed her hand on the bunkhouse door.

The screen displayed the name *Terry Overholzer*, her boss.

"Hi, Terry!"

A chuckle. "Hello, Quickdraw. How's vacation treating you?"

Vacation, hell. It sure didn't feel like much of a vacation to her.

A jumbled silence hung heavy while she tried to figure out what on earth to say. A typical man would have filled the void after a few seconds, but the senior brand inspector just waited her out.

"Is that what they call this? Anyhow, you probably wouldn't believe me if I told you. You callin' to make sure I know when to come back?"

"Something like that," another chuckle.

Her words came out in an unintended rush. "My dad may, or may not be embarking upon a geriatric romance..."

"Whoa, whoa, whoa. You'd better watch those words you are flinging around. We like to be referred to as sexy senior citizens."

She shook her head. "What's in a label, right? But one of our neighbors got shot, and we're all trying to figure out what happened. And hire a new cowhand. But yes, I'll be back. The day after tomorrow is my plan."

Now it was Emory's turn to wait out his confounded silence on the other end.

She could almost hear him thinking.

"What happened with the neighbor?"

A sharp inhale through her nostrils as she realized that first part slipped out. "That's the ninety-four-dollar question. He drove here for help, and someone shot him. There were three shooters, to be exact."

"*Three* shooters? That doesn't sound good at all."

"No. Can't say that it does."

A pause. A very long pause echoing with a whole lot

left unsaid. "If you can't come back because you're needed there I'd understand, but…"

"No," she cut him off. "I'll be back in time. Whatever this mess is, it's not our fight."

She brightened. "Hey, the National Western is kind of, like, my first rodeo…as a brand inspector, that is."

She meant her words as a joke, but the brand inspector on the other end of the call didn't laugh. "Are you OK?"

That unexpected sympathy caused her eyes to well up.

"Sure." Then stronger. "I'm fine. You don't know anyone who's reliable and looking for ranch work in the Colorado mountains, do you?"

More silence on the end. "Not right off the top of my head, but I can ask around."

"Thanks, and I'll see you on Thursday. Say, Terry? Kai's going to stay up here while I'm working the stock show. That way my dad can take care of him and it won't fall to your wife."

"She wouldn't mind, but it sounds like a good plan. Stay safe and in one piece."

"Yeah, I'll try." Emory didn't hang up. "Oh, and one other thing. If you come across a steer or cow head, um…*unrefined*…could you bag it up for me?"

"What the hell for?" Now he sounded incredulous.

She thought about lying, claiming it for a craft project that would never come about, but the request was simply too strange to pull off a lie about crafts or normal uses.

Come to think of it, there were no "normal" uses for discarded skulls. Not in its natural state with meat, membrane, and skin still attached.

"In all honesty I'd rather not say, but it's nothing illegal."

Silence. He wasn't going anywhere until she leveled with him.

"Alright. If you must know, it's for the back gate to the BLM land. A warning of sorts."

No sound and no words were forthcoming.

Emory could guess Terry's expression as he searched for an answer and a way to provide reasonable help in the circumstances. Predictably, in this instance, he came up short. "I'll see what I can do, but I'll be straight. I don't like the sound of any of this. Sounds like a modern-day range war brewing."

And that wasn't a question, but a statement.

10

THE HERD INCREASES

NOTHING COULD MAKE THAT HOLLOW FEELING OF THE unvarnished truth go away.

That's what their actions amounted to—staring down a range war that they didn't understand. Emory didn't exactly have any knowledge or histories about true range wars, but in all likelihood one side started something, and the other side responded in kind. In the past, the participants might not have even seen it coming—as in their particular case. True, she could go to the library and start reading, but that idea had two strikes against it. One, it felt fairly passive. Two, she didn't have spare time to spend wading through books and fragmented interpretations.

She stared at the old bunkhouse and thought about the laughing ghosts. Something lingered in there, all right. Information or relics beyond the vented hide. The hawks no longer circled in sight, having been scared off by that Paulson woman. *Linda.* Maybe the redtails had flown away because they led her to where she needed to be and figured their job well done.

Phone in hand, she typed *old bunkhouse* into her notes, adding the *new bunkhouse*, which amounted to little more than a fifty-year-old modified boxcar.

Cade's old digs.

While interesting contents lurked in the old bunkhouse, she remained drawn to Idella's house. But Idella's house pulled the strongest. Curiosity might prove a fine thing, and her longing pressed hard. She could disguise that notion as a simple task of reconnoitering. The oldest buildings held the most interest for her by far, but dutifully she made note in her phone of *all* the structures as she passed.

Old bunkhouse
New bunkhouse
Horse stable
Hay shelter
Chicken coop (disused)
Main storage shed
Seven corrals (repair needed)
Old cattle chutes—two (unusable)
Modern chute (fine)
Smokehouse
Root cellar
Idella's house
Blacksmith shop

In the earlier days of the valley's settlement, the Lost Daughter was considered a huge concern with plenty of sons and daughters to run it. Over time, the drive and ability faded away as times changed and the once-sprawling family declined. Some of the old untended buildings came across like the next strong wind could blow them right on over, but they'd been in that condition for years.

No doubt a lot of upkeep on the ranch slipped away from them. Always something to attend to, those chores didn't include shoring up disused buildings. No matter that those buildings contained a lot of history within. Time whittled away the memory, and the wind dispersed the shards. In all likelihood, they would end up casualties of neglect and disuse.

Emory paused her inventory taking as she neared the faded footsteps in the snow. She glanced from the impressions to look back up at Idella's house, lording over the battleground—tall, proud, and defiant on the outer perimeter.

Idella of the red hair.

This new fixation on a hitherto little-known ancestor marked a new development. Perhaps she fixated on Idella because she never would have abandoned her family. Not like Emory's own mother had done, a fair long time ago when Em reached the age of eleven.

That blot on history, *her history*, would ever remain a wounding truth. The underlying pain could never be erased in its entirety, and she knew as much. No matter how much her father growled, or how much she pretended that it didn't matter.

It did. It mattered a great deal.

Trudging forward and scanning the snow and the surrounding area, she kept an eye out for blood stains, searching for whether they even still remained. Emory sidled over to the approximate location where blood spotted the snow that previous night, next to a random shed whose purpose had disappeared through the years. Just a faint rust-colored stain remained in the melting snow. In another day or so, even that trace would disappear altogether.

But the disquiet continued to reverberate.

Squinting, a newly installed lock stood out on Idella's door.

Of all the dang times for her father to be efficient.

Still, she walked over and chuckled. While the latch had been mounted, all right, the padlock hung unfastened. She unhooked the lock, pocketed it, and opened the door to the building where she had been certain one of the marauders sheltered. In the morning light, the windows dimmed by years of grime still let enough light in. Thick dust lay everywhere and covered everything. The only visible disturbance remained her boot tracks from the other day.

She stood in the middle of that room near the old, scarred table, trying to remember what stories she could recall about Idella. Something concerning how she rode fast and stuck in the saddle. Gave as good as she got and a bit more besides. No doubt she tried her best to keep her boys in line (whatever that might have meant in those early days and circumstances). Nevertheless, it felt doubtful that she even worried about notions such as propriety.

No, as Emory stood in that room, she figured Idella would have worried more about the ranch hand's actions and honesty, and the neighbors who helped themselves to straying Lost Daughter beeves.

Just the same as the modern-day Crosses themselves did.

Lost in thought, it took a moment before Emory realized her father's truck approached. She cast a glance at the aged sink set against the back wall in the kitchen area, complete with an old-fashioned primer pump. That might have passed as a modern convenience back in those days. The rotting fabric curtains still hung in the windows, faded by the strong sun and brittle with age. A box staircase rose along the western wall. By all outward appearances, it appeared sound enough.

She'd have to wait for another day to give it a try.

LANCE CROSS'S PICKUP TRUCK, pulling up to a stop in the ranch yard in front of the house, marked her father's return as she slipped out of Idella's house.

She threaded the lock back through the latch leaving it just as she found it—unlocked.

When he emerged from the cab, Emory used her range whistle. He turned his face toward the sound and raised his arm in greeting as he strode over in her general direction. She retraced her path to meet him and they met up by one of the derelict corrals.

"How's the banker?"

"I intercepted him on the street as he parked his car." A dry laugh. "I sure got the feeling he wasn't too pleased to see me, alright, but I hung on as he tried to dodge me by going into the bank."

Emory wagged her head at the image presented. "And?"

"He acted kind of snakebit. Anyhow, I explained that there was this notion circulating about cash deals and unlikely buyers. For a minute I thought he wasn't going to say a damned thing, but then he got all riled and about scattershot what he knew."

"Mr. Wright did?"

"He did. Guess he's been in a bother for a while now, saying how land's getting sold but it ain't going through the bank. Guess that means they don't get their cut. Anyhow, he flat-out said it sounded like money laundering to him, but he didn't want to get shot over it. I guess in banker school they teach them to be on the lookout for that kind of deal."

"Getting shot," she teased.

"Money laundering."

A serious accusation. Emory wanted the law to be involved. The regular law, and not the range version they favored. "Did you ask him if he spoke to the sheriff about any of his concerns? Seems to me that he should."

"Funny you should ask that. I did. He said that money laundering's a federal crime, and he doubts our local law enforcement has experience in such matters. Obviously, something's not right, but heaven only knows who we'd be taking on."

"Other than they wear tennis shoes in the snow."

"That, and the sheriff's got the results from the bullets gathered from the ranch. Anyhow, afterwards I went to see Iver again."

"Oh?"

"Seems when he sold off the back end of his land, the buyers paid cash. He finally came clean and admitted as much. He knew he shouldn't have done that, but cash money is a hard thing to turn down. According to him, the same broker's been proffering other cash deals. That fits in with what Evan said."

Emory nodded.

"Anyhow, Iver's got something for you."

She felt her eyes narrow. "What do you mean?"

"A mustang going by the name of Outhouse." Her father shook his head, as if the notion wounded him.

"*Outhouse*? What kind of name is that?"

Lance Cross offered his crooked grin. "Before you go

getting all excited, he's probably a $300 special from Canon City. But Iver said he appreciated our help. Guess the horse is a payment of a kind."

Emory laughed. "Don't suppose we can change his name..."

"Hell no," her father replied. "That might just confuse him. Besides, I kind of like it. The mustang named Outhouse."

"Is he broke?"

"Didn't ask. Sounds like a project for you to do on one of those next *vacations*. Something to keep you turning up, so your old man don't get too lonely."

Her conscience stabbed like it ought. "That Paulson woman stopped by."

Her father stopped goofing around. "And?"

"She said she hadn't heard from you lately. Are you sure that saddle in the barn fits her? Looks kind of small..."

"Hey! I'll thank you to keep your opinion to yourself. I like a woman carrying a bit of meat on her."

Emory smirked. "She's got that...anyhow, Terry called to make sure I'm coming back. And I'm not sure I need another project, or another horse for that matter."

Her father's mirth drained away. "What did you tell 'im?"

"Why, that I'd be back, of course. But I also asked if he knew of someone good who might be interested in working up here, but he didn't know of anyone off the bat. But he'll keep on the lookout."

"Now," her father paused, ominous. Inserting the kind of pause that meant issuing an edict of some variety. "Before you go on getting how you get, I already called Monty."

"Monty?"

"My second cousin once removed, or however the hell that all goes. He's a bit rough around the edges, but he can handle himself and he knows what he's doing. Better still, he sure as hell can shoot."

It was Emory's turn to pull up short. Random second cousins didn't sound on the level either. "Where's he been hiding?"

"Up in Wyoming, getting blown around by the wind. He'll be down as soon as he can—don't know if that means days or weeks. He's got some loose ends to wrap up, or so he says." His tone ended the matter, although chagrin lingered. "He can be eccentric at times."

Emory grimaced and made certain her father took notice. "Where's he going to sleep—do I need to clean out that old guest room? As in the guest room that hasn't seen guests in at least forty years?"

"He'll sleep in the bunkhouse. Hell," Lance Cross halfway barked, "I don't even know if he's house-trained."

About the last thing she wanted to hear, but she still held her tongue. Family remained family, warts and all.

Another practiced gun on their side, these days, was nothing at all to turn down.

"I guess I'll go give Linda a quick call. Why don't you go ride your horse?" He acted like she remained a child at times, and this, apparently, was one of those times. He displayed the effrontery to wink at her as she stood among the buildings and the rusted castoffs. He jogged back to the house, heaven help her.

Kai lifted his head at the sound of her voice and called.

"I'm coming, Kai." Yes. She might as well ride.

EMORY WALKED over to the pasture gate, grabbing the halter hanging on a hook to the side.

Good old Kai, he ambled toward her. Obviously, he didn't bear a grudge for her failure at not having ridden him near enough during the last couple of days.

Emory unhitched the gate and walked up to him, slid the noseband over his nose nice and easy, and flicked the poll strap over his head left-handed, and threaded it through the loop, tying it into a D knot.

He grunted.

"You're a good boy, Kai. I'm going to miss you while I'm working. But you'll be better off here. Just try not to let the fat lady ride you." She rubbed his soft nose before leading him back into the barn.

The previous day the thawing ground churned to mud, but overnight froze it back solid. Footing turned precarious. She hung on to Kai to help steady her, as she led him back into the barn to tack him up, glaring at the Paulson woman's saddle as they passed by.

She tied the lead rope to the Blocker Tie Ring and went to get Kai's tack box. She brushed the mud from his legs, curried his back, chest, and throat, and picked his hooves. He always acted difficult about getting his hooves picked. He stamped, pulled away, and made her work for the privilege.

"Kai! Listen. You won't like it if you have rocks stuck in your hooves and we go riding and you end up lame. Settle down, would you?"

A few more stamps, which earned him dirty looks from Em, and he finally settled down enough to let her check all four of his feet. Afterwards, she tossed on his saddle blanket, positioned the saddle on top of his spine, tightened the cinch, and slipped on his bridle, latching all the buckles.

Kai, in a full winter coat, nickered.

"You look like one big furball," she told him, and he tossed his head in agreement.

She stuck her left foot in the stirrup and swung up into the saddle, riding him out through the open barn doors.

"Let's go out to the back gate," and pointed him in that direction, "and see what we can find."

THE WORLD unfurled differently on horseback. That perspective of five feet above the ground changed the view in remarkable ways. Kai's ears tilted forward, and licking and chewing, he acted happy to be once more out on the trail. The rimrocks warmed in the cold winter sun. The underskirts of the snow melted, slipping from the trees and the outbuildings with solid thuds. Kai spooked the first time snow slipped off an old roof, but he soon got the hang of the landscape and conditions.

"Just snow, Kai. Snow melting off roofs. Definitely not an avalanche."

That was the thing about even the most stable and steady of horses. Their wide range of vision took in more than a human's...and a wide range of vision often meant more threats were detected.

She patted his neck.

Their plodding pace acted well to get him warmed up, the sun shone down flattening some of the contrast but boldening the colors. Kai picked up speed, content with a job to do. Emory faced where she wanted to go, and he followed sensing the movement of her head. She clicked her tongue and simply thought the word *trot* and he understood.

Together they picked up pace toward the back gate, Emory evening out the ride, the pair of them moving in tandem. In time she nudged him into a slow canter to see how he would respond, then slowed him back down after a few hundred yards. Her tension drained away, she inhaled and sighed. Kai blew in response. *Unfettered* felt more than fine.

As they headed out toward the back gate the snow glistened, and the cloudless blue sky opened wide and fair, devoid of any hint of the madness humans inflicted.

THE SNOW DEEPENED on the northwest facing side of the road as the BLM gate came into view. The two stone pillars her father built stood sentinel on either side of the trail. From horseback height—she hadn't noticed it before—she noticed that each pillar had holes drilled into the tops. Holes where poles could be inserted for a slender crossbar.

Or more likely pikes, crowned with rotting cattle skulls.

Kai picked up his feet nice and jaunty, looking past the barbed wire fence to the BLM land beyond.

"I don't know that we have time to go out there," she murmured to the horse.

Nevertheless, they rode up to the gate to peer over. Smothering misgivings, she unfastened the latch and chain, and they passed on through.

The snowmobile tracks remained visible; a patch of yellow snow stood out where the shooter peed.

Of more interest were the different sets of tracks— the person who drove the snowmobile, and two other sets, presumably boots belonging to the sheriff's office.

But how could she be certain? Those boots dismounted snowmobiles, after circling the original set of the person of the yellow snow.

Uneasy, she turned Kai around, scanning the horizon in all directions.

The wind caught in the sage and in the distant brush alongside the river, and the cottonwoods groaned.

A sudden flutter as a white piece of paper flew by them. Kai shied and did a slight crow hop. She rode the buck. "Whoa, Kai. It's just a scrap of paper, silly boy."

A piece of paper that blew into the scrub, caught.

Eyes upon it, she dismounted figuring it would be nothing more than meaningless trash.

She grabbed the slip and turned it over.

A receipt.

From a restaurant in New Jersey, of all places, and dated three days prior to the shooting.

She stuck it in her vest pocket and decided to follow the tracks a bit more. Two sets of tracks climbing and returning down the slope. She followed them for a ways, but in the end, turned Kai around to head back to the ranch.

She experienced the uncanny sense of hostile eyes watching her.

Again, she scanned the horizon and saw nothing. But she didn't want to be caught out there alone.

They trotted back to the ranch.

Emory considered where the skull ought to go, and all of a sudden, having a second talisman struck her as a fine idea.

A very fine idea.

HER FATHER WORKED on chores when she rode up and dismounted.

"Found a receipt out back," she announced. "More than that, I got the feeling I was being watched. That's never happened before…well, not like that."

"Not like how, exactly?" He stiffened, eyes raking over her, searching.

"It wasn't the ghosts," she replied, pulling out the scrap from her pocket. "Here."

He unfolded the scrap and read it, frowning. "Might not mean anything. Then again, it might mean a good deal."

"Did Sheriff Preston ever say that he found the shell casing? There were three sets of snowmobile tracks. The shooter, and then two more sets that circled where the shooter parked."

"He said the shooter was smart enough to pick up the casing. This receipt might be all there is."

Emory, bothered, uncinched Kai, and pulled off the saddle and blanket and stuck them both on the rack.

"I don't think I should just leave you here with a range war brewing—because that is what it feels like to me."

"You read too many books," he replied. "You go do your job and let me do mine. I'll call you if I need you."

She stared at him to see if he honestly meant his words.

He winked. "I've got your number," he crooned.

Yes. And she had his.

PART II

11

THE BEST DRAWN OUT
SIXTEEN DAYS IN JANUARY

LIKE ANY OTHER RANCH KID IN THE STATE OF COLORADO, Emory had been to the National Western Stock Show in Denver. And it was a *big* deal. It was a big deal then, and it certainly felt like a big deal to participate as a working adult, although viewed through different eyes and in a different manner.

It wasn't so much a place that the Lost Daughter ever bought or sold livestock, but it provided a notable celebration when they'd had a good year. As every rancher knew, working and celebrating amounted to two different things entirely. The "Best Sixteen Days in January" stretched out longer when people worked the National Western. Then those best sixteen days became more like the "busiest twenty days" of January for the brand inspectors and the people who provided the infrastructure. Fanfare, setup, stock sales, loading and unloading, and keep-everything-moving types had their hands full and more than enough work to go around.

Everyone, from the highest commissioner to the

fellow shoveling shit, knew the drill. Get the job done with a western twang and a smile on your face.

Denver counted on them all.

THE SPECTATING crowds wouldn't arrive for another three days, but the livestock would trickle in—or flood—during the next day or two. The brand inspectors occupied a trailer where she'd been instructed to report, set up behind the stock pens. Up and ready at three o'clock in the oh-so-dark morning, she didn't feel exactly good about leaving the Lost Daughter. At that pitch-black hour, her bedroom light did little more than to illuminate the dinginess and shabbiness of her old room. Most of her possessions were in her apartment in Greeley anyhow. Looking around her bedroom, it now seemed an empty shell of a place, and a discarded shell at that. She'd never really had that much in the way of possessions anyhow, but now it looked down-right poor, and that deficit twanged. Her father, the land, and the Lost Daughter were what she held most dear, and she knew that she had best keep that in mind. Dingy paint, worn carpeting, a few wire hangers and empty shelves didn't mean that much to people like them.

It was the disquiet she felt.

Both she and her father knew their way of life was coming under threat, and there she was, poised to head out—leaving the ranch largely unguarded, except for the efforts of her father.

The ranch demanded more than one person to keep it running.

She couldn't help but wonder if she was doing the right thing and felt fairly certain of the answer.

No.

HER FATHER'S bedroom door was open, and she passed down the hall. She peeked in, but he wasn't in bed. He'd risen to see her off. She found him in the kitchen.

"Dad, I've been thinking," she said, coming into the room.

"That's dangerous," he replied with a manufactured sigh.

"I don't think I should go down to Denver. Not right now."

"I didn't think I raised a quitter," he replied.

"You didn't," she replied. "That's why I think I ought to stay here."

"Bullshit," he replied. "You just think I can't cut it anymore. Ain't that so?"

"No," she replied with care. "This ranch has never been run by just one person. You know that."

"I'll call you if I need you," he replied, steely. "No go do what you're paid to do."

Thus ended the argument, but it didn't mean the misgivings went away.

A MAN at one of the lot's entrances motioned for her to stop as she pulled into the back lot of the National Western.

She rolled down her window.

"Good morning," the man said, sounding like he meant it. "Who are you here for?"

Smirking, Emory showed him her badge. "That remains to be seen."

He chuckled. "It usually goes pretty smooth. The brand inspector trailer is over there."

He pointed in a vague manner, but she thought she understood where he meant. She pulled her grandfather's battered Ford F-150 behind the trailer and next to a marked brand inspector's truck.

One trailer over, a door opened, and the senior brand inspector stepped out.

Close enough for horseshoes, she figured.

She opened her door, and halfway to standing yelled over the top of her truck in the finest barnyard fashion. "Am I OK to park here, or should I move?"

"Move your truck behind the trailer," Terry called back. "Although there looks like a lot of room, it gets filled up. Let's get you situated."

He waited outside of the trailer, and she hustled up to him. "Is Dave in there? Man, I've missed you guys."

And she truly had. She just hadn't realized how much until that exact moment.

"He sure is. How's the neighbor?" The question posed wasn't frivolous, and Terry expected an answer.

"Iver? He'll pull through. Dad says he's even giving me a horse named Outhouse. What a name."

The bit about the new horse flitted right on by. "You all figure out what that shooting was about?"

"Not yet," she sighed. "Iver thinks dirty money is coming in, but it's not our battle, even though it ended up at our door. Still, I won't lie to you. I didn't feel all that great leaving this morning, but Dad won't have it any other way."

"Stubborn, huh? That still don't sound good." Terry eyed her, displaying a well-founded caution.

She could read between those lines furrowing on his forehead but didn't exactly want to. Instead, she opened the door and stuck her head into the trailer. "Hey, Dave!"

The lanky older man remained seated at the small table, papers and catalogs spread out before him and covering the tiny surface. His eyes twinkled.

"Hey, yourself. We were worried you might not be coming back, you taking so long on your *vacation*."

Emory laughed. "Hawaii would've been a better choice than Stampede, that's for damn sure."

"No beaches, huh? There's over fifteen thousand head of whatever floating around here, and that ain't including the two-legged variety. We probably pay better than your *vacation* spot, too."

Emory leaned against the trailer's doorframe, including Terry in the general conversation.

"Last time I checked, Dad didn't pay. Well, he doesn't pay me at least. He's got some second cousin coming to help for a while, and he'll have to pay him something... I'd guess. One never knows. I still think we need a 'regular' paid hand, so if you guys hear of someone dependable that can handle himself...that's turning out to be a very real requirement."

Dave's eyebrows lifted at that last part, recognizing the words for what they meant. Terry, still standing outside, put his hand in his back pocket and spat.

"The Wild West is alive and well and living at the Lost Daughter, is that the story?"

"Pretty much. It got real western there for a bit. Now, I'm here to work. What do you need me to do?"

Safer ground to steer the conversation toward. Not that it fooled anyone. Not even for one split second.

Thankfully, the men decided to let the matter drop.

THE NATIONAL WESTERN Stock Show lived up to its reputation dating back to when Denver's reputation amounted to a glorified, cow town bolstered with gold from the mountain mines. As when it started in 1906, the stock show proved no small enterprise or undertaking. The pens alone sprawled over a vast distance remarkably near the center of the city. Those barren pens and stalls would soon fill to the brim with bawling cattle, spitting llamas, bleating sheep, pigs, goats, bison blowing, and whatever else livestock-wise a body could conceive to breed and show.

It never stayed quiet for long, or so common knowledge ran.

The pens provided for the business side of the operations while the rodeo and shows offered all the flash and glamor. Everything about the National Western drew in serious money, and as of late, she'd grown understandably cautious about serious money. Serious money attracted serious problems. Money changed hands between not only those buying and selling legitimately but could lure in another element as well.

"What'cha reading there?" Emory tossed the question out for anyone who cared to answer—those "anyones" being Terry or Dave.

"Auction catalogs. That way we know what we're looking at and looking for," Dave slid one over to her.

Glancing at it, she shrugged. "Maybe a bit later. What do we do when people are unloading?"

"Just check their transport papers. We'll get down to the specifics later once the buying and selling starts."

She nodded as if she knew, but she really didn't.

"Have either of you ever had any trouble out here? At

the show, I mean." The question might have been offered in a casual manner, but it hit a tender mark.

Both men shifted slightly. "What kind of trouble are you asking about?" Dave frowned.

"Anything that I need to be aware of. Like drugs or fencing, to name a few."

"Every now and again, something comes up," Terry admitted, sticking his thumbs in his belt loops and stretching back. "We pretty much stay within our lines, but it's the prostitution that comes in when the show starts. I don't think I've ever seen anything—or not around the pens for heaven's sake. But if you see young girls who look troubled, might be being held against their wills, that type of thing…report it in through your radio."

The predatory element. The element never considered in conjunction with the flag-waving, anthem-singing stock shows before.

He turned and grabbed a radio off the small sink counter and held it out for her.

"It's kind of cramped in here," Emory noted, taking the radio and clipping it on to her vest.

"It serves good enough for getting out of the wind and weather. Time will tell if we get the traditional stock-show blizzard," Dave grinned.

Pretty much everyone in Colorado knew about stock-show weather—and if the attendees didn't, they might just have the chance to find out.

THE NATIONAL WESTERN produced a published schedule for the events and a published schedule for the various livestock producers with staggered delivery and set-up times and dates. Inside the trailer, paper copies circulated, and a whiteboard kept tally. Each inspector had a schedule, and each folded it into quarters and stuck it into a pocket for later reference.

The first arrivals were scheduled for 8:00 a.m. on the Tuesday.

"It may *say* eight," Dave drawled, "but they'll start lining up well beforehand."

"Em, we get here at six," Terry clarified, scowling a bit at Dave.

"That's fine," Emory shrugged. Everyone bringing in livestock were ranch and farm people. They all knew how to get up in the morning.

The truth of the matter was that the logistics behind setting up and running a stock show of this size, or almost any size for that matter, proved an endeavor dealing with many competing demands and priorities. Established rules had to be followed, lest the entire production descend into one roiling and heaping mess of chaos.

The sheer size of the National Western staggered the imagination, hence the need for maps and diagrams. There were twenty acres of pens on asphalt, cement, or old bricks from the early 1900s. Of those acres of pens, there were day pens and night pens making a whole lot of pens and livestock to keep straight right there. Not to mention the fact that the pens could be reconfigured to expand for a larger outfit unless they wanted the dividers kept up. There were fifty-six sale display pens, chutes for loading and unloading, and 180 wash stations. Not to mention exercise areas, working facilities, tub scales, and alleys for moving livestock—haltered and unhaltered.

It almost went without saying, moving parts abounded.

When Emory absorbed what she could, she felt her eyes widen and her stomach tighten.

"That's a lot to keep track of," she stammered.

"Here's the thing," Terry offered. "You know those games of wiles we occasionally play? The one where the stray brand is loaded into the sale barn shipment to see if we catch it proving we're on our toes? That type of thing don't happen here. They're bringing in the best of their best. We just stay visible—but do your job and keep an eye out for the brands. Mostly, you'll be checking transportation papers and counting heads."

"Yes, sir," she replied.

12

RHINESTONES AND DIAMONDS
ARE TWO DIFFERENT THINGS

TRUE TO THEIR WORD, THE TRUCKS ALREADY LINED UP AT ten to six that following morning.

That first wave of arrivals was for the cattle yards. The next day would be for the cattle housed in the barn area. The sheep would come that same day.

Terry summed it up right. There proved a river of transportation permits to inspect, heads to count, and a whole lot of general checking going on.

Time passed quickly to the tune of cattle bawling and sheep bleating. All the inspectors had their hands full, and there wasn't time to watch out for anything more sinister than loading, unloading, and waiting while misplaced papers were found. On the surface, everything certainly ran as it should after over a century of practice.

BENEATH ALL THAT all-American pride and confidence, a darker element lurked. *The criminal undertow.* Once she heard about it, Emory swore she could feel the notion grip her stomach. Maybe she felt determined to root out what she could in Denver, because she couldn't help at home. She kept her mouth shut, having worried them enough with the hints and innuendos concerning the Lost Daughter's latest saga of Iver's shooting.

She turned her attention to what she could control.

Emory wouldn't have been human if that praise-worthy determination hadn't faltered in the face of all the excitement the stock show brought with it. The National Western wasn't called the "Best Sixteen Days in January" for nothing. Come blizzard, plummeting temperatures, or sun, on fine days the National Western remained something to be proud of, all right—a genuine piece of Colorado history waited right there for the taking.

But she wasn't exactly a surface-type of gal.

Dave caught some of her turmoil. "Don't worry, Em, we'll make sure you have a bit of time to go shopping or to see a rodeo. We remember what it was like to be young. Don't we, Terry?"

"Speak for yourself," he replied.

Despite the inspector's levity, Emory recalled those migrant shacks that she and Terry had passed by in the fall. The theory haunted in the back of her mind—the worry that some of those dilapidated shacks housed women who were used as prostitutes.

If you see something, say something.

That covered plenty of ground.

THE WORK STARTED RIGHT IN. Time meant money at any stock show. Truckloads of livestock rolled in, and before long, the air carried a strong feedlot smell. Paperwork flowed in a continual stream of brands, flanks, and signatures. The back lot amounted to a sea of churning heads in pens. If most of the people were there for the rodeos—which Emory sorely wanted to see—the real money came in the livestock sales proving the National Western hadn't become a legacy enterprise. It still performed its original function started all the way back in 1906 and the drill remained the same.

Get that livestock moving. Get that livestock sold. Improve the breed. Bring in the money to save the ranch.

It boiled down to how the trappings came across as fancier in modern days.

Emory stood alongside Dave by the indoor pens where the prized bulls were displayed, and those going up for sale waiting before auction. No run-down outdoor stalls for those high-priced guys.

Dave studied the pages on his clipboard while Emory studied the bulls.

"Angus," she commented. "Now how much are the prize ones going for?"

Dave flipped through his bags. "Highest sold last year at near $85,000. Now where is that Texan?"

"Texan?" She tried not to act interested, but she knew who Dave meant.

"Hugo Werner," Dave deadpanned. "Ain't he the fella that came to watch you skinning the steer?"

"Yeah," she still tried to come across as disinterested, but got the distinct impression that Dave saw through the act, like he did on most everything else that he came across. "Thanks for reminding me. Not my finest moment nor the impression that I want *anyone* to remember, by the way."

"Au contraire," he droned. "That's French, you know."

She stared at him flat-out. Dave chuckled and returned to consulting his clipboard pages.

"What are we doing here, other than me listening to you speak French?"

"Apparently waitin' on Hugo," he murmured.

Eyes narrowing, before she could even ask, she caught sight of the Texan. Limping in their direction.

A wide grin shone as he hobbled over.

Dang. He was good-looking. But he had never called since that time they met up at the dance hall.

"What happened to you?" The words shot out of her mouth before she thought it through. She managed, however, to catch Dave's brief scowl at the periphery.

"Hello to you, too, Em. Dave," Hugo thrust out his hand in Dave's direction. "Got kicked in the leg. It was either me or a little kid standing where he oughtn't, so... I'm gimping around. Damn that smarted! Better a leg than a head."

"When did that happen?" she asked, hating how she probably sounded like a mother or a nag.

While she hoped she got points for being concerned, her delivery left plenty to be desired and she knew it.

He grinned, a bit sheepish. "Yesterday when they were unloading. It's nothing much other than a big bruise."

"Hope the parents thanked you," Dave sighed.

"Hell, they didn't even notice," Hugo laughed.

"Figures." Dave paused, turning something over in his mind. "This is Em's first National Western as a brand inspector, probably yours, too. Why don't you two walk around and get the layout? I can handle the paperwork and inspections on my own for now. Em, meet me back at the trailer at 10:30?"

"She can come along, but I've got shipments to check," Hugo explained.

"Take her along! She's good at reading brands."

"These one's brands are cleaner than clean," Hugo's nod took in all the prize pens.

Dave's attempts at matchmaking were none too subtle.

"I'm standing right here," Emory groused.

"And so you are! Now git a move on. Daylight's burning," Dave replied, turning and walking away.

Hugo grinned.

TOGETHER THEY AMBLED a distance through the pens, in silence. Hugo still grinned, and Emory felt...off balance.

"Well," he broke the ice and waded in, "how've you been?"

She stopped in her tracks and turned to face him square. "You mean to tell me that you haven't heard anything at all?"

He stopped. Stopped grinning and stopped walking. A blush spread from the base of his neck up into his cheeks as he struggled to find words. When no easy ones were forthcoming, he toe-poked the arena dirt. "Oh, pretty much everyone's heard something about the shooting."

Just great.

"It's all probably blown out of proportion," Emory countered, a trifle on the defensive side. "I've been up at the ranch, burning some vacation days before working the stock show. Did you go home for Christmas?"

"Just a quick trip to see my dad. Mom died a while

back. The drive wasn't too bad, at any rate. Seven hours each way."

His eyes danced—evading or struggling. "You think you might want to go dancing some time?"

Nope. A proffered date wasn't the source of his discomfort. And if he truly wanted to go dancing, he would have asked her before now.

"What is it that you heard exactly?"

Looking away, he scanned the pens and their contents, but the contents didn't really register. She didn't know him that well, but she sure as hell could see that much.

He wanted to resume walking for lack of anything better to do. She stayed rooted in place.

The pair of them got the eye from some of the passersby. Sympathetic glances thought they witnessed a lover's tiff, but they interpreted the unfolding scene wrong.

Hugo deflated, eyes fixed on one of the steel girders above. "I heard you killed a biker."

She nodded. "He tried to kill me for what it's worth."

"Now, Emory, I didn't mean it that way. But that's a big thing. *Killing* a man. Not to mention the guy you winged at the sale barn…"

"And skinning calves."

"You were right about that one," he agreed, nice and fast and a little too enthusiastic.

"Thanks." Her budding reputation wasn't the one she hoped for. That familiar flash of temper rose up along her spine.

"What's that poker game you play in Texas?"

"You mean Texas Hold 'em."

"Here the game is Colorado Shoot 'em. You don't have to be in this state, you know."

"Whoa, Nelly…" he reached out and clasped her arm. "I didn't mean it that way, Em. You asked what I heard, and I told you straight."

It took a moment, but she regained her composure.

"I'm sorry. I didn't mean to snap at you. Now come on. We're supposed to be working and you've got brands you're supposed to be checking and I'm just stringing along for the hell of it."

She started hoofing it, he lingered behind. She refused to turn to see if he planned on catching up or not.

In a moment, he returned alongside, looking puzzled. "Is everything OK, Em?"

To her horror, tears welled up. "Not really." She held up her hand to stop him. "No sympathy. Sympathy always makes me cry."

Bemused, he raised both hands in surrender. "No sympathy here. No, ma'am."

Troubled for the rest of their pass around the arena and pens, each retreated within as they neared his inspection point.

"You know," he said at length, pulling to a stop and breaking the stalemate. "They're calling you Calamity Jane. I said it was more like Annie Oakley, if that helps."

She didn't break her stride but kept on going, figuring to escape back to the trailer to leave this conversation behind. "It doesn't."

"What I'm trying to get at," he raised his voice and aimed it between her shoulder blades, "is that if you need help, say so. Texas wasn't settled by wimps, you know."

She paused at the obvious point he made. The same could be said for the rest of the West, too. However, everyone knew that Texas's history proved harder than most.

His offer was genuine. She knew that much. But what she didn't want was sympathy, nor did she want pity. She hadn't been offering empty words about that point.

The Crosses and the Lost Daughter prided them selves on self-reliance now and forevermore. She wouldn't let their side down. Not if she could help it.

EMORY HAD NEVER SEEN SO many damned buckle bunnies in her entire life, but then again, the pro-rodeo circuit would be the place drawing them in like flies to shit. Since everyone at the stock show dressed up in their best finery, Emory found it difficult to tell the "real deal" from the "fake," and that inability to distinguish unsettled her to a degree. Boots provided the best indication. People who rode horses displayed those rubbings along the insoles if they rode in a particular pair. But there was nothing to say that riders and muckers couldn't put on their dress boots, all shined up and clean, when the occasion came around.

The National Western certainly lived up to the definition of "an occasion."

In an attempt to cut to the chase, Emory took the stance that she hated anyone who wore rhinestones, as simple as that. Of course, professionals didn't allow any traces of hostility on such a benign issue. Rhinestones or no, she slapped on a smile as best she could and stuck into the tasks given.

The most irritating fact of all remained crystal clear; although each and every one of the brand inspectors were all working their asses off in the pens, she couldn't help but notice the admiring glances cast in the Texan's direction when he worked nearby. All-American and squeaky clean. The kind of starched-and-pressed cut that people approved of.

Usually, mud splattered and hair escaping, the same could and would never be said of her. Although that stung, too, she was the product of a working ranch.

To make matters worse, since Hugo worked out in the pens the same as the rest of them, it stood to reason that he likely dealt with the real deal. Not that the distinction mattered all that much, because he could fall in love just as easily with one as the other.

But it mattered to her, damn it. If she were to be truthful, she wanted Hugo to fall for her. Knowing that he could end up falling for some buckle bunny or Denver chick, it would be damned near intolerable and a hard thing to swallow if he set his hat on a girl who hung around the stalls harboring a misguided cowboy infatuation.

Those types tended to wander off when literal shit, or manure, happened.

Emory must have missed a beat in keeping count because Terry's voice snapped her back into the here and now.

"You two have a lover's tiff or what?"

A stab. "No...I mean, what are you talking about?"

"You don't lie very well, and your counting ain't so hot either."

"Sorry, Terry."

The senior brand inspector finished up taking notes and filling out whatever form required completion.

True enough, Hugo stood there smiling down at some hair-twirling blonde who was the real deal since she owned, or brokered, cattle to sell.

Terry handed the sale records to the rancher they were reviewing and came over to her side and followed her gaze. "Who's that cute little girl the Texan's talking to?"

He meant his question to rub it in, and it sure did.

Emory half reared back. "How the hell should I know?"

As luck would have it, Hugo took that moment to look in their direction. He tipped his hat, and his eyes locked into Emory's before he returned his attention to the girl who beamed up at him.

"Shoot," Terry drawled, surveying the situation. "Aren't you going to do anything about it?"

"Like what? Tell him to keep his mind on his work?"

Terry guffawed. "Hell, I could say the same to you. Why don't I just call him over here to get his opinion on something."

"Don't you dare, Terry. I mean it…"

"Then keep your mind on the job at hand. Go check out that pen of steers over there. And keep your wits about you. You can get hurt, you know."

Surely, she knew. And likewise, she knew that she could be hurt in more ways than one.

13

COWBOYS WHO NEVER SAW SUNRISE FROM THE BACK OF A HORSE

THE DAY PASSED IN A FLURRY OF RUMPS, BRANDS, AND paperwork. Plenty of paperwork requiring completion.

"Feeling any better?" Dave asked stepping inside the trailer and angling onto the bench on the other side of the table from her.

"Didn't know I felt bad," she countered, daring him to add anything further along those lines.

Dave stretched, unbothered as well as unrelenting. He decided to try another tact, as was his MO. "You've got the run of the stockyard and all the pens, and your badge will get you in to any other place that you choose, and that includes the rodeos. Terry's the boss, but I say you can do it."

Emory felt drained, but not too drained to be interested. "You want to go check out the rodeo pens?"

"You don't need me along, and I'm not sure that I'm referring to the pens. You could watch the rodeo. Come seven o'clock, I'm going to head to the hotel, clean up, get dinner, and hit the rack. The morning will roll around mighty early for me, but don't let that stop you from having some fun. Besides, you don't need an old geezer hanging around you. Might give people the wrong idea. Like I'm your father or something."

"Or something," she reiterated. "Speaking of old geezers, where's Terry?"

"I'd watch that old geezer talk where he's concerned if I were you. Over by the prize pens. He'll be along any time now."

As if on cue, the door opened, and Terry's bulk filled the doorway. Having the three of them in there together after a tiring day made the tight trailer interior cramped and claustrophobic.

His pensive expression and slight frown made Dave and Emory quit the banter.

"What's up?" Dave asked, settling back as he tended to do when things were poised to turn serious.

Terry chose his words, taking his time to formulate his thoughts and impressions. The same as always.

"This is likely of more interest to Emory, but it doesn't hurt you to hear it as well. Talk is making the rounds about a group from New Jersey buying prize bulls for their ranch up in the Stampede area."

New Jersey.

"That's odd." She shrugged, but her mind whirled. "New people are moving in, but bulls aren't that common in the area, and especially not prize ones."

"The point I'm making is," he paused to make sure he secured her attention, "that this concern is using brokers to buy."

Emory bit her lip and shrugged, waiting for him to continue.

"It seems, according to one of the brokers I happen to know, that these buyers don't appear to know a darned thing about bulls or cattle. They're making general pests of themselves and driving up prices for no real reason."

"That's odd. Hope they hired a good foreman to go along with their investments," Emory quipped, shaking her head as she felt another tie to the past straining—people moving in to play at ranching. People who didn't know the first thing about any of it. Bulls were a distinct case in point, but whoever wrote the checks for their purchase possessed plenty of money to toss around.

"Is there a name or address he can share?" she asked.

Terry hesitated. "I didn't ask. Since it's your part of the state, I think you might want to talk to him, Em. He said he'd wait around if you want to walk over, and I'll introduce you."

"And it's close to the rodeo chutes," Dave prompted with the hint of a smile, which passed as a grin for him.

Terry looked at Dave like he'd lost his mind.

OUTSIDE AND ONCE THE door to the trailer closed, Terry resumed.

"Now, this guy's name is Frank LaChase. Normally he's not prone to talking about clients, so something about this deal isn't landing square with him."

Walking into the prize pens area, Terry spotted him right away. "Over there," he said, indicating the general direction by a nod of his head.

Around the man gathered prospective buyers or hangers-on, and Mr. LaChase sure acted the part as the last of the good old boys. Terry and Emory hung back at the fringes of the group standing enough apart to attract the man's attention.

The broker latched on to their presence like a trout

snapping insects, and held up two fingers in their direction.

A few laughs erupted as conversations concluded, and handshakes and some backslapping passed all around.

"I see some people whose good side I need to stay on," he said as he stepped aside, breaking away from the live-stock buyers and hangers-on.

Once his banter ended, the people peeled off and dropped away.

"Frank LaChase, this is Emory Cross, our newest brand inspector."

Frank held out a wide, meaty hand. "My pleasure, young lady."

Emory shook his hand, making sure her clasp was firm. "Nice to meet you."

Terry cut the pleasantries off at the pass. "Emory's from the Lost Daughter Ranch outside of Stampede. I mentioned that you're dealing with another broker who represents an...interesting client. They've had a bit of trouble up that way."

The broker's eyes first turned beady, then bothered. "What kind of trouble?"

Emory sized this game up as an *I'll show you mine if you show me yours* type of exchange.

She calculated how much to share. "Oh, like every-where else, land prices are through the roof, and that brings a whole raft of new problems. The thing is, the prices commanded by some of these remote ranches are astounding. What's more, not all of them would be considered prime locations. Some of the land is going for stupid amounts of pure cash. Cash offers in the millions. We don't understand the how and the why of it, but it can't be considered good."

The man took her at her word, but his guarded expression said he would make her work for any information she might receive. "Could just be a load of wealthy people looking for investments," he spread his arms wide and theatrical, "in the clean mountain air."

She paused, face poker still. Emory locked into his eyes for several seconds before responding so that she got her point across—that playing her wouldn't work.

"Ranchers are selling unused high pastures; some are selling their entire spreads for what they consider a windfall. Tax evaluations rise for the rest of everyone else, making it hard to pay. Beyond that, the land these people are buying may not even have good water sources. That's a real issue, whether they know it or not, that ought to devalue the investment, but it doesn't seem to be working that way. We always figured, wealthy investors aren't wealthy because they're stupid."

"Which brings us," Terry inserted, "to why I wanted to introduce the pair of you. Frank, do you mind telling her what you told me earlier?"

Caution swept over the man's florid face. "I guess I could...provided we keep this between us."

Emory nodded. "You have my word."

"The broker's client is buying some mighty expensive bulls. They're going to be shipped up to Rimrock County. No loans—just EFTs." He glanced at Terry. "Electronic fund transfers—like wire transfers of cash. Their instructions are to buy the best, which means in their minds *the most expensive*. They're paying me a percentage of the purchase price to obtain a level of confidence that I point out the best...in this case, meaning the bulls with the largest price tags. Their broker takes it from there."

He implicated himself right there, and he knew it.

She had the good graces to pretend not to notice, although they all did. "Not many ranchers keep bulls in our area. How many are you talking?" A warning zinged up Emory's spine.

The broker quirked his head and eyed her. "They're not going by the number of heads. They're going by budget. Now you see why that's striking me as a remarkable condition?"

She did.

"I can see that frown inside of your head," he lowered his voice and leaned in. "Their budget is $1.5 to $2 million all in."

Emory blinked a few times, astounded. "The entire state of Colorado would know about an operation like that."

"Hence, my point," the broker replied with a firm nod.

"Don't suppose you could provide a name or an address, could you?" she asked as the three of them stood there, locked together in a private conversation, backs positioned to keep intrusions at bay.

It didn't entirely work.

"Frank!" A pair of ranchers walked up, breaking the moment into two.

Terry and Emory made their excuses as they turned away and left Frank LaChase to conduct his business and jolly prospective buyers along.

"How well do you know him?" Emory cast a glance over her shoulder, registering the fact that the broker didn't miss a beat. Already he regaled his newest arrivals with whatever he wanted to sell, but he'd make them certain that it all came down as their idea first.

"Well enough to know that he knows what he's

looking at, and don't make mistakes with numbers," Terry replied.

Emory chewed on those notions, uncertain and worried. "I thought about going to the rodeo tonight, but it can wait."

"There's a rodeo on every night," Terry offered to soften any sting.

"A name or address sure would help. Could we look and see if any of those shipments are already in the computer?"

"They aren't. The sales started going through today. Chances are they'll ship them all together, so all we have to do is look for expensive sale prices going to a combined destination. I'm heading home for the night. I'll check today's results again first thing in the morning."

"That's a lot of driving," Emory said.

"Yeah," he admitted, "and I'm tired. Just don't like being away from home too long. See you in the morning."

"See you then," Emory replied, sensing a new threatening facet had taken up residence in their district.

That conviction made her even more uneasy along the base of her spine. She needed to talk to her father.

BONE-TIRED, Emory returned to her hotel room and felt adrift. Perhaps she ought to have returned to her apartment in Greeley, but she took the offered hotel room for convenience and as a result, felt unsettled.

Sterile, clean surfaces, neutral colors with a pop of green, and a crisp made bed may have been nice for most people, but they put her on edge. Considering the grime wedged underneath her fingernails along with the dirt and dust caking her jeans, the call home could wait for a few moments. She jumped into the bathroom for a quick shower, unwrapped the flimsy hotel-sized soap and turned the shower on high and hot.

She never could get the water that hot at the Lost Daughter.

Better after the grime washed away, she dressed in clean clothes and picked up her cell, with a fifty percent charge. Pretty good, for her.

"Hey, Dad."

"How's the stock show shaping up?"

"There's enough work to go around, that's for sure. Has anything happened since I've been gone?"

"In four days? I would have called you if it had. Geez, you're like an old mother hen. No, nothing's happened. Other than Linda said you weren't exactly friendly toward her."

A pregnant pause fell between them as she twitched her mouth to the side. Nevertheless, words sprang forth.

"Linda Paulson. What is it that you want me to say? I don't really *know* her...and it wasn't exactly the time to be paying social calls. Not considering all that had happened."

"She wouldn't have known that, Em."

Irritated, she pressed ahead. "Anyhow, I've learned something that's important." Other than Linda Paulson's feelings one way or the other. "There's a group out of New Jersey buying expensive bulls and they are shipping them to Rimrock County. They're buying the most expensive champions and have a two-million-dollar budget to spend, or something along those lines. Have you heard anything about that one?"

The silence on the other end told her plenty.

At length her father spoke. "Bulls you say?"

"Yeah. *Expensive* ones. It's more than seventy-five miles from Denver to there, so they'll have to have transport papers. I'll see what I can find out and Terry's going to check in the morning, but the people down here are acting spooked. The deals are straight cash passing through a couple of sets of hands. See the problem?"

"Yes." Her father's clipped tone in his one-word answer expressed displeasure beyond the bulls. He expected an apology out of her.

She thought about it and didn't feel much like apologizing. Deep down she knew her father went forward with his life and had developed a new interest, potentially shutting her out. She relented a degree owing to the fact that he remained her only living relative that she knew. Her mother might still be alive, but Emory didn't know where she was and didn't exactly care to find out. Anyone who would just up and leave a child...

"You can tell the historical preservation lady that I'm sorry, if you must, but since when do people just come onto the ranch for social calls?"

"Since I invited her." Her father's voice had an edge to it he didn't normally use with her.

"At least it wasn't as bad as the time you ran them all off at rifle point. I take it you're going to file for that grant money?"

She didn't need to see his eyes to feel them narrow at her choice of words. "That remains to be seen. Just because I like Linda don't mean that I go for all her ideas. Anything else?"

No. No there wasn't. And their conversation ended upon that sour note.

EMORY SPIED the girl in the early evening hours on the third day the National Western was open to the public—a waif wearing an off-the-shoulder blouse, flowered miniskirt and ill-fitting cowboy boots about a couple of sizes too big. The full impact of her outfit was somewhat blunted by a winter parka—a *man's* winter parka—far too large for her tiny frame.

Whatever the case, it wasn't an outfit to wear in Colorado during the month of January by any stretch of the imagination.

The girl halfway posed, leaning against one of the pen posts, brown hair tangled across her face. Bright, overly shiny eyes peering through the locks and sized up the men as she hedged her bets.

She got attention, all right.

A few nudging elbows and some guttural laughs as the men swung wide, none of them caring to come any too close in case whatever the girl suffered from might be catching.

Emory watched for a long moment, before a big rancher lumbered over to her side.

"What do you suppose that is?" Emory asked.

The rancher didn't have to ask who, or what, she referred to. "That's one of them camp followers."

Emory shook her head. "Camp follower?"

"Prostitute. I'd be willing to bet a dollar on it, but I don't want to." He held out his paperwork.

Exactly what Terry told them to be on the lookout for.

Emory glanced at the girl from under her brim and weighed out the options. The man needed his papers signed off. That was her first job. *Inspect the brands.*

Pointing her concentration, she moved over to get a better view of the steers hindquarters and their markings. One came across as mottled. She eased her way around in the pen, staying calm and unhurried, fully versed in how cattle sensed stress and worry. She had no reason, nor did she want to, churn them up.

The steer displaying the wonky brand eyed her, and she eyed him back. Part of the brand stood out clear.

"What happened here?"

The rancher moved over to her side as she pointed.

"That came out as a botched job—my grandson's first attempt at branding. I told him he done good, but he didn't hold the iron quite square. Need me to hold the steer so you can get a better look?"

Emory shook her head, still staring at the brand. "That won't be necessary. Half of it's there but I'll make note of that for clarification."

"He's gotten better," the old man claimed, a trifle on the defensive side.

"We've all gotta start somewhere," Emory smiled, thinking of the vented hide at their ranch.

She jotted down a few quick notes and held out the paper for the rancher. "Now, about that girl over there. What can you tell me?"

He frowned, disapproving. "She seems to have staked out her spot, by the looks of things. I'm too old for that kind of behavior. Not that I ever paid anyone, you understand. Still, she shouldn't be here, being a family-type event and all."

"You see her around yesterday? She looks cold." Indeed, there wasn't much meat on her, and her skin came across as tinged a bluish-pale.

"Yup."

Emory pursed her lips. "She's turning tricks on the showgrounds?"

"No, I wouldn't go that far. I'd say that there's a fake cowboy in brand-new Western wear and tattooed knuckles prowling around in shiny, clean cowboy boots. I'd bet he has her working for him."

A man conspicuously trying to fit inside the rancher crowd who didn't belong.

That put things in a whole new light, and she wasn't sure she wanted to travel down that road again. Still, she waited the rancher out.

Unaware of Emory's recent history, the rancher studied the paper in his hands, considering matters beyond her signature and deeper within. Taking his time, he deliberately folded the document and stuck it in his billfold. Still troubled, he returned the billfold to his back pocket with a fair amount of deliberation.

"I'm not sure, but I'd say she takes them off the grounds, but hell. Trailers are all around, ain't they? No good will come of it, I'll say that much. I wonder where her parents are."

Warning bells jangled, loud and clear. "Maybe they weren't very good parents in the first place. Not everyone comes from a good family."

"True," the rancher lamented, before lumbering away. "Either that, or she's breaking their hearts. I'd wager she ain't no more than nineteen."

Another rancher intercepted her, and by the time Emory finished examining his livestock and paperwork, when she turned back to check on the girl, the girl had vanished.

Halfway relieved as the wind blew in cold from the north, she snapped a picture of the pen number so the location wouldn't get lost in a flurry of numbers and brands and competing demands.

Nevertheless, she took it all for a bad business and tried to shake off the sense of dread that lingered.

Like the Red Sea parting, the milling people veered aside at just the right time to reveal Terry standing straight ahead. Standing in plain sight, he wrote on his clipboard and made small talk as he jotted down information.

She kept her eye on him, intent on keeping him in her sight.

"Terry!" she called out from about twenty yards.

"Hey, Em. What's up?" He didn't give her his undivided attention. Not even a quarter of his attention. No, occupied with doing what she ought to be doing—looking at brands, clearing sales, and signing off on transportation papers—he performed his job.

"Could I have a moment, please?"

The use of the word *please* got his attention, all right.

He finished his task and handed over the paperwork, before coming over to her. "Problem?"

"Maybe. Remember how you asked us to keep our eyes open for trafficking? I'm pretty sure I found a prostitute. A nearby pen's rancher thought so as well."

Terry chewed on that piece of information, tipping back his hat and scratching his forehead.

"You don't say."

"I meant to go talk to her when I finished up, but she had gone."

"*Talk* to her? No one ever said anything about talking to them. We'd call the number they gave us."

"How else am I supposed to know if she's being held against her will?"

"Whoa, whoa, whoa," Terry held up both hands, and clipboard. "I guess you do have a point, but still."

Emory put her hand on her hip, annoyed. "How do you want me to go about it, then?"

Ha. He hadn't thought that far.

He eyed her. "Given your past history, you above most others should know how play can get rough. I think we should leave such issues to those who handle vice, don't you?"

Based on her very recent experience, Emory didn't see any reason for pussyfooting around. "But if we're supposed to call for *trafficking*, I don't think we'd want to call the number for a plain case of prostitution. Do you?"

"Listen to you—*plain case of prostitution*. I think we should do our job and let the vice officers do theirs."

"Maybe," she conceded.

He doubted that she would follow his advice, and he himself didn't know enough to make that call. Nevertheless, he wasn't surprised because he had no reason to be. The plain fact of the matter held that Emory tended to find her target.

"Change of conversation. Did you find out anything about those bulls headed to Rimrock County?" Emory asked.

"Sure did. Transportation papers list a group called Blue River Ranch. Heard of it?"

Emory shook her head. "Maybe the name's changed," she muttered, feeling her world tilt more than comfortable.

"The buyer is listed at Smith and Associates, Toms River, New Jersey," he added.

"That doesn't mean a thing to me," she replied. "Yet."

Perhaps events unfolding were all further signs that time had a way of wearing down the staunchest resistance. Deep down, it felt like they were losing control.

14

THE RODEO'S BRIGHT LIGHTS

THE MUSIC BLARED IN THE DARKENED ARENA AS THE Westernaires thundered in on their horses, replete with Day-Glo accessories and the spotlight upon the American flag. The crowd bounced along to a western hip-hop song repeating the lyrics:

If you're ready to have a good time, say hey!

"HEY!" The crowd shouted back, excited and revving as the horses thundered around the arena in skilled precision riding.

The riding and formation slowed as the American flag took pride of place. Hats were removed as they sang "The Star-Spangled Banner."

Then the Westernaires and the music revved right back up as the hip-hop tune returned. *If you're ready to have a good time, say hey!*

"HEY!" Echoed around the coliseum's arena.

The announcer's voice boomed over the loudspeakers as the flag rode off in a thundering exit.

"Ladies and gentlemen, it's about time to BUCK 'EM!"

The crowd roared. That night marked the run-up to the rodeo finals, and their group of brand inspectors had the night off—Dave and Terry stood at Emory's side as the spectacle built, loud and boisterous.

Activity surrounded one of the chutes in particular, the chute leading off the bronc riding event. Three handlers struggled to adjust tack and manage the chute as the cowboy lowered down onto the thrashing horse, wrapped the rope around his right hand, and leaned back. Left hand held up, tentative and cautious. At his abbreviated nod, the gate swung open.

Left arm raised free and fingers pointed skyward, the cowboy rode the buckskin horse as it turned out of the chute. The announcer's voice boomed as the horse cleared the chute's confines and bucked toward the open arena.

"Alright, Dustin, let's see what you've got!" the announcer challenged.

Five big bounds, springs, and crow-hops until the cowboy found his rhythm enough to spur. Left arm raised higher and confidence building, his ride strengthened all the way up to the point where the eight-second timer sounded.

Mission accomplished and ride ended, the cowboy quickly snatched the rope with both hands and the pickup man pulled his horse alongside. Grabbing the pickup man's waist, the rider swung off to the crowd's applause. He took off his hat and raised it to the crowd.

The brand inspectors glanced at each other. A fair ride, it scored a seventy-two.

"It took him a while to get settled," Emory remarked.

"You ever ride a bucker like that?" Terry asked, and it was no idle question.

"Never," she admitted with a laugh. "Can I ride a

buck, yes. Do I want to do that? No. That pounding hurts if you didn't know already, and don't let anyone tell you any different."

The next contestant readied. The electronic timer on the scoreboard reset to zero.

"This next cowboy also hails from the state of South Dakota, Jake Plummer," the voice announced.

A flurry of activity at the chute conveyed problems. By all indications the horse wouldn't settle enough for the cowboy to lower to be seated. Flashes of the horse's arched back as the men worked to steady him made it clear this would be no easy bronc to ride. The struggle continued. The cowboy climbed over the top chute rail and eased himself onto the horse's back. One arm on the chute's top rail and one hand grasping the rope. Still, the cowboy hesitated.

"That's one feisty horse," the announcer drawled, to cover the drawn out time.

The cowboy spoke to the men hanging on to the chute, and one of the handlers adjusted the tack. The horse refused to hold his head up.

This drawn out process took time. The spectators squirmed.

"I'd really like to have that horse's head up before that gate swings open," the announcer said, like he could actually do something about it.

The hype and momentum drained.

Right arm up and the rider gave his nod, the horse bucked clear from the chute—lovely arched back and mane flying. The cowboy spurred in perfect rhythm with the bucks.

But then a bit of daylight became visible between him and the saddle. Unseated, he flew clear, landing in the dirt.

He didn't make time.

Score, zero.

He picked himself up off the ground and limped over to the side.

The next rider readied himself; a rider from Utah.

He nodded, and the gate swung open. That horse crow-hopped, bucking a jagged pattern. The bronc never traveled far away from the chutes but bucked high once he got going. The cowboy rode well and made the time.

Seventy-nine points.

Two more cowboys rode and went flying, landing scoreless.

The second to last rider climbed the fence and waited to crawl over to sit in the saddle. The horse, a big paint, struggled and fought in the chute. It reared up high on his two back legs, towering over the upper rail. The handlers had their hands full to get horse and rider arranged. In fact, the cowboy jumped off the rails and down to the ground behind, while the handlers brought the horse back under control.

It wasn't the best of signs.

But the cowboy wasn't about to give up and reclimbed the fence, lowered down and nodded. The gate swung open wide, and the cowboy held on, loose arm snapping to bucking rhythm, and well away from his body. It wasn't a fancy ride, but it did the trick, and he made his time.

Seventy-two points.

The last cowboy got ready in his chute. A guy from Wyoming, but Emory no longer listened to the announcer. Her eyes caught on a flash of something not quite right—tattooed knuckles and big old biker's rings —standing behind her in the sea of cowboy hats in his brand-new Western wear. True, a whole lot of people had on new Western wear. It was something of a miracle that she had spotted those tattoos.

Before the buzzer could sound, the crowd moaned.

Emory didn't hear the thud of the body hitting the ground, but she instinctively glanced over in time to see the cowboy getting to his feet, clutching either his shoulder or his arm.

A hazard of the trade she figured, wry yet deep down, sympathetic. Broken bones were no laughing matter.

Swiveling back to where she thought she saw the tattooed knuckles matching the rancher's description, all she found was a churning mass of cowboy hats and blue jeans and nary a man's ring big enough to attract attention.

"Em?"

She turned back to them, just as Dave said something about cowboys.

"I thought I saw that girl's bully," she said, low and guarded.

Dave's head swiveled around—as did Terry's. Dave used his height to stretch a bit taller, peering over the crowd as best he could. "He's headed for door number four if I've got the right one."

"I'll be right back." Emory brushed past them before they could argue, jogging toward the exit, dead calm and intent.

People milling around were not all that easy to thread through in an expedient manner. She wove in and out, brushing shoulders and offering a few scant apologies.

Bird-dogging.

Outside in the cold January night air, breath turning to a cloud, she scanned the lot in front of her but saw nothing at all unusual. Nothing that she shouldn't.

Terry and Dave turned up right behind her.

She glanced at them. "He could be anywhere."

"Not sure it's such a good idea for you to be chasing after him, regardless," Terry chastised. "I kinda figured you might have learned your lesson by now."

"Yeah—but I guess I didn't. Let's go down the stairs into the back lot." Emory didn't mean it all to come out as clipped as it did, but she could apologize later.

Without waiting for them to either agree or decline, she turned around and picked up her stride, crossing the cement walkway, and rushing down the outdoor back stairs into the edges of the floodlit loading area.

The floodlights, although far reaching, left shadows between. City shadows that covered or obscured any number of things out in the dark spaces that held different threats than those in Rimrock County.

Squinting into the darkness without success, the two brand inspectors huffed up behind her.

"You did say to keep an eye out," Dave reminded Terry in that flat way of his.

The senior inspector snorted, ill-humored, in response.

Emory turned her attention in the direction of the pens, taking special note of where the girl staked out her turf earlier.

"I don't think he went this way," Emory admitted at length.

The sound of the rodeo drifted outside, catching on the night air. The contrast couldn't have been more pronounced. Inside the arena were the bright lights and the spangling family entertainment. Outside, in the shadowed back lots, another primal existence played out.

Each one of the three of them knew there were far

more ways to lose than there ever were to win. Emory felt the basic truth most keenly.

THE FOLLOWING MORNING, bright and early, the stockyard roused itself from the festivities and business of the night before. The morning sun hung low on the horizon in the watery winter sky, the dawn painting in yellow and purple pastels to the east.

No matter how pretty the sky, it didn't exactly make up for the fact that she hadn't slept well at all. Her dreams ran disturbed, featuring the man whose tire she shot out from under him while he aimed straight at her, riding seventy miles per hour.

Just another event that she'd try to outrun. She thought she had, too. But the previous night brought those memories slamming back.

Emory went through her routine, displaying a desperate diligence, checking paperwork against the brands and signing off. She didn't *want* to see that girl, but she kept watch. Every time she had call to pass by that patch where the girl set up shop, she'd look. And hoping against hope that she didn't find her.

So far, that hope worked just fine.

And it remained a cold January morning in Colorado, almost like any other.

HOURS PASSED BY, and the early pastel hours brightened and melded into the afternoon, which in turn, drifted into dusk. Hugo worked in the same approximate area as Emory, so he stopped by to chat, coming up to the pen where she checked and signed, draping himself over the top rail to watch. Watching her work and knowing enough not to crack any jokes.

Their last encounter left them both uncertain and off balance, but not so fractured that she couldn't feel his presence before she even turned to look.

She tried to paste on a pleasant enough expression, but when she turned, she caught sight of the waifish girl standing a few yards off behind him. Plain as day and as unwelcome as locusts. That girl had resumed her previous day's location at the back corner of pen 253.

"Hey, Hugo," Emory said, never taking her eyes off the girl. In fact, she backed up a few steps to reach Hugo.

"Hello, I'm over here," he said.

"You see that girl over there?"

Her eyes darted to his face, then back to the girl.

"I do…" His voice came out slow and uncertain.

"Would you do me a favor and walk by and tip your hat at her?"

Shock rippled, strong and pure. "Oh, I don't think so, Em. That girl's a…a…"

"Now, we don't know that for certain," she corrected in her most persuasive voice. "All you have to do is walk by and tip your hat at her. You said that Texas wasn't settled by wimps."

"Hell, Em. Then what?"

"We'll see what she does or says. Didn't you get the same notice about how we're supposed to look for signs of human trafficking? I'd say that is one sign right there. I think she even has a pimp."

By this point, Hugo's eyes went truly bug-eyed at the notion. He sized up the girl, then sized up Emory.

Apparently, he decided Em was the scarier of the two.

"Have you seen anyone looking like a pimp around

recently?" Hugo sounded unhappy about the entire proposition.

"Of course not," Emory said, offering cold comfort. "The thing that stands out are tattooed knuckles and notable, huge biker's rings, if I've got it right. And I'm pretty damn sure that I do. If you see anyone looking like that, well…"

"And what do I do if he comes outta somewhere, and heads straight for me?"

"Relax. I'm wearing a gun. If he confronts you, as I see it, you've got two choices. You could say you were just being polite, or we could try to arrest him. I'll cover you. What do you think?"

"I think you're insane, and obviously I'm not much better. If I get in a fight, you owe me a steak dinner. A *good* steak dinner." He tried to crack a grin, but it didn't exactly work. His eyes darted, worried.

He watched the girl and scanned the crowd. Then he took a deep breath and shoved off. "Here goes nothin'."

He walked over in the girl's direction, and plenty wide of his mark, tipped his hat.

She opened her jacket and flashed her bra.

He shied like a spooked horse and legged it on by. Out of the shadows, the tattooed cowboy she'd just seen emerged.

The girl, reacting to Hugo's skedaddle, called out. "I won't bite, unless you want me to!"

Hugo didn't even break his stride. If anything, he picked up his pace—flicking the back of his neck with his fingers as if trying to get something unpleasant off him.

The girl, for her part, glanced back at the pimp and shook her head.

The pimp faded back into the shadows.

Neither noticed Emory standing there, watching the drama unfold.

That was creepy, how the man emerged and faded back into the shadows like a mountain lion, stalking the girl's prospective customers like prey.

Emory would have to wait for another chance, or a better opportunity.

It struck her as strange, to think of speaking to a prostitute in terms of an opportunity. Of a sort. Although the girl's actions solidified their assumptions to a large degree, there remained one very important missing piece of information. The distinction needed to be made as to whether the girl found herself forced into prostitution or chose her path voluntarily.

As far as the Texan's participation went, the only conclusion that Emory could reach on that count was that Dave might be better suited for that sort of caper than Hugo proved to be. Not to mention, judging by the way the Texan hightailed it out of there, she'd probably seen the last of him for quite some time.

But they hadn't accomplished all of what she had set out to do. What all of them were *supposed* to be doing.

Just as Emory decided to try to locate the pimp from a safe distance, another rancher approached, papers in hand and a job to be done. Reluctantly, Emory turned back and followed him to his livestock to check the brands and sign the transportation documents.

HUGO CAME to chew on her a couple of hours later.

"And that is the last time I tip my hat at your command," he drawled.

Emory did her best not to laugh in his face. "Looked like she scared you pretty good from where I stood."

"Maybe she did. Nothing like a large helping of sleaze to make a man decide to swear off being polite for a while."

That part made Emory's conscience twinge and her tone softened. She didn't want to ruin Hugo's manners, and all on account of people breaking the law. "Thanks for doing what I asked of you."

He nodded, still wary. "But I don't get the purpose of it all."

"The purpose of it is to determine whether or not she is being trafficked. I guess we got the prostitution bit verified."

"Shoot," an embarrassed grin. "I can honestly say that that was the first time a woman has showed me her bra out in the open, and in daylight, too. But my basic question still stands. What are you planning on doing?"

At that precise moment, Emory caught the sense that Hugo would tell Terry that she overstepped the bounds.

For her own good, of course.

She considered at Hugo's strong, square jaw. Blond-haired, blue-eyed, and clean-cut. Jeans hugging in all the right places. Straight as an arrow if a girl showing him her bra made him flustered.

Once again, the old insecurities about being a Cross trickled on in.

"Human trafficking is a serious issue," she ventured.

He stiffened, digging in. "How do you know she hasn't chosen her…profession…by choice?"

She hadn't an answer for that question because she'd never had the chance to talk to the girl, trail the pimp, or do anything much of use at all. Maybe the *trailing the pimp* idea wasn't so hot.

"Does she look happy to you?" Emory demanded.

"I wouldn't care to venture a guess," Hugo replied, equally dug in. "Now, I've got to get back to work."

Hugo stalked off to safer ground.

That time, he didn't give Emory a backwards glance, a tip of his hat, or even the hint of a smile.

15

WHAT ARE YOU DOING?

HUNTING DOWN A PROSTITUTE MIGHT HAVE BEEN OF secondary importance to her actual job, but it came first in Emory's interest. Drawn into the shadows, the brand inspector couldn't help but wonder what would make a girl willfully choose such a way of life. If she were in it for the money, there didn't appear to be that much of it going around—at least not judging by her getup.

The waif-like girl, skin-and-bones thin, shivered in the cold—although she tried to suppress her shudders to come across as hardened.

As to the pimp—Emory held no sympathy at all.

If the girl proved held against her will or forced to turn tricks—those yet unknown distinctions provided the impetus for much of Emory's attention.

Prostitution lived along those gray margins—like the Crosses themselves did plenty of times. Not with prostitution, but they traded along the gray margins featuring land grabs and livestock appropriations.

But that was then, this is now.

The inevitable comparisons rose between the two

young women. Deep down, Emory wanted respect, plain and simple. That girl likely didn't care what anyone thought at all—but what had happened? Deep down everyone wanted love, but if that were the case for the nameless girl, she went about it the wrong way.

Maybe, although she hated to admit it, Emory went about it the wrong way, too.

The young brand inspector watched for either the prostitute or the pimp, who predictably kept to the shadows.

Either he was very good at staying out of sight, or else he saw Emory coming before she saw him.

Badges tended to have that effect on certain types of people.

MORE BRAND CHECKING and corresponding paperwork to verify said brands.

She hadn't seen the sale or transportation papers for the expensive bull shipments come through, and that struck her as another oddity that required follow up.

During a lull when she had time to catch her breath, she seized the chance to track down Mr. LaChase. Terry held him in high enough regard, but salespeople always made her skin crawl.

Still, a conversation needed to occur.

Knowing it a knee-jerk reaction, she felt like holding her wallet as she approached. It might not have been fair, but she labored under the distinct impression that professional sellers told a person what they *thought* the person wanted to hear, instead of the unvarnished truth.

Many a goose chase started out in such a manner.

Emory found him holding court the same as when

she first met him, and about in the very same location. Again, she waited on the sidelines as he wrapped up his conversations and dealings.

Remarkably, he found her important enough to cut a few conversations short.

He walked up, cautious around the eyes.

"I don't think I told you, but I have a daughter about your age. She goes to CSU. We're hoping that she finds a job and works hard. Like you. Anyhow, what can I do you for?"

A college girl.

Emory would have liked to have tried that and supposed she still could. "Oh, just checking back. How's the show treating you?"

It wasn't as idle of a question as she made it sound.

"It is proving outstanding, but then again, it always does. I wouldn't do this if it was any other way."

Behind all of that forced joviality, something else lurked.

"You haven't heard anything else affecting Rimrock County, have you?"

"Funny you should ask. Now that I know its prized brand inspector and prettiest young lady, I've kept my ears and eyes open. There's a party planned for some time in February. Of course, the likes of me are not invited, but it sounds like one big whale of a shindig."

"And you heard this from…"

"No darlin', I don't reveal my sources. But let's just say that they're planning on a bachelor gathering—meaning no wives are allowed. And that usually means a couple of things—mainly bad behavior that they don't want getting spread around is at the base of their actions. From there it goes into drugs, booze, broads, and bulls. Oh my, that last part must have slipped right on out."

"I didn't hear a thing," she teased, sensing that was the very last she would hear of the matter.

"Do you know when they're planning on shipping their livestock?"

"At the end of the show, darling. Those bulls are still on display. Why don't you go have a look. Oh, and Emory? Someday I may need a small favor from you."

Emory smiled, her answer a slight shrug.

"Smart girl," he replied. "Never commit yourself to something that goes against your own interest. What the favor will be is that I'd like to know when the purchasers are getting ready to sell those bulls onward. That's how I make my money—brokering deals, and you and I both know that it'll only be a matter of time. Here's my card."

Emory took it and pocketed it with attention. "As long as the favor is legal and above board, I have no problem."

He shook her hand. "I'll be in touch."

She didn't doubt it. Not for one second.

———

THAT WASN'T A HALF-BAD IDEA, going to check out the bulls.

Emory went over to the prize pens and took a walk through the winners. Bulls were large, and in Emory's opinion, intimidating. *Dangerous.*

The showstoppers stood in their pens, for the most part uncaring. She read the paperwork hanging on the pens for the world to see. A fair number of the animals were purchased by the same outfit.

B.F. Helman, LTD. Saddle River, NJ.

Emory clicked a photo of the information and moved away in a fluid motion, hoping that no one had seen a damn thing.

EMORY HADN'T COME across the girl or her pimp for a couple of days, as the stock show activities led up to their final crescendos. It was as if they had vanished into thin air, and truth be told, Emory found herself more than a bit relieved at the possibility that the problem had simply gone away.

Late on the final Thursday afternoon as the shadows lengthened, Emory made her way back to the brand inspector's trailer. She skirted a group of pens nearer to the service trailers.

The girl.

Like most problems, it hadn't gone away at all. The problem merely shifted locations. This time the girl stood at a different pen corner, jacket slouched down, and bare shoulder showing.

Emory searched the area conscientiously to see if she could locate the pimp but didn't see him.

Now or never, came a voice inside her head, so she took her chances.

"Hello," she said, coming right up to the girl.

The girl eyed her with plenty of hostility and latched upon her badge. "You gonna arrest me...*brand* inspector?"

"My name is Emory. And yes, I'm a brand inspector, but no, I'm not going to arrest you." *At least, not right now.*

"What do you want?" The girl no longer posed but tensed like she was fixing to spring.

"I wondered if you need help...if you're being held against your will."

The girl snapped her head back at what she considered an outlandish question. "You're a do-gooder, huh? You have no idea what you are talking about."

"I have an idea that you are turning tricks. I just want to make sure you don't need help."

"I don't need help turning tricks."

Emory hesitated.

"Get lost," the girl tried to shoo Emory away. "You don't need to be involved here. Just turn a blind eye, like the men do."

Emory didn't like being shooed away. Maybe it had something to do with the badge, maybe it had something to do with the fact that Emory knew positively that she could outmuscle the hooker in a fair fight. "You're doing this for money, aren't you?"

"You checking brands for money, ain't ya?"

"I am. But no one is making me do it."

Something in the girl folded a bit, and she scanned around. "Look. I know you mean well but stay out of it. OK?"

Emory searched the surrounding people. "The man with the knuckles and the rings. Does he work with you?"

"I work *for* him. Now please go away before he comes back and sees us talking. You know what those knuckles say? *SLOW BURN*. If you wanna help me, I'll tell you what. Go away and pretend that you don't notice a damned thing where I'm concerned. *That* would help me."

"I take it you're afraid of him," Emory prompted.

"Never said that," the girl snarled, but something in her eyes said otherwise.

"You aren't conducting business on the stock grounds, are you?"

"No. Just finding customers. Now go. *Please.*"

THAT ENCOUNTER left Emory irritated and put out. She hadn't accomplished a dang thing at all.

In fact, she had even allowed the girl to chase her away. *Slow burn* her ass.

At the time she hadn't wanted to put the girl in danger —worried that the pimp might give her a beating. But now upon second consideration, she felt like she hadn't done her job at all, or anything else that she set out to do.

Returning to the brand inspector trailer, she sat down at the table, distracted and bothered. Emory had one night to either figure out the situation or leave it behind. Tomorrow she would rotate back to Greeley to handle their routine business.

She knew what Terry would say if she told him of her idea.

Shift done, technically she could be off the clock anytime she chose. She could at least try to trail the girl to figure out where she took her customers, and maybe she would learn a bit more besides. The idea gnawed inside of her as did the girl's fate. Emory would be stepping out of bounds—she knew that. But fighting *real* crime took a bit of doing. That often meant not playing by the rules. That one, fine point seemed to be the part that most people overlooked.

As the sun lowered behind the mountains to the west and the evening chill set in, the shadows lengthened, and she weighed her options.

It would all be a moot point if the girl wasn't where she could find her in the first place.

She slapped the table's surface, moving out from behind it, clamped her cowboy hat down a bit firmer, and headed out of the trailer prepared to do some trailing.

The wind had picked up, cold and from the north as the evening turned dark gray. Leaning into the wind and hand clamping on the crown of her hat, she set forth nodding greetings as she scanned the pens. More precisely, she scanned the people lingering around them without a clear, stock-driven purpose.

On account of the cold wind, people didn't act inclined to stop her for a chat or an exchange of pleasantries. The cattle themselves could have cared less about the weather.

Emory passed down one stock aisle and rounded the corner where the girl staked her turf, or at least where she had until Emory had blundered up all helpful and completely unwanted.

No one and nothing stood there, other than for a corner post and a patch of dirt.

She pulled up short, thought about it. Pursed her lips, hard and unhappy.

"Looking for that tramp?" came a female voice.

Emory turned. "Don't know that I'd put it that way exactly...but yes."

"Something ain't right there." The voice belonged to a heavy-set ranchwoman who'd probably seen her own fair share of grief and hard times. But something in her eyes cared, despite her choice of words.

"No," Emory agreed.

The woman's eyes sparked at Emory's badge. "I'm

down about four pens. I've been watching myself. Don't like it."

"What do you think is going on?" Emory kept her tone neutral.

"Well, hell. The same thing as you do," she shot across. "It's cold, she ain't dressed right, and she goes off with men. It's not too hard to figure."

"I asked her if she needed help," Emory sighed.

"And I'll bet she said no," the woman countered.

"Have you noticed the man with the tattooed knuckles and rings?"

"Sure. Anyone would have to be blind not to." The woman eyed Emory up and down. "How'd you get your nose busted?"

"Smacked a fence rail when I came off a horse," Emory chuckled, somewhat put out at the memory, and the fact that the break remained noticeable. "But that was a long time ago."

"Be prepared for another something broken if you go chasing that man and that girl around. I seen her giving him her money. That pissed me off royal."

"We were told to keep our eyes open for human trafficking."

Judging by the woman's expression, she didn't recognize that term.

"Prostitution," Emory clarified, to nail down the topic in no uncertain terms. "Against her will. That type of thing."

"Huh. I just don't like to see women handing over their money to men, and the men acting like they were entitled to it. Like the women were property." The rancher turned to leave.

She proved the first person that Emory came across who seemed to care, one way or another. "Wait. Here's my card and cell number. Could you give me a call if needed?"

The woman reached out for the card—the two women connected by a thin rectangle of paper as both hung on and neither let go.

"She ain't dressed for this weather," the woman said as Emory released.

"If she needs help," Emory replied, "I aim to see that she gets it."

The woman nodded her agreement and walked away with purpose, heading back to her livestock and her livelihood.

Emory had a job to do. For that matter, so did the girl.

16

EITHER A JOB'S WORTH DOING —OR IT ISN'T

DAVE AND TERRY WAITED INSIDE OF THE TRAILER.

"There she is," Terry said as she came in.

"The wind is blowing cold," she offered by way of an unneeded explanation as both of the men's skin blanched, tired and chilled.

"I went to see if that girl worked her patch," Emory explained.

"Nothing you can do about it, Em." Terry folded his arms over his chest like that settled matters once and for all.

She tried another tactic. "Are you two heading out and getting dinner?"

Terry didn't look fooled, but Dave smiled—curious as to what she planned. "Sure are. You wanna come along?"

"Sure. Where're you guys going?"

Terry shrugged. "I don't much feel like going downtown, unless either of you two really want to."

"It doesn't matter to me," Emory answered. "Just find me a big, juicy cheeseburger and I'll call it good."

"Restaurant in the hotel?" Dave asked.

"That works," Terry replied, decided on that specific matter, if not Emory's intentions.

THE RESTAURANT ATTACHED to the hotel didn't look like anything to write home about, but it would get the job done. They chose a table in the half-empty dark cavern, near enough to the lounge singer if they wanted to listen, but far enough away to hold a decent conversation should that prove the better option.

"Think I'm gonna have a beer tonight," Dave announced, sounding exhausted.

Terry stretched out, watchful but tired. "I might join you in that. Em?"

"Coffee," she replied. "I think I'll have coffee."

Suspicious, they eyed her.

"I got chilled, what can I say?" Emory met their eyes. *The road to hell was paved by partial truths.*

Terry's half-shoulder shrug, didn't mean that he didn't see through her intentions to return to the stockyard. Not for one second.

Emory turned with a manufactured interest to pay full, undivided attention to the singer, who chose that precise time to launch into her own special rendition of "Rhinestone Cowboy."

"Didn't know that song was still popular," Emory muttered.

"It's probably not," Dave intoned. "They bring in entertainers and tell them to cater to the stock show crowd, I guess."

Everyone catered to the stock show crowd, one way or another.

A lot of them didn't know what they were doing. But

that girl's pimp sure did. "I'd say she's a couple of decades late on that song being popular, but whatever. It's kind of cool in a vintage way."

Before either man could respond, the waitress came up.

"Three beers," Terry said, before she could even ask. His smile couched his emphatic response.

"I wanted coffee," Emory corrected, nevertheless.

The waitress locked into her, discounted the two older men, and didn't hesitate.

"Coffee it is," she replied.

Good for her.

Terry smiled, and although it wasn't exactly sincere, the waitress's backbone was still appreciated. "Sorry. Habit," he lied.

He waited for her to walk away, then faced Emory square.

"I don't want you going back to the grounds."

"Getting me to drink a beer wouldn't change any of that. If you're worried, you could come along."

Terry sighed.

Dave stretched out and locked his fingers across his stomach. "You did tell us to keep our eyes open. Doesn't seem to make much sense not to do something about what we find."

The beers and her coffee came.

"I forgot to ask if you wanted cream or sugar, so I brought both," the waitress said, still wary to the point where Emory felt she owed the woman an explanation and smiled to put her at ease. "Thanks. We're brand inspectors, and I'm just going to go back out later tonight to check on things. Beer would make that a bit more unlikely to occur."

The waitress relaxed. The hotel staff had obviously

been told to be on the lookout for trafficking as well. And although she hoped she didn't look the part, a man ordering beer for a woman who wanted coffee seemed a tad suspicious right there.

"Do you all know what you want for dinner?"

The men ordered steaks, rare of course, and Emory ordered her cheeseburger.

"Another beer, please," Terry said, nodding to Emory. "Since you're driving."

MEAL FINISHED, both Dave and Terry looked done in to the point where Emory felt almost guilty.

"Shall we?" Dave asked.

"Wait," Emory said. "Let me tell you what I'm going to do, and then you can decide if you really feel the need to accompany me. I'm going to try to locate the girl to see where she goes. I've been told it is away from the show grounds, and in one of the adjoining neighborhoods. Then I think we would call the regular police once we are certain as to what is actually going on. Correct?"

"You plan on wearing a gun?" Terry remained on edge and not completely sold. "Prostitution is a far cry from checking brands. Why don't we just alert the regular police and let them deal with the entire thing? The girl and her pimp are breaking the law—plain and simple."

She considered both questions for a moment.

Terry set his jaw. "You haven't figured that far?"

Emory sniffed and shifted in her seat. "I guess I'm just used to handling problems when I find them. I can go armed if you like—that's not an issue. If I go alone, I'll carry the rifle in the truck, and will wear the .45."

Terry shrugged. "What do you think, Dave?"

"I think a couple of things. If we tell the police, we're only handing them part of the equation, aren't we? I'd suppose if we're going to get involved, we can do better than that. Second point, I don't see how anyone is going to exactly *drive* to where this girl is taking her customers. I mean, you're following them on foot, ain't you?"

"That's the plan. I mean, sure, we can turn it over to the regular police, but won't the pimp see them coming? Even plainclothes ones would likely stand out in our crowd...wouldn't they? Chances are that the end result would amount to the girl getting arrested, and the pimp scuttling off, free and clear and able to set up business again. I vote we go after the root cause."

By the way the two men held themselves, they agreed with her latest root-cause argument. Plainclothesmen standing out like sore thumbs was a notion they understood. She pressed ahead. "You two—Dave you only drank half of that beer—follow as best you can in the truck. I'll stay in contact by cell phone. What do you think?"

Terry considered and took his time about it. At length he said, "Let me see your bars."

Emory held up her phone for inspection. One hundred percent charged and ready to go.

"You've got to admit she's getting better about it," Dave said, rising.

And that was as close to a compliment as she would get on the matter.

———

EMORY TOOK THE WHEEL, the three of them cramped in the single bench cab.

"Your grandfather owned this first, right?" Terry folded himself into the middle as the labeled brand inspector's truck was a nonstarter for this mission. "What year is this, 1950?"

"Don't be ridiculous. 1985."

"Hope it doesn't conk out tonight," Dave sighed as Emory drove back to the stock show yards—the city streetlights passing by in a blur.

Halogen lights became less frequent the closer in they drove to the grounds.

Pulling up along the fringes of the parking area swathed in the shadows, Emory hopped out, tossing her hat into the cab for Terry to catch.

"Best to make myself as small as possible," she remarked as Dave switched places, taking the steering wheel and pushing back the seat.

"Call me now," Terry said from the passenger seat, and Emory dialed his contact. Terry's phone rang. "Now, you leave this on."

"Yes, sir," she replied.

When he nodded that they were set, Emory plugged in her ear buds and jogged off into the dark shadows that the yard lights failed to reach.

The sounds of the rodeo threaded on the night air. Most people were inside at the performances or vendor booths—only a few singular ranchers remained out in the yards, tending to their stock in the night pens.

"Coming up to where I want to be," she said in a low voice, pressing forward.

She dodged a few shoulders, nodded a few brief greetings, but her pace made it clear she wasn't there to shoot the breeze or kill time. Most people didn't want to stand out in the cold night air without good reason. No one tried to stop her as everything played out.

January nights earned the deserved reputation of low, clear nights and frigid temperatures.

Almost in view of the girl's patch, Emory craned to see...nothing. She pulled up short.

She stood there figuring out her next move. "She's not there," she said low.

"Then come on back," Terry replied, decisive.

Emory stood there, weighing her options. Just as she turned, a wisp of a skirt caught her eye.

"She's back," she whispered, scanning the crowd. "Looking for the pimp before he locates me..."

He likely remained inside the arena where it was nice and warm.

Footsteps came up behind her. Emory placed her hand on her gun and turned...

To find the rancher woman.

"She just came back. I've been watching for you," the woman said. "That just flat-out pisses me off."

"You didn't talk to her, did you?"

"Hell no," the woman's eyes widened. "What would I want to do a thing like that for?"

"You wouldn't," Emory agreed. "Did you see where she goes?"

"Now that, I did. Tonight she's taking the men down along the outer boundary toward the east. I happened to go down that way in the daylight. Sure enough, there's an old gate in that direction that nobody uses, well...it doesn't look much used at least. Other than for *them*."

Emory spoke into her phone. "You hear that?"

"Sure did," Terry replied.

The woman's eyes widened. "Is this one of those stakeouts like on TV?"

"Something like that. That's why I'll need to ask you to keep this to yourself."

"I already told my husband...He's keeping his eyes open, too."

Emory hadn't counted on that. Through her ear buds, Terry counseled. "Tell her that's just fine. Just let her know that the fewer people who know, the better."

"That was my boss talking. He said that's just fine, but the fewer people who know, the less the word gets out, if you know what I mean."

"I've got it," the woman replied.

"You don't know where that pimp goes, gets the men, or takes them, do you?"

The woman scrunched up her face. "I've seen him leading men over to her, but I don't know where he gets them from. All I know is that I'm staying away from him —he looks like a piece of work that I don't want to tangle with. Then the three of them will go down that way I told you about. Or at least today they do."

"Staying well away is a good idea," Emory replied.

"I'll leave you to it," the rancher woman said, "but I'll still be watching."

No doubt she would, and that wasn't an entirely bad thing.

THE GIRL CLAIMED her newest patch, standing on the cold ground, eyes darkened from too much makeup and her hand on a bone-thin hip and intentionally showing off her goods despite the frigid temperature.

Two men walked by, and she turned sideways lifting both her coat and her skirt, revealing an skinny thigh rising up to the curve of her ass.

She slapped her hip in suggestion.

Probably that slap solved two purposes, one to get

her point across, and the other to keep the blood moving.

The two young men reared back, then continued on their way jostling each other as they laughed.

Undeterred, the girl just waited for the next opportunity to pass her way, confident that one would come.

They always came.

17

THE STAKES RISE BUT THE
GAME IS RIGGED

THE PIMP EMERGED FROM THE SHADOWS, A MIDDLE-AGED man in tow.

A prospective male customer who did his best to come across ready for almost anything carnal in the big city of Denver. Stomach protruding well over his belt buckle, he sized the girl up and down, leering. She opened her coat advertising her goods. Greed and lust carried the motion—the john nodded and the three of them headed toward the outer perimeter.

"Told you," the ranchwoman hissed, materializing back at Emory's side, never having crossed the distance to return to her livestock pen.

No doubt she found the unfolding drama enthralling, more so than anything ever encountered on her ranch or farm.

Emory raised her hand with a dual purpose—a gesture of thanks, but also a signal meant to hold the woman off as she spoke into her cell.

"I'm moving," Em advised the brand inspectors.

"We're driving as best we can in that direction," Terry

replied. "We'll let you know when we see either you or them."

"Over." Emory paralleled the trio's movements, stalking from the shadows, leaving the ranchwoman behind.

The floodlit outer stretch of the stockyards didn't offer much in the way of cover. The shadowed margins were claimed by the trio, an obscurity that did a fair job of concealing their actions. Mirroring their movements one aisle over, Emory did her damnedest to remain undetected, and succeeded where at least the three perpetrators were concerned.

As to whether or not other people noticed the strange comings and goings in and out of the old, disused gate remained debatable.

Considering the appearances of the pimp and the prostitute, it seemed unlikely they would pass undetected.

But ag people sometimes kept their opinions on the actions of others firmly in the "none of their business" zone.

As the ranchwoman claimed, at the back end of the lots stood an old, forgotten gate in the shadows where the lights failed to reach. The three of them passed through, into the deeper darkness.

"They left the grounds," Emory advised into her cell, voice low and urgent. "They'll see me if I go through that way as well."

"Tell her we're on it," Dave's voice came from the background.

"You hear that?" Terry asked.

"On it how?" Emory cast around, still trailing behind but closing in on the gate.

"We're driving on an old frontage road near the train

tracks. Good thing this is an old truck we can drive without lights."

"Very funny," she hissed.

"They're crossing a vacant lot. We're pulling over to watch."

Emory saw their faint outlines in the darkness. "Do you think I can get out the gate without them noticing?"

"That one's a crapshoot." Terry didn't sound convinced either way.

A crapshoot analogy seemed pitch-perfect in this case.

The rusted gate, old and disused, led to nowhere more interesting or important than a vacant lot in an industrial area as far as Emory could tell. The faint outline of a footpath crossed through the dark expanse to an even darker trough between two old manufacturing buildings. At one point in time, this probably marked the outskirts of Denver proper, but the city overtook the stockyards and grounds, swallowing it whole.

Although it went against the grain and everything Emory had ever been taught about gates, she didn't latch it closed when passing through for fear of a metal clink carrying.

The silhouettes of the three were outlined faint against the light streaming from a few nearby porchlights—lights feeble in strength and not offering up much in the way of hope or illumination.

The sound of the cattle lowing in their pens threaded on the cold night air and carried. Emory's breath puffed out visible before her in a cloud of white vapor.

The bulk of an off-loaded semitrailer came into view, and indeed, that box marked the spot where the trio headed. Standing in plain sight that everyone nearby could see, and likely no one ever bothered to question.

Always measure up your surroundings as best you can.

That was another old gunfighter's rule her father drilled into her.

She didn't see any vantage points for shooting in either direction, as far as she could tell.

One thing remained for certain, she didn't have any cover.

The disused lot looked like a victim of an economic downturn. The passing footprints packed down a well-worn track in the snow, molded by the comings and goings of them and whatever customers they lured in. Emory found it hard to believe the people in the nearby houses failed to notice the happenings at the semitrailer. There was always the chance that someone had called it in, but it certainly didn't feel that way.

Maybe the police didn't even care.

Out of caution, Emory hesitated in the shadows. Looking upwards, a now glassless streetlight reduced to nothing more that steel might have once illuminated the vacant lot, but any light offered had died long ago. The girl, her john, and the pimp entered the semitrailer. After about two minutes, the pimp reemerged, and lumbered over to the warmth of a nearby house.

He didn't have to knock at the door. He just turned the knob and went straight on in just like he owned the place.

Maybe he did.

Asshole.

Emory shivered, but whether from the cold or the circumstances would be next to impossible to pinpoint as she watched and waited in that dark, vacant lot.

"They went in the semitrailer, and the pimp went into a house across the street," she whispered into her phone. Indeed, the pimp's profile stood out, backlit in a picture window. "Do you see where we all are?"

"I do, and we're calling the police now," Terry assured her, considering the episode as closed.

In the background, Dave spoke into his phone.

Terry continued on, heedless. "You hightail it back into the stockyard and back over to our trailer. We'll pick you up there because we can't get to you from here. The frontage road dead-ends into a drainage ditch."

"Don't you think we should wait to see what happens?"

"Absolutely I do not," came the response. "And that's a direct order."

Then she heard the scream.

A crash.

Terry's voice still came through, but his words no longer registered.

Sounds of a knock-down drag-out argument and a physical fight stole all of Emory's attention. Cautious of knee-jerk reactions, Emory searched the picture window across the street. If she once hoped that the pimp kept careful watch and would step in, she was sorely mistaken.

But not only had he *not* heard the altercation, he'd moved away from his surveillance spot.

Another scream followed, and Emory made a split-second decision.

"Going in," she announced to the brand inspectors on the other end of the call.

"No!" Terry's voice came through emphatic. "Emory…"

She stuffed the phone in her back pocket, muffling Terry's voice. She pulled out her gun and ran toward the trailer.

"Terry, please stop talking," she asked between breaths.

Raised voices. The girl's cutting through.

"Does that make you feel like a man, you—"

The crack of an open-handed slap, as Emory reached the corner of the trailer.

Gun held in both hands and pointing upward, Emory paused to take that all-important steadying inhale.

She sprang at the door, locked into place on the outside, trapping both customer and hooker inside.

That was one hell of a way to keep track of time and payments.

The two swing-out doors were latched but unlocked and Emory seized the handle, yanking it upwards.

The door swung open wide.

The girl laid on the floor, arm raised up to ward off another blow. The john's fist was clenched, raised, and poised to come crashing down upon her head.

Emory shouted her identification. "Officer! Stop! If you make another move, I swear I will shoot!"

The girl, recognizing Emory, collapsed back down onto the floor.

"Are you alright?" the brand inspector asked, gun still trained on the man.

"This asshole is crazy," the girl shouted.

Judging by the strength of her voice, she'd live.

"Hands above your head," Emory barked at the man.

The girl rolled over on her side and struggled to get up. Crouched toward standing, her thin, bluish arms covered her naked chest.

The man raised his hands skyward, pants missing and in his undershirt.

He didn't make the most attractive of pictures. And

now scared and about to be arrested, he came across as pitiful.

The sound of a truck pulling up reached them all.

Emory stepped to the side, her back hugging a wall. There was no sense in getting jumped from behind if she could help it.

And she certainly didn't feel like getting jumped by the girl's pimp, wherever that lazy no-account sack of shit hid.

She assumed the sound belonged to her truck, but she didn't catch the motor's cadence well enough to be certain.

"Brand inspectors," Terry's voice rang out.

Sirens approached in the distance.

"In here, Terry," Emory replied.

"Can I put my clothes on?" The girl's eyes, unnaturally shiny were dark and something in them pleaded.

"As long as you stay away from that man," Emory cautioned.

The girl dressed with her back toward the door. The sirens approached, louder. Terry stepped into the trailer, gun drawn.

"Is everything OK in here?" he asked, pointing his gun at the man as well. "Kneel down," he commanded.

The man fell to his knees.

"She tried to steal my wallet," the man pleaded. "I have a lot of cash in there."

"Liar! I did not," the girl challenged in response, but Emory didn't believe her, and the girl could see it—on drugs or not.

"He hit me!" she accused for the second time.

"Damn straight I did! I did that because you were stealing my money."

"Where is the wallet?" Emory asked.

"Probably in her hot little hands," the man replied.

The sirens pulled up right outside.

"Police!"

"You've got two officers in there, and two others," Dave's voice remained calm and distinct.

"Come out with your hands up," one of the policemen barked.

"That means you go first," Emory said to the john, "and you follow out after him, hands up high. Again, I'm asking you, where is the wallet?"

As the girl went to lift her hands over her head, she held it in her hand and tossed it over to Em in a surprisingly casual manner.

Smart enough to let it sail on past, the billfold thwacked on down to the ground. Emory kept her gun trained level to cover the pair of them.

That was another old range lesson. *Never catch something thrown at you while you have a gun in your hand. It gives the opponent the chance to draw and fire. Never EVER take your eye off your target.*

Outside, the police handcuffed both the hooker and the john.

"My wallet," the man whined again.

"She threw it over to me," Emory explained to one of the police officers, "but I didn't catch it."

Together she and the police officer went back inside to pick up the wallet. The officer opened it and thumbed through the bills. "That's at least a couple of thousand in here," he commented, shocked.

"Livestock can bring in a lot of money," Emory explained.

And the cop grinned. "Shoot. Might be I'm in the wrong line of business."

Back outside of the trailer, the pimp remained

nowhere to be seen as the police bagged the wallet for either evidence or safety. Emory didn't know which, nor did she care.

"Her pimp went over into that house right there," Emory said, pointing out the building.

The police called in for backup. This time the cars came rapid and silent.

And all they found was an open back door and the signs of a hasty departure.

———————

NEEDLESS TO SAY, Emory got a tongue-wagging the entire way back to the hotel, but underneath all the words and admonishments, Emory could tell that Terry was proud of her. That said, defiance of direct orders still rubbed him the wrong way. Chances were he'd give her the tasks that no one else wanted to do as a punishment—a punishment for being right and essentially doing the right thing.

Her cell rang.

Ranch.

"Hi, Dad."

"Hi, Em. Bet you wonder why I'm calling you."

She laid down on the bed to listen, tired. "OK..."

"Iver's son dropped off Outhouse for you. That's one thing. The next thing is that Iver's son said someone is making calls to Iver and hanging up on him. Guess he's gotten pretty spooked. The next thing is that Monty has been a bit delayed on coming down from Wyoming. Which could be a good or a bad thing, depending upon how one looks at it..."

"Dad..."

"Guess I'm rambling," Lance Cross admitted.

"You sound tired."

"You do, too."

"I am." And she was. She felt bone-tired. "A prostitution bust went down today."

"Branching out, is it? Well, here's a new branch for you. A local branch. A branch holding out a group of people it's hard to strike a bargain with."

Emory sat up in the bed and swung her feet down square onto the floor.

"What are you saying?"

"I'm saying that I need you to come home when you're done working in Denver. Just for a quick break. People holding strange ideas are moving in. Need I say more?"

Yes. Actually, he did, but his limited explanation would have to suffice. For now.

WORD of the prostitution bust thankfully didn't spread throughout the National Western grounds, proving something of a miracle.

The next morning, Emory went to work checking brands and filling out paperwork, grateful that everything was in the process of winding down. She went back to the ranchwoman to satisfy the woman's curiosity and to thank her again.

"That all should be over," Emory explained.

"About time, I'd say," the woman replied, although she offered a smile.

"I don't mean to tell you what to do, but the less said the better."

The rancher woman nodded. "Darn straight. This is

supposed to be an all-American activity. My lips are sealed on the matter. And good job, by the way."

With a smile and a nod Emory left, thinking how the woman didn't know the half of it, and even better, didn't want to know.

And sometimes, not knowing would prove the smartest course. Maybe that was a lesson that Emory should learn.

WORK PASSED by in the standard flurry of brands and paperwork. She only saw Hugo from afar. He remained angry about being "duped"—as he most likely considered it—and getting flashed in the process.

Still, they needed to keep their eyes open for the pimp. There was nothing certain that he only had one girl working for him.

In time, Emory decided she could stand it no longer, and approached the Texan. Of course, there were a couple of girls lingering about, admiring him and giving him those big, dumb cow eyes of admiration.

"Could I have a word?" she asked, making it sound professional.

The girls didn't scatter like she hoped that they would.

Hugo took an inventory of his bevvy and finished recording and signing. He handed off the paperwork finalized by a nod.

He seemed to have a particular interest in one of the girls, and acted reluctant to break away.

Probably served her right.

"Sure, Inspector Cross. Hang on just one second."

Inspector Cross? That was one way to keep his distance.

"No problem," she replied, clipping her tone.

He took his time to come over to her.

"What can I help you with?" he asked in a professional manner, playing like he held the upper hand.

"Come this way, please." She turned her back to the girls but had no way of making him do the same.

"I wanted to thank you for helping me earlier with the prostitute. She and a customer were arrested last night, but the pimp remains at large. Unless you already heard all of that from someplace else, that's what I thought you ought to know. We're trying to keep events under wraps. Maybe she's held under duress, maybe not. Likely, we'll never know for certain."

Hugo dropped the act. "No kidding? Well then, I guess it all worked out for a good cause."

Emory eyed him. "Hard to tell."

"No hard feelings?"

"No hard feelings on my part," Emory's eyes, however, strayed over to the girls in the distance.

He mirrored where she looked.

"They're just a bit of fun, Em. You're kind of hard to get close to, you know."

"What if I buy you a steak dinner?" Her question surprised the both of them.

He grinned. "I wouldn't say no."

"Will you then?"

"Will I what?" Now he was messing with her.

"Join me for a steak dinner. Tonight. If you don't already have plans, that is."

"I don't have plans, and believe I will," he offered another striking grin. "In fact, I thought you'd never ask."

Her heart jumped a bit, and she could feel a blush rise.

18

STRAIGHT LINES AND
CROOKED PROSPECTS

As time for the dinner rolled around, Emory felt butterflies in her stomach and a bit jumpy besides. Truth be told, Emory hadn't dated much at all. Young men never came to the Lost Daughter to pick her up for fear of getting run off at rifle point.

But that version of her life discounted Cade and his role—a stinging memory best left in the past.

Cade aside, in the past she arranged to meet her prospective boyfriends in town at the local park or the Cow Palace Dairy Delite, but even those occasions proved few and far between.

As to the spelling of the word "delite," it stuck right up there with the Kum 'N Go as far as those things went. Standards were slipping to hell and Emory rebelled at the basic assumption that poor spelling came across as quaint. As soon as she learned how to read and to spell with any proficiency, those butchered spellings rubbed her the wrong way.

The underlying assumption that people didn't know

how to spell in the mountains or rural Colorado felt like a losing prospect when they did it to themselves.

But back to her date with Hugo.

Unlike Cade—shit, she did it again—Hugo even insisted upon picking her up at her hotel whereas Cade would never have even thought to offer. Oh sure, if the pickup truck had already pointed toward town, he might have thought to offer a ride...but nothing further or more substantial.

Absolutely nothing to do with manners.

"I'll be there at seven," Hugo informed her when finalizing their plans.

The twinge of the truth still niggled. She had asked him out, but at the time he seemed just fine with the prospect.

Nevertheless, that invitation left plenty of room for Hugo to find her pushy. If she acted as nonassertive as possible, maybe that way he'd end up liking her a bit better.

All of which, she figured, amounted to stupid on her part.

He already knew her—knew she could willingly skin a calf to check the brand, and far more seriously, knew that she had killed a man.

Acting coy or demure belonged in the dust heap by this point in time.

Nerves twanging as she debated the best way to act that evening, she worked herself up into a ball of confusion in the process. Halfway toward putting on a dress, she changed course over to her makeup and took a half step back again toward the dress when her cell buzzed.

She stopped dead cold, caught halfway between her dress and the waiting makeup.

No doubt, the call came from Hugo. The brand

inspector figured out he couldn't make it for one reason or another and called to tell her as much. He'd explain how something unexpectedly cropped up causing their evening plans to change.

Edging over to look at the phone laying on the bed, the display flashed the single word, *Ranch*.

Which might have even been worse than Hugo calling, all things considered.

"Hi, Dad," she answered, picking up.

"How's the stock show treating you?" His voice held strong, but she felt the undercurrent.

"I've had about enough, I'll say that much. This is one long haul."

Her father chuckled in commiseration. "Hey, there's a reason why I'm calling."

"Never doubted it for a second." And she hadn't. Her father simply didn't make social calls. It didn't occur to him, for better or for worse.

"You see," he paused, gathering his words and thoughts, "Iver's truck got run off the road."

The shooters still roamed free. Whoever they were, they continued to go after the Holsteads for one reason or another.

"Is he OK?"

"Shaken up. But there's more. You know that the Double X Bar's sold, right? Again, no money went through the bank and it turned out a hefty selling price —another one of them cash deal specials. I wonder if those bulls you were talking about are destined to go there."

The Double X Bar covered at least ten thousand acres, on flat enough terrain. That made it a distinct possibility to house those high-priced cash bulls.

"Terry found something going to the Blue River Ranch. Heard of it?"

"No," Lance Cross replied. "People change ranch names to suit themselves, you know."

"No word on the shooters, I don't suppose?" Emory asked, already knowing the answer.

"No. I'd have told you."

"All cash deals are suspect. Like the bulls I told you about."

Her father warmed to the subject. "Get this—there's a sudden uptick of people from New Jersey around. They talk funny and they're hosting parties. One of them parties got a bit out of control. Drugs passed around and some girl OD'd on whatever they snorted or shot into their veins."

Odd. "Did she die?"

"Rumor has it—but, that's another strange part of the deal. You see, there's no body. True, they might have buried the girl somewhere out on the back range or dumped her down an old mine shaft, but one of the locals would have had to help them do that. Otherwise, she'll be turning up sooner or later."

Her heart hitched and she could feel her eyes widen at the notion, and none of it good. "Ah, that's sounds a bit extreme. Calling an ambulance would be easier."

"Sure seems like, but maybe they didn't want to answer questions."

"That's fairly brutal."

"If it's the truth, it sure is. No need for it in today's day and age."

Emory let the rumor swirl around in her brain. "It all might be a coincidence, and a tall tale. Where'd Cade sign on to after he left us?"

"Who cares? I don't know if he's on the old Kittleson

place or that Blue River outfit. Both spreads are in the same general direction and might share a fence line."

"Chances are they know each other."

"With all these comings and goings, I wouldn't put it as out of the question."

Emory took a deep breath, trying to fit the pieces of the fragmented stories together. "How'd you even come to hear a thing like that in the first place?"

"Not from Sheriff Preston, and that's for dang sure. Linda said that a report was filed from one of the guests of the guests. A woman who said that something bad happened. Linda heard all that in town. So did Monty. He said the exact same thing, and how the word is getting out cautiously. Very cautiously."

Bad. On multiple counts. But now wasn't the time to debate the Paulson woman or his cousin.

Logic. Emory needed to stick to the story and apply logic. Not go chasing after girls who simply might have left a party in the dark of night. "Does anyone know the woman who reported the crime?"

"That's part of the problem, you see. Apparently, no one can get hold of her either."

"Not good."

"No. I'd say it isn't. Obviously, *they* didn't want anyone to know their business, or that they had drugs and things got out of hand. Sure hope nothing happened to her as well, but it all sounds suspect to me."

His words hung in the air, churning.

Emory concentrated on the fundamentals as they applied to the Lost Daughter. "None of our neighboring ranches are thinking of selling up, are they?"

"That's what I'm now trying to figure out. After the Western Stock Show, I need you at home for a bit. You go talk to the neighbors to see what you can get out of them. They don't like to see me coming."

"How'd Monty hear about the girl?"

"Now that one came courtesy of Cade and the Ace High. He don't think much of Cade, I can tell you that, but he seems to like the Ace High just fine." A dry laugh followed.

But Emory didn't find a whole lot to be amused about. "Did either of you bother to tell any of this to Sheriff Preston?"

"That's what I'm struggling with here. If he's any good at law in this area, he should already know these things."

"That's a 'no.' Did Iver tell him that he got run off the road?"

"Don't know. That's Iver's business, not ours."

Sure. If everything ventured along normal, run-of-the-mill business lines. "Sounds like whoever *they* are, that they might have run Iver off the road because he got us involved."

Although she couldn't see him, she could feel her father nodding. "That's what I'm thinking, but I ain't got any proof."

"Um, Dad? I've got a dinner at seven. Is there anything more that I need to know right now?"

"Not unless you need to know that they shot up a place along the creek."

She blinked a few times and felt even colder. "Why didn't you say that first?"

"Guess I was working my way up to it."

She asked the question she dreaded. "Are you OK, Dad?"

A pause. "Yeah, we're fine. We might be the only ones that are. People like you, Em. I can go around askin', but that don't mean that they're going to be tellin'. Still, you'd have a better shot than me or Monty."

"Fine. Let me digest all of this, but I've gotta run. I'll call you after dinner or in the morning. How late are you going to stay up?"

She could hear him shaking his head at her question.

"Nine o'clock," he said firm and decisive. "Same as always."

"I'll call you in the morning then. You're sure this is serious, right?"

"I'm sure," he replied.

How, after all he had told her, could it be otherwise?

HUGO CALLED from the lobby at seven right on the dot.

She let the phone ring three times for good measure. Just to prove she wasn't anxious.

"I'll be right down," she said, a bit breathless when she picked up.

She could hear the unspoken question on the other end. "Great," came as the single word offered.

The elevator opened straight into the lobby. Hugo stood waiting all starched and pressed, clean and tidy. Even his boots. Emory glanced at them expecting to find traces of work, but no.

His eyes sparked when he saw her. "Wow, you're wearing a dress!"

She didn't have the desire to tell him that her black dress remained the last of the clean clothes in her case. Instead, she smiled and fluttered the hemline a bit.

"Did you pick a restaurant?"

"I sure did," he replied. "Even made a reservation because this is a city, after all. The truck's out front."

Even his truck came across as spick-and-span. "Are you from a ranch or a farm?" Emory posed her question for reasons other than making simple conversation.

"Why?" He glanced over at her as he drove.

"Everything's so clean," she admitted, feeling the Lost Daughter's shoddiness in comparison.

He laughed but took his time in answering. "Yes and no. We owned a ranch which we sold out when I was fifteen. Then we moved into town."

"Why'd you sell up?"

He sighed, turning into the restaurant's parking lot. "There was a bit of bad business and double-dealing. In short, Dad lost the ranch because he couldn't make the payments. However, on the brighter side, my grandparents kept theirs. I never lost the hang of it entirely."

As he parked the truck, Emory muttered, "I hear you on that front."

He eyed her and made no move to get out of the truck. "You sounded kind of strange when I called from the lobby."

She stared out the window into the parking lot beyond. "We're having a few problems and bad business of our own."

"Sounds like an interesting conversation for dinner." A smile played at the edges of his mouth.

She watched those lips and the tug of his smile; half afraid she might just kiss it.

Emory shook her head to get hold of herself. "Aren't we supposed to talk about pleasant and trivial matters?"

Hugo got out of the truck. "Hang on a second."

He came around his truck and opened the door for her in another display of good manners. She keenly felt how unaccustomed she was to receiving and accepting what most would consider a commonplace courtesy.

"You don't strike me like the trivial type," Hugo added, closing her door once she stepped out.

"Hope you're not one of those calling me Calamity Jane," she teased.

"Like I said, you're more akin to Annie Oakley, but I certainly don't refer to you as such."

"Better," she said, teasing. "But not good enough. In case you didn't know, she was actually quite small."

"Either way, I'd consider it a compliment if I were you," he said. "As a matter of fact, I call you Emory Cross."

She nodded, and her voice came out weaker than expected. "Thank you."

SEATED with a glass of wine in front of each of them, their eyes locked over the tops of the menus. Conversation hadn't exactly flowed.

"Oh, and by the way, Em, you aren't paying."

She set her menu down. "Like hell I'm not. A deal's a deal."

"I just wouldn't feel right. Especially considering how I…earned this steak dinner. Tipping my hat at someone I clearly knew worked…on the game."

He did look pained.

Still, Emory laughed. "Let's just see how the dinner goes, but maybe I'll let you pay the next time."

"If that's the case, you have yourself a deal," he replied.

Over their half-consumed dinners, the talk turned a bit more serious and less lighthearted. "You asked why I sounded a bit off when I answered your call. I had just gotten off the phone with my father, who asked that I come straight home after the National Western."

"That a fact?" Hugo's fork stopped midair, and he set it back down on his plate.

"There's talk about money laundering." She conveniently failed to tell him about the shooting. For the moment. She wanted to see his reaction before she divulged too much. "Brokers come in with plenty of cash, and ranchers sell off their back pastures, or maybe even the entire ranch. No one knows who's behind the cash."

His eyebrows raised, but he held his tongue.

"A neighbor got shot over this—or at least that's his version. His name is Iver. He ended up shot on our front porch."

"Holy cow, Emory."

She nodded, miserable. "You're allowed to ask, 'What's with you people.' I won't take it hard. Promise."

She tried to laugh, but it came out kind of strangled.

Hugo refused to be deterred. "Why your family?"

"Haven't you heard? We're the ones that people warn their children about."

Hugo didn't laugh. Not at all. He eyed her, unconvinced but wary.

"In all seriousness, our history runs long and hard. I guess that's the best way to phrase it. We're a legacy ranch and a centennial ranch to boot. Over time, we've learned to keep to ourselves, largely out of necessity." She shrugged. "Dessert?"

"Maybe in a minute." He eyed Emory. "Why?"

"Why what?"

"Why have you all learned to keep to yourselves?"

Emory didn't rush to answer. Instead, she assessed the other people in the restaurant, wondering what kind of conversations they held. It took a moment to turn her attention back to the man seated across the table from her.

"People say suspicious things take place on the Lost Daughter, so named by a suspicious death. The Hapless Susan—that's what we call her at least— died back in 1889. Story has it that she drove into Stampede for one reason or another one summer day. She had to cross the river to get there. The team, still in their riggings and attached to the wagon, were found on the other side of the crossing, completely fine and waiting. Susan was never seen again, nor her body found."

"That's troubling," he replied, long and drawn out, "but I understand. Sometimes strange things happen that can't be understood. Anything could have happened to that girl."

"Maybe. There's no way of telling. She doesn't have a grave because there's no body. But that didn't mean our reputations didn't grow. Now, I'm not saying that there weren't some shady dealings with appropriating mavericks, maybe altering a few brands, and fighting our share of the fights that it takes to keep a ranch. Hank Cross, my great-great-grandfather, was a tough old bastard by all accounts. He outlived his first wife—his second wife outlived him. There were children from both marriages, and the bloodline continued. The willingness to fight."

"And you?"

"Ha. I read plenty of books about Calamity Jane claiming she was an unfortunate drunk who probably meant well. Beyond that, she was also a whale of a self-promoter. Do you think I'm like that?"

"No," he stretched back. "No, I don't. Not unless you

start slinging back that wine you've barely touched and start taking potshots."

"And, like you've said. You've seen the Annie Oakley part, haven't you?"

"More like I've heard about it."

Emory dipped a shoulder. "Well, then. Have I scared you off yet?"

"Maybe that question ought to go the other way around. In truth, I can't help but get the feeling that you're giving it your best shot. Scaring me off, that is."

Emory flinched inside. "That's not true—not intentionally. But you've got to admit that we are different from each other. You're so clean-cut and I'm..."

A haunted look came over him. "What's that supposed to mean?"

"Nothing. Nothing."

The waitress came up. "Would you care to see the dessert menu?"

"Oh, no th—" Emory started.

"Absolutely," Hugo held his hand out for the dessert card and made a big show of studying it.

The waitress handed a card to Emory as well, who glanced at the selections. That was another whole other gauntlet to run with precious little experience. Women ordered first as a rule. She knew that. What she didn't know was whether she should order something large, or something small and dainty. It would be embarrassing to order a huge mound of molten whatever and then have him say he'd pass, that he'd just have a coffee.

In the end, she decided to take the safest course possible. "Apple pie, please."

Hugo chose the same.

Crisis averted.

She squirmed in her chair. *Still, she'd given too much away.*

"Back to our earlier conversation," Hugo said taking a sip of his wine. "I'm not going to let you get out of it that easily. Now what did you mean by saying that I'm clean-cut and you're not."

She toyed with the saltshaker. "Like you said, Hugo. I've killed a man."

"You never asked me if I've killed anyone." His blue eyes were bright and burned with a strange intensity.

"Alright," she played along. "Have you?"

A vein throbbed in his cheek at the turn she hadn't expected.

"Yes," he said. "Yes, I believe I have."

She waited him out.

"I was in the army before brand inspecting. I did one tour and we got ambushed. We were pinned down, and I assume I killed at least one of the men firing at us." He swallowed. "It took me a while to readjust. My best friend was blown to bits right beside me." Hugo looked away. "Blood, clumps of flesh, bone fragments, shredded Mylar." Again, that absent gesture of him flicking the back of his neck with his fingers.

"I'm sorry."

He looked across the expanse of that table at her, focusing on her and away from his memories. "That's what brought me to Colorado. A change of scenery. And for what it is worth, I'm sorry for you as well."

Just then, the waitress came out of the kitchen with their plates.

"Saved by dessert," Hugo claimed in a hearty voice that never once reached his eyes.

The waitress sensed something wrong.

"True," Emory cracked, to cover for him. "And there I

was, worried that one of us might go away hungry."

Meeting each other's eyes, they burst out laughing.

The waitress tilted her head and the moment passed.

But that marked the time Emory started to worry a bit about Hugo.

DISHES CLEARED AND CHECK PAID—EMORY insisted and in the end, won.

"Fine. Have it your way," Hugo said as he gave up on the argument. "But this means that you have to let me buy the next time. Say, next Saturday night?"

He wanted to see her again!

But then her heart sank. "I'll be up in Stampede. My dad needs me to come home to help."

"I didn't say the dinner had to be in Greeley, or anywhere else for that matter. I planned on taking a few days off myself. Why don't you pick out a restaurant up there?"

Emory blinked as her mind whirled with problems and complications.

He can't come up to Stampede—he'll want to see the Lost Daughter. There are no good restaurants. What will he find out about us? Dad will scare him away in no short order.

And then the last thought. The most important thought. *He knows how to fight.*

She met him square in the eye. "How about you buy me another glass of wine in the bar, and I'll tell you what is going on regarding that count. Then you can decide whether you want to come up to Stampede or not."

"I can do that," he replied. "Shall we?"

And her hand linked under his arm and they walked to the bar.

19

ONE SPUR SHORT OF A
FULL SET

DRIVING HOME AND EMERGING THROUGH THE WESTERN end of the Eisenhower Tunnel, the valley opened wide and Emory thought about the future. Hard. Having a boyfriend like Hugo Werner would lend her a legitimacy she didn't have wandering around on her own. She and her father weren't a team in the strict sense that they once were. First came the advent of Linda Paulson, and then came the addition of the cousin blowing down from Wyoming—whenever he managed to arrive.

Of course, her father forgot to tell her any details about Monty's arrival.

All of which meant that she potentially held the role as the odd Cross out in more ways than one. In the most important way, she trumped them all. It remained down to her to keep the bloodline going and the Paulson woman didn't appear to be of childbearing years.

Thank heavens for that small mercy.

In due time, the Lost Daughter would be hers.

To her surprise, fortune intervened in such a way that it felt as if respectability might actually be within grasp.

And there she plotted—figuratively counting on strands of history to arrange themselves in the form of a lasso—a lasso that would snare a prospective husband.

Toward that end and with reluctance, she agreed that Hugo could come visit but she made sure she sounded positive about the visit.

Which might not have been the best of ideas, but it was too late to change anything about it now.

She pressed the accelerator down harder and the truck picked up speed.

The purple mountains rose in the distance, growing as she neared. The sagebrush passed in a blur. Driving always turned her mind to abstract thoughts, and this time proved no different. She did her best to keep her immediate concerns at bay and focus on notions that wouldn't change the outcome of anything at all, like thinking about authors. Zane Grey again, to be precise. Hugo Werner could prove to be her Lassiter—if he had the stomach for it.

At that point she determined that she didn't want to think any more about Hugo. It was bad enough that he would see where she came from.

No, she thought about that other book. *The Homesman.* The one about the women who went crazy on the plains and that one woman, whatever the hell her name was, who got saddled with dragging them back East when they proved that life was too harsh in the West.

Emory, in part, understood why.

The other part of her rebelled against the notion. Women, in truth, were seldom weak. They might act like they were, or they might even believe it. But deep down, somewhere along their spine, most women knew that they could survive damned near anything once they set their minds to it.

She stomped on the gas harder, all but screaming into town.

Of course, she missed the posted speed limit that she'd seen every damn time she ever drove along that stretch, no matter the direction.

A second too late, she caught the patrol car out of the corner of her eye.

He pulled out after her, the red-and-blue lights switched on, flashing. He provided a small mercy when he failed to turn the siren on.

She pulled over to the side of the road.

Damn.

Checking the rearview mirror, none other than Sheriff Preston himself sat behind the wheel—not that it came as such a surprise, but the sheriff usually assigned the deputies to handle the speed detail.

She rolled down the window, watching him approach in her rearview mirror.

"Emory Cross. How are you?" he said upon reaching the window.

"Driving a bit fast by the looks of things. Sorry about that."

"Guess you forgot how things run out here," he laughed. "Slow and then some."

She sniffed. "You gonna give me a ticket?"

"Don't need the revenue today," he replied, making a joke of it. "But since you're here and somewhat captive, I do want to talk to you."

She laughed at his description, wanting to speak to him as well. "About?"

"Oh, about any number of things." He leaned against the roof of the truck and eyed the town.

"Shoot," Emory laughed. "That sounds bad."

He drew his attention back to her. "Things are changing out here. Like you know. You hear anything?"

"Yeah. I've heard a bit," Emory shifted in the truck. "Did you ever get anywhere on who shot Iver, or aren't you allowed to say?"

"Between you and me, officer to officer, there's some talk and a few leads, but no. We're not really getting anywhere near where I would like to be in the investigation. People are afraid to talk."

She had figured as much. "What do you know about a new outfit going in that is buying bulls? Smith and Associates from Toms River, New Jersey."

"Bulls?" he echoed.

"A lot of them. Expensive ones, too. They'd need shelter up here, I'd say. No one around here deals with bulls to any real extent. Their growers would need to know what they are in for."

The sheriff knew that as well as anyone. "They can make a lot of money."

"Sure can. Especially selling bull semen. Big money. *Legitimate* money. Catch my drift?"

"I do. What I can tell you is that the latest sale of note is the old Hodges place. It ain't the entire old Hodges place any more. They sold their upper pastures but kept the house at the bottoms. Still, it's another piece of history slipping away."

"That upper land isn't fit for bulls—they'd break their legs in nothing flat. You haven't seen any new barns or outbuildings going up, have you? Someplace now called the Blue River Ranch came up."

"Could be any number of places, but I'll look into it," he replied. "And thanks for the tip."

"Does Dad know about the Hodges sale?"

"Emory, I don't know what your father knows. Never

have and likely never will. Maybe that's a good thing in the long run, but it's why I'm talking to you."

Em laughed. "And here all these years I thought you liked me."

He smiled, softening. "You know I do. But you're also the best route to communicate with Lance. The only route, some might say."

"He asked me to come back home for a bit. Don't know how long I'm supposed to stay. How's Iver doing?"

"Spooked."

Emory met the sheriff's eyes. "Don't blame him."

"Nope."

She stared at what she could see of the town, parked by the butcher's where she got pulled over. "You get the sense of a range war brewing? Because that's how this all is setting up as far as I can tell."

"I sure do, Em. I sure do."

He patted the top of the truck and started back to his car.

He tipped the brim of his hat and kept on walking and got into his patrol car.

The shipment would have already taken place. She'd call the local brand inspectors to pass on what she knew, and to hear what they had to say.

AFTER THAT NEAR brush with a ticket, Emory killed her speed and drove into town at the same rural pace she grew up with. At the stoplight, the Kum 'N Go still lorded over that end of town from the crest of a hill—Emory noting that yes, gas prices remained forty cents higher than they were down in Denver. She shook her head at that irritant as the light turned green and she made the left-hand turn to rumble down Main Street, which also turned into a highway number further on. Nothing much had changed since she saw it last. True, that was only three weeks back, but she'd seen a lot in that short period of time.

The old buildings on the southern side of the road remained empty as ever—for the last few years back, but that new furniture shop spoke volumes. Shiny, trendy, and well-kept, it sure wasn't for the likes of the ranch people who bought a new piece of furniture once every decade or so. No, that shop aimed squarely for the newcomers with money. And by the look of things, their business thrived.

The town park stood the same as always, waiting for better days that never seemed to arrive. Barren in the winter, the tree limbs reached for the warmth of the sun. The old beaten-down motels hunkered down on either side of the road, remnants of the 1970s. Back in the day when people might stop for the night, and then keep on moving. The meth head's battered and illegal fuel pump remained next to the old landmark restaurant. A huge FOR SALE banner draped across the entire false front making it clear that the current owners, this time, weren't joking around.

Never mind that the food varied between good and bad—that didn't mean she wanted to see the change of ownership, or to see it fold altogether.

The Ace High endured changes of fortunes as a matter of course. It looked dingy in the daylight hours. Her truck rumbled on by as she wondered about the current fortunes of Cade Timmons.

Something about him still lingered that she couldn't quite shake.

Passing by the second overpriced gas station, she

might later stop in to see what Josie might know, but for right now, she headed home.

Headed home to do damage control before Hugo arrived.

Once and for all, she needed to let the notion of Cade go.

―――――――

THE SAGE and scrub waited for spring, winter brown and brittle. Snow remained on the ground, scattered in patches on the high valley floor. The lower mountains sloped upwards and away, as if keeping their distance. The scrub and snow alternated as their palette melded with the distant high mountains—the higher elevations slate-colored.

Clouds drifted and swept across the vast winter sky, uncaring.

Emory passed beneath the talisman skull, still menacing all comers foolish enough to travel that way.

Its mere existence would make one hell of an impression on the Texan, as it would anyone. Its message was bound to send any alarm bells that hadn't already rung into full timber.

Hardly the impression she wanted to make.

To make matters even more precarious, she hadn't told her father that company would be arriving in the form of a decent prospect.

Down the rutted road, the ranch's setup stood locked in history and time.

She pulled up to her usual place, put the truck into park and hopped out. Kai waited in the nearest pasture, and he whinnied to her.

"Hi, Kai! I'm home!" Another horse ambled over to his side. *That must be the mustang they called Outhouse.*

"Hell-o," Emory called, taking three long strides toward the fence.

Her father came out from the house. "Oh sure. You have time to say hello to the horses, but not to your old man."

She wouldn't give him the satisfaction of laughing or responding. "Is that Outhouse?"

"One and the same."

"Is he any good?"

"Got a clubbed hoof which they told me about. I took a look, and that's about the size of it. Other than a general once-over, I haven't had too much to do with him. I figured it's your job to see what you think, because he's *your* horse, not mine."

"Clubbed hoof? Which one?"

"The back left."

Emory eyed the mustang, liking the looks of him. She turned back to her father. "Company's coming. And before you go getting excited and your hopes up, just *don't*."

Her father's eyebrows shot up high. "What are we talkin'?"

"A friend from work."

She claimed his full, undivided attention with that one. "Does that just-a-friend happen to be male?"

"From Texas. He says Texas wasn't settled by wimps. We'll see." She pretended a fascination with the landscape that she didn't feel at that moment. She just didn't want to deal with the curiosity that would rise in her father's eyes, but she had to say something. "He fought in Afghanistan. It didn't sound good."

Lance Cross, somewhat unremarkably, latched on to

more practical matters. "Probably not," he said, letting the silence fall. Moment over, he then added, "I hope he don't mind sharing with Monty."

The second cousin. "I don't know, but I guess not. What's Monty like?"

"You'll see for yourself, because here he comes."

Sure enough, a shiny new red truck headed in their direction. It sure didn't look like any ranch truck to Emory. She gave her father one of *those* looks.

"Stands out like a sore thumb, don't it?"

"Sure does. Does he have money?"

"Nope," her father rocked back on his heels a bit. "Said he won it in a card game, but I don't believe him."

"He lies, then?"

"More like he makes up tall tales." Her father bit back a laugh. "I'm assuming they are tall tales—and sometimes they're pretty good. Just wait until you see him."

None of this sounded promising at all. "Great. Can we take some steaks out of the freezer?"

"Sure. They're all slow elk."

"Dad," Emory stopped, dead serious. "You gotta stop saying shit like that."

He rolled his eyes.

"Just you wait," he droned on, unbothered.

Emory ducked back into the house and pulled four steaks out of the freezer and set them on the kitchen counter to thaw.

She hurried back out front in time to watch the shiny pickup truck come to a full stop.

A strange old curmudgeon stepped out and his spur clanked. Just like something out of a spaghetti Western. His gray hair flowed long and loose, he had on 1960s blue oval glasses like the Beatles might wear, and most remarkably wore a spur. Only the *single* spur.

"Why, this must be little Emory," the apparition exclaimed.

"Little? I don't think I've been called that in a long time," Emory countered, feeling her eyes widen at the notion, and all five feet nine of her. Yet she stepped forward, hand outstretched.

"Last time Monty saw you, you was probably about three," her father offered, kind of puffed up and proud. Proud of *her*.

"Don't you remember me?" the wizened man asked. "I usually make more of an impression than that." And no doubt he did. He clasped Emory's hand and pulled her into a big bear hug. For a skinny old buzzard, he seemed strong and solid.

Emory broke free and did her best not to stare at any particular feature of this newfound cousin, but that courtesy proved difficult to uphold. "Looks like you've lost a spur somewhere along the line."

"Don't wear it. Just need the one."

Odd. Downright odd. And before her father could stop her, she asked, "And why would that be?"

"Em—"

One-Spur Monty cut him off. "It helps with my aim! You see, it goes like this. There came this night in a Laramie bar and…"

As soon as she could disentangle herself, Emory left her father to deal with Monty and went over to the pasture to introduce herself to Outhouse. All the horses were in the large pasture. Horses are herd animals and as such, always preferred to be at least in sight of each other. She called to Kai, and he ambled up to her. She rubbed the side of his face and his muzzle.

"I've missed you, boy," she told the horse, whose eyes conveyed that he understood, and that the feeling was mutual. "Who's your new friend? Is that Outhouse?"

Remarkably, Outhouse flicked his ears in her direction, listening. Intelligent eyes sure looked like he knew his name.

With a final rub for Kai, Emory picked up the rope halter and lead, slinging them over her shoulder nice and casual. She approached Outhouse by his side. The bay mustang grunted and moved away.

"Playing hard to get, is that it?"

She tried again. This time he let her lay a hand on his neck for a moment, before darting off.

Unwilling to be caught at that precise moment by a stranger, the mustang needed coaxing. Emory sludged through the frozen, uneven mud peaks and troughs to reach the barn for a handful of horse cookies which she stuck in her pocket.

Back outside, she gave Kai a cookie first, so that Outhouse could see him enjoying the treat. He noticed, all right. She held one out for the mustang. Still cautious and distrustful, eventually his stomach won over. He approached at an angle and nibbled it from her hand, almost dainty.

Without making any sudden moves, Emory slipped the noseband with the knots over his muzzle. She threaded the tie loop and finished it off with a D knot.

Now that she had hold of the horse, she led him into the circular working pen.

Outhouse didn't resist the lead—a very good sign— and she grabbed the lunge line which she fastened to the lead line loop. Picking up a crop, she pushed him on a slow trot circle, paying close attention to his clubfoot. It didn't appear to be giving him any trouble, but then again, he wasn't carrying a rider's weight.

That could make all the difference.

When Emory felt satisfied with the effort the mustang made, she retrieved a saddle blanket, and placed it on his back to see how he would react.

Both men came to the rails to watch.

"What do you think?" Her father watched her work. One-Spur Monty didn't appear all that interested, but maybe those blue glasses made things look different. That, and the fact he kept scanning the horizon.

"How long have you been here, Monty?" Emory asked, still working the mustang.

"Three nights, two days," he said, decisive.

"You like the view?"

The mustang relaxed visibly and stretched out his neck as he trotted a bit. Another good sign.

"Yes and no," he replied.

Emory glanced at her father, who met her eyes.

"Think you might want to tell her why that is?" Lance prompted.

"Don't know that I do," the cousin half sang.

Emory frowned and stopped the horse. She patted Outhouse and gave him another cookie.

"You know, if you keep feeding him treats, you're going to have a cookie monster on your hands, and that ain't good," Monty offered.

"You train your horses, and I'll train mine."

"Huh," he said, then spat.

She eyed her father, who didn't seem predisposed to help her understand this strange relative.

"OK, I'll bite," Emory began. "Most people come here

and start gushing about the scenery. What don't you like?"

"People'll want it. That's what. Lots of places to hide out. I ain't surprised you lot got pinned down. I am here to help out on that count, but that don't fix the base problem. You have something that people'll fight over. Sometimes it's best just to have a bit of scrubland no one would look at twice and consider you crazy for living there in the first place."

"I don't know how much you and Dad have talked…"

"Enough," Lance Cross inserted.

"Which brings me to my point," One-Spur drawled. "Ain't you law enforcement?"

That old note of caution rang. "Brand inspector. If you think I've got forces at my disposal or backup to summons, they're over in Greeley and are more senior than I am. Whatever you're thinking…"

"What I'm thinking," Monty interrupted somewhat exasperated, "is that we need to track down every last person in the vicinity who hails from New Jersey."

She'd thought something very similar, and along those same lines. "And how are we going to do that?"

"License plates," he pronounced, decisive.

"And if they're driving rental cars?"

That complication stumped him.

"I told you she was smart," her father drawled.

Monty walked off, single spur jangling, presumably to find another angle to the identification issue.

20

THE WAY TO MAKE AN
IMPRESSION

EMORY SPENT ANOTHER THIRTY MINUTES SHE COULDN'T really afford getting to know Outhouse better by walking up to him from different angles, taking his saddle blanket on and off multiple times, lunging him and trying to *read* the mustang in general.

But the knowledge that Hugo was already driving in their direction made her aware that time ticked on by. Instead of hanging around the corral playing with the horse, she needed to check the condition of the bunkhouse before the Texan arrived. She'd make up his bunk, provided Monty hadn't somehow destroyed the place.

A voice niggled at the back of her mind; she must have been insane to allow Hugo to visit in the first place.

Nevertheless, regrets at that point didn't amount to a hill of beans.

Leading Outhouse out of the circular corral and into the pasture, she shut the gate and threaded the chain through the eye for an extra measure of security.

The battered bunkhouse waited off to the side and had never looked worse.

She walked over to Cade's old digs...or make that *One-Spur* Monty's and knocked on the door, uncertain where the curmudgeon lurked.

He didn't answer.

"Dad," she shouted over to her father who worked on seating a fence rail into the post at the far side of the house. "Where's Monty?"

"Riding the fence line or checking on stock. Why?"

She covered part of the distance, so she didn't have to yell as loud. "I need to check the bunkhouse. Can I just walk right in?"

"Hell, I don't know." Her father barely looked up at her.

"Do you think you can call him?"

"I guess." With a sigh, he abandoned the fence and pulled out his cell. "Yo. Emory wants to go into the bunkhouse to make sure it is... Hell, I don't know."

Her father listened some more. "Yeah. OK."

He turned to Emory. "Monty ain't happy about it. I've been instructed to go inside with you."

"What for?"

"I ain't sure. Now come on. I don't have time to be running a guest ranch." Lance Cross already strode toward the bunkhouse.

"He's a brand inspector, not a dude."

"Whatever he is, daylight's burning. Now do you want to put him in the bunkhouse or in the regular house? Your choice—but make it quick."

Emory fell in step alongside him. "Let's take a look to see what your cousin has or hasn't done, as the case may be."

The door swung open.

Lance Cross whistled low through his teeth. "That's a lot of firepower. No wonder he didn't want you in here."

Emory stopped where she stood, slack-jawed. Nothing less than an arsenal confronted them. "Are you sure he's not unhinged?"

Her father frowned but didn't answer, caught up in looking at the array of firepower.

And with good reason. There were rifles propped up against the walls, handguns on the table, and an AK-47 leaning up in a chair. Danger aside, whatever the case, Monty'd been oiling and cleaning his guns—and what appeared an old sheet spread out on the table caught the droppings, splattered and smeared with fluids.

Emory took a closer look. "Is that one of the *new* bedsheets?"

Her father lifted his hat, scratched his head, and clamped it back down. "I did tell you that he might not be house broke."

"We don't use AK-47s," Emory groused.

"Apparently, he does. Never tell a man the type of gun to use. Goes against the grain."

Emory set her jaw at the mess. Coffee cups needed washing, Monty's clothes lay scattered about, but the guns and the ruined bedsheet clenched the deal in her mind.

"Didn't you see him unpacking all of these weapons?"

"Well, now, no. No, I didn't." He sounded relieved to be able to claim as much. "He brought some gym bags and one or two rifle cases. But I left him to it. I mean, it's not my job to go through his things."

"The door stood unlocked. Anyone could come in here and have a field day. Hell. We'd be sitting ducks if intruders took control of this arsenal."

A nerve throbbed in her father's cheek.

"I guess we'd best put your friend in the house. Shit. You'd better go get that room ready."

The sound of a horse's hoofbeats approached, followed by the jingle of a singular spur.

Monty clanked on up.

Poised to let him have it, Lance Cross put a restraining hand on Emory's arm.

"You sure have a lot of weapons," her father started.

Monty pulled up taller. "Damn straight."

"Emory's put out about the bedsheet."

"Shit," the old cowboy replied. "I don't have need of those."

Again, her father put a clamping hand on Emory's shoulder, holding her down. Or back. It didn't much matter which.

"Is that an AK-47?" her father asked, halfway toward changing the conversation.

"I've got company coming," Emory muttered.

Monty squinted from Emory to her father and back again. "Sure is. You said a range war was a-brewing, and I came prepared. Problem?"

Emory turned on her heel after giving him a dirty look.

The old man guffawed. "Shit. Your scowls don't scare me none, girl."

Emory turned back and walked up to Monty, her eyes cold and mocking. In a clear voice that echoed through two men, she said, "Then, you best think on that again."

She turned to her father. "You brought him here; YOU figure out what to do with him."

She stalked off, leaving the men behind.

USED AS ANOTHER STORAGE ROOM, the empty room in the ranch house proved cluttered and dusty enough to be hopeless in the time remaining.

Her father came up the stairs to help her look at it. "Kind of hard to know where to start," he said.

"Get Monty to help, since this is his fault. I don't care where you put these boxes, but they are leaving here and we're cleaning out under the bed. Maybe you'd better call your sidekick now."

True to his word, Lance Cross called the one-spur wonder and he came clanking up the stairs. Together he and Lance carried down four boxes and returned for more.

Seven trips later, the room stood cleared out enough to start cleaning. The clock read two o'clock. Hugo would arrive around three.

"I'll change the sheets on my bed, and he can sleep there, and I'll deal with this mess."

"She ain't gonna make us go up and down again, is she?" Monty asked.

"You'd better ask her. Next time don't use sheets for cleaning guns and then you might not have this problem."

That concept appeared to be a revelation for the cousin right there.

She stripped the bed and gave the sheets to Monty. "Here. If you insist on using sheets for your guns, only use these. Deal?"

"Deal," he replied. "Can I go now?"

"Sure. If Hugo drives up, you'd best put on your manners, assuming that you have any."

"Now she wants manners," the old cowpoke muttered going down the hallway and down the stairs.

Her father handed her sheets from the linen closet and she sniffed them.

"These smell old and dusty," she complained. "Fine. You vacuum and I'll throw these in the wash."

"Now I know why we don't have company. Too much damned trouble," the elder Cross bitched.

Emory didn't care who complained about what. They were going to get the job done, and get the job done on time.

HUGO PULLED up to the house about three that afternoon.

Emory felt more of a sense of dread than anything else when he pulled up. She hurried down the stairs to greet him, but her father beat her to the punchline.

"Welcome to the Lost Daughter Ranch," Lance Cross boomed, hand extended.

"My pleasure, sir, and I thank you," Hugo replied. "Is Emory at home?"

She made it out of the front door just then.

"Hi, Hugo," she said, suddenly turning shy under her father's watchful eye.

The Texan tipped his hat in her direction, but he watched her father. "I brought something with me. It's in the back of the truck."

All three of them glanced over at the tarp covering the lump in the truck bed.

Just then, Monty chose to make his appearance from the bunkhouse, wearing that damned single spur.

Everyone marked his jangling approach.

"This here is Cousin Monty," Lance Cross offered,

like he was a prize to be proud of. "Monty, this is the guest."

"How do, Guest," Monty extended a gnarl-fingered hand with long, ragged nails.

To his credit, Hugo didn't flinch but met him square in the eye and shook his hand. "Pleased to meet you."

Monty's mouth quirked up. "It's been a while since I've heard that one."

Emory and her father locked eyes. Emory broke away first and smiled at the two men as if nothing at all struck amiss.

"As I was saying, I brought a relatively fresh steer head…" Hugo yanked the covering away with a snap, revealing the severed steer's head.

"I'll be damned," her father beamed. "Outstanding," he slapped Hugo on the back as he went to lift out his prize.

Resting on a plastic garbage bag, a vacant-eyed steer's head waited, skin and all still attached.

Her father chuckled and nudged Emory.

For his part, a baffled Hugo covered any misgivings well. In fact, he did his best to act as if the rotting gift could be considered commonplace.

"I was told that you wanted a steer's head. One was in the lab at Fort Collins for a necropsy, and the tech said I could take it."

Monty ambled up to peer over the side of the truck bed. "Hell, you might fit right in. Wanna a shot of whiskey?"

Hugo laughed and stuck his hands in his back pockets. "A little later, I wouldn't say no."

Lance Cross stared at the vacant eyes, sizing it up. "This'll do the trick."

Pleased, Hugo moved a few steps over in Emory's direction, still more than a trace baffled. "Hope you don't mind me asking, but what exactly do you plan on doing with that?"

Her father cut in. "Did you tell him all that's been goin' on over here? Anyhow, I want it for the back gate. Guess I'll just set it on the porch for now. Need the bottom tarp? If you do, we've got others laying around."

"No. Go right ahead. Need a hand with that? It doesn't bother me."

That impressed her father like nothing else would. If Hugo set out to make friends with the menfolk of her family, he was off to one hell of a start.

Monty watched the proceedings with a close interest. "Let's think about this. We could just take it out to the back gate right now. I believe in flying my colors, especially if all hell is going to break loose."

Emory corrected him. "All hell isn't going to break loose."

Monty's eyes narrowed. "You got proof of that?"

"I believe Emory mentioned something about the troubles the other evening." For his part, the Texan appeared steady and unruffled.

Her father stepped in. "Em, did you have any plans for Hugo right now?"

"I planned on showing him the ranch, and then to grill some steaks."

Monty acted like a dog with a bone. "Hell's bells, Emory. He'll see part of the ranch out to the back gate. Now Lance, how do you plan on affixing this thing?"

Lance Cross picked up the skull, flipped it over and examined the underside.

"Guess we can drill holes in it and mount it on a pike," he concluded.

"Yep," Monty agreed, "and we'll set him out there and let 'im rot."

NOTHING PROGRESSED ACCORDING to Emory's plan—not that she followed a plan per se, but she never once counted on Hugo hauling up a steer's head and all the *men* joining up forces to go put the damn thing on display, leaving her behind with the steaks and a smoldering temper.

He was her guest, dammit.

They hadn't even allowed Hugo the time to remove his belongings from his truck.

Her cell rang. *Dad.*

"If someone's drill bit broke, don't be askin' me to bring one out there," she snarled by way of a greeting.

Her father chuckled at her expense. "I'm gonna do you a favor and not respond to that. Say, this all is workin' out real well. I'm calling to let you know to set an extra place at the table. We're going to make a party of this."

"Who's that extra place for, *Dad*?"

"Linda. Problem?"

"I'll manage."

"Glad to hear it. Now, we're finishing up out here, and we'll be coming back in. Maybe you can take Hugo riding or something until dinner time. I can handle the rest from here."

A pause. "OK. Thanks, Dad."

"You are welcome," he shot back, just as happy as hell.

—————

THE MEN CAME BACK SHORTLY THEREAFTER.

There were plenty of grins and camaraderie, which shocked the hell out of Emory.

Table set and the salad made, Emory stepped out onto the porch. The snow had melted to a large extent but judging by the slate-gray clouds rising in the northwest sky, more storms strengthened and built and were heading their way.

Emory cast a practiced eye at the threatening sky, then at the pickup truck barreling in her direction.

The truck pulled up to a stop, and the men alighted. Hugo appeared amused, which meant he was hanging in OK.

"Hey, Em," he called out. "That was something. I'd sure as hell stay away from that back gate."

The men guffawed, well pleased with their handiwork.

"I'd say that earns more whiskey. I've got a bottle," One-Spur crowed.

Emory hadn't counted on the afternoon devolving into a drunken spree. "Not so fast. Hugo, what would you like to do?"

Hugo took a few steps toward her. "Whatever you like," he said with a grin.

"I can saddle up two horses and we can go riding, or I can show you the outbuildings the preservationists are so interested in—apparently you will be meeting one of them tonight—or I can drive you around…"

He shrugged. "I guess now is as good of a time as any to tell you that I don't ride horses."

That pulled the Crosses up short, and Emory thought she hadn't heard right. "You don't?"

"Nope. We didn't have any but the two old fellows at my grandparents." Again, the start of a blush, and that bashful grin that tugged at her heart.

"Do you want to learn?" she offered. "I can put you on Kai, and I can try out Outhouse."

"Outhouse?" He blinked.

"A new horse a neighbor brought over for Em," her father supplied.

"That's quite the name," Hugo replied.

"Yes. Yes, it sure is." Emory smiled, still caught on the fact that he didn't know how to ride.

"I vote for drinkin' whiskey and eating dinner," Monty blustered.

And that's exactly how it came to pass.

PART III

REAL WESTERN

21

A LIQUOR-FUELED FRIDAY
NIGHT

MONTY MANAGED TO PUT A GOOD-SIZED DENT IN THE bottle by the time Linda Paulson pulled up in her danged Jeep.

"You show her the blood stain on the porch?" Emory asked her father under her breath.

"You gonna be like this all night?" The question offered didn't require an answer. In fact, he didn't wait for any further opinions from her but went to the door and flung it open wide.

"There's my girl," he called out.

Those words stabbed. She was his girl. Not this...this woman.

Linda arrived with a Tupperware covered box holding something to eat.

Lance gave her a peck on the cheek, and she giggled like a schoolgirl as she held out the offering for Emory. "I made cupcakes. Hope you don't mind."

"Thank you," Emory replied, a bit clipped as she took the box. "Let me introduce Hugo Werner, and I suppose you've already met Monty, there."

Monty tipped his sweat-stained, old, gray Stetson in the woman's direction.

"Of course," she replied, still gushing all over the place.

Emory took the cupcakes to the kitchen, setting them on the counter. Upon second thought, she put them on a plate so Hugo might not think they were heathens altogether.

With a smile she wasn't certain she felt, she called to her father visiting in the front room. "Are you ready to start grilling?"

"That's my cue," he joked, springing to his feet. "How do you want your slow elk done?"

"Dad!" *How many damn times did she have to tell him?*

"Just kidding. Emory gets sensitive about things like that. Seriously, any preference, Hugo? Linda?"

"Ladies first," Hugo responded with that Texas charm blazing.

Another girlish giggle from the plump Paulson. "Medium, please."

Inwardly Emory chuckled. Her father would have to share his steak with his guest, and he hated his meat brown in the middle. Nevertheless, he nodded at Hugo for his preference.

"Rare to medium rare—bloody in the middle is a fine thing."

"That's my man," Monty chimed in. "But I want mine as rare as they come."

Emory shook her head finding his choice predictable, and she didn't even know him.

"Take it you want medium rare as well?" Lance Cross looked over at his daughter.

A strange haze of manners came over her. "How about medium? Linda and I can share."

Her father's head snapped back a little at her effort, a delighted Linda relaxed and smiled. "Us girls have to stick together, don't we?"

"Medium it is," Lance half sang, walking out to the kitchen for the platter of steaks and out to the grill beyond.

***

THE DINNER PASSED PLEASANTLY ENOUGH, Monty displaying at least some traces of table manners. Rusty perhaps, but deep down, they were there.

Cupcakes rounded out the meal, with coffee turning into the drink of choice. At least for everyone other than Monty.

Linda and her father started nestling along together, the preservationist all but cooing.

Remarkably Monty seemed to have the good grace to make himself scarce. "I think I'll go clean my guns."

"Not after you've been drinking," Emory cautioned.

"Oh, pish," came his toned-down reply as he rose to his feet. "Thanks for the dinner and the cupcakes," he replied, more curious about Emory and Hugo. "What're you two going to do?"

"I thought we might go into town to the Ace High. That would give Hugo the chance to see some local color and me a chance to talk to people. That is, if anyone of interest comes in. What do you say, Hugo?"

"Sure," he replied. "Do you want to go now?"

"Let me go freshen up. I'll be right down."

Monty hesitated in the doorway. "Don't suppose..."

"No," Lance Cross cut across. "They don't need you acting as a chaperone."

"Hell, they'd be chaperoning me," Monty boasted.

"But yeah, I git yer point. Three's a crowd." He nodded at Hugo. "Here's somethin' that we never got around to. How are you with a gun?"

"Fine," Hugo replied with a trace of humor. "I don't need it in the bar, do I?"

Emory paused on the stair, eavesdropping on the conversation below.

Monty took that question in all seriousness. "You shouldn't on a normal night, but things ain't normal right now. If you've got a permit, it might not be the worst idea you've ever come up with. If you have more questions, you'd have to ask Emory. She seems the type that gets off-color when someone does her explanin' for her."

With that, the front door opened and closed. Exhaling, Emory headed on up the stairs to get ready for a night out on the town.

HUGO HELD open the truck's door for Emory even though she insisted on driving. "You've been drinking whiskey with the guys. I'll drive and you ride. Deal? Besides," she smiled, "I know the roads."

"You've got a point on that road part. My last sip of whiskey was two hours ago." Hugo jogged around the truck and slipped into the passenger side.

Emory started up the engine staring at Linda Paulson's Jeep and checking that the lights went on in the bunkhouse.

Hugo followed her glance. "Why is it that Monty only wears one spur?"

Emory groaned at the question.

"What?" he asked, half laughing.

"Why don't you ask him. He'd be more than happy to tell you. But before you do, let me add that it makes no sense to me. He thinks it improves his rifle aim."

Hugo stared out the truck's windows into the dark-velvet night beyond. "Sure is dark out here. Beautiful. No wonder you love it. And your family is real nice, too."

Emory glanced over at him to see if he was pulling her leg, but he came across as sincere. "They're a bit rough around the edges at times."

"Maybe so, but that's how you know they're genuine."

"They like you."

"And I like them." He settled back into the truck seat. "No problem."

Silence carried for a long moment. Emory could tell that he turned a more delicate notion over in his mind. "Does your father really think a mounted steer head is going to scare people off?"

Emory thought about his question for a moment. "Don't honestly know, but it sure sets the tone."

"Yup. That's one message received loud and clear." He paused for a moment. "Just how rough is it getting out here, that Monty actually thinks I should be carrying a gun into a bar? And by the way, I'm not. Carrying, that is."

His admission caught her.

"Oh?"

Maybe she ought to turn around.

But she didn't. She didn't for fear of how those actions might make Hugo feel. Instead, she sought to offer an explanation of a sort.

"There was one very rough night out here, but I don't think that had anything to do with the Ace High—for the record. The night Iver got shot. That's the reason why Dad sent for me. I'm home to help figure out what is going on, and to root it out or contain it. 'Them's the rules' as he would say."

Hugo's head bobbed a few times, as if he bounced along with music only he could hear.

"What *is* going on, anyhow?" He turned to face her.

"Money laundering put simply. People selling off ranches for higher prices than makes sense, and sometimes getting cold feet in the process. That's where the bloodshed came in, and these new people are playing rough. We're guessing that's what happened to Iver—the man who got shot on the porch. He almost died over it. I need to log on to the computer to locate that shipment of expensive bulls. Should have done that before now."

"Why don't you call back to Greeley and ask about it? Terry and Dave will want to hear from you, you know."

"You're right. Those guys worry a bit."

Hugo nodded like that much was a given. Especially considering her history. "And how rough is this bar?"

"In theory, it shouldn't be rough at all, beyond the occasional bar brawl. Just a local bar. But there's now an undercurrent. I don't go in there all that much myself, and never have. When strangers come in these days, it can set the locals off in one way or another. Probably you're wondering why we are going."

"Now that you mention it…"

"Beyond getting out of the house for a while, people in there may know bits and pieces that we don't. In theory, it never hurts to ask, or to try to read between the lines."

They turned off the dark ranch road onto the equally dark two-lane highway. That two-lane highway, in the stretch of a few miles, would be called Main Street.

Stampede didn't come across as much in the nighttime. The streets stood empty and deserted, and the sidewalks rolled up, as the saying went. Especially during the winter months. The ski traffic shot on through and left the locals to their own devices in times past. But the times, as they all were aware, were a-changing—and changing fast. As it stood that night, the few signs of life centered around the Ace High's 1950s neon sign, all lit-up and ready for action.

RANDY TRAVIS'S "Forever and Ever, Amen" threaded through the opening and closing door at intervals, cutting through the cold town's silence with a wink and a promise. Hugo held the door open for her, the warmth of the packed bar vanquishing the sharp winter night's air. She'd always liked that song, but in her heart of hearts, wondered about her odds. Such musings swept aside at the sheer volume of packed bodies, all vying for a patch of turf on that mangy carpeting and hoping for a smile.

Emory never knew that the place filled up, packed to the gills.

With a glance to catch Hugo's overall reaction, he didn't seem bothered.

If the stench of the beer-soaked carpet, wet wool, and what passed as a good time struck him any way at all, he sure didn't let on.

Just another Friday night gathering steam in Stampede, or so it seemed. Plenty of voices raised to carry over, or through, the din. But there were the silent ones—those more interested in the bending of elbows to drink their boredom away.

"What would you like to drink?" Hugo asked.

Several sets of eyes traveled in their direction, with

more than a few admiring glances tossed in for good measure.

"Coors Light," she said. "I see an empty table over there. How about I go grab it?"

He nodded, and she slipped over to the booth, just as another woman tried to do the same. Emory proved the quicker of the two. Score.

The other woman, not a local, acted put out and as if she thought Emory should, for some undeclared reason, offer her the prized vacant table.

Which, of course, Emory refused to do out of principal, if for no other reason. Besides, she was on a date. A bona fide date as far as that woman needed to know, and her loss of a table was just how such matters went.

Hugo returned with the beers and nodded at the woman. Of course, she smiled and went a step further. "Hello, Sweet-Cheeks," she cooed, hanging a bit on his arm.

He didn't smile and stood ramrod straight, eying the stranger with uncertainty.

"Forgive me for being rude," Emory began, "but this is a private conversation."

The woman, catching the drift, wasn't about to go without a final dig. "But how interesting could it possibly be?" the woman asked, turning to Hugo with a dazzling smile. "If you decide you tire of the local color, come over and find me."

"That won't be happening, ma'am." He set the beers on the table and slid into the seat across from Emory.

"Pity," she replied walking away, adding a fair amount of extra wiggle in her ass.

"What the hell," he muttered. "Guess she isn't a friend of yours. And I'm not going to tip my hat at those ladies in the next booth, so don't even think about asking."

"Never saw her before," Emory replied, reaching for one of the beers. Nevertheless, she glanced over to see the girls that Hugo referred to—and sure enough. Their faces were cast in masks of good-time determination, but the hardness in their bearing came right on through.

"She probably has more money than I'll ever see," Emory sighed.

Hugo puffed up, valiant. "Money doesn't keep you warm at night."

Again, she just couldn't help herself. "It does if you need a coat," she cracked.

Uncomfortable, Hugo kept glancing over his shoulder.

"If those...ladies...are bothering you, just don't look at them."

He shrugged his wide shoulders, sheepish. "Don't like sitting with my back toward the door, that's all."

"Is that from the army? Trade me places then," Emory said, sliding out of her side of the booth.

"Guess it might seem odd," he said, swapping.

"Or maybe not," she replied. "I'm a strong believer in gut reactions." She scanned what she could see through the crowd, over near the pool tables.

He watched the direction her eyes traveled, curious.

Rearranged, she sat back down remembering she was on a bona fide date. "I'm trying to see who all is in here—if there's anyone of interest who might know a thing or two. But maybe you'll think I'm being rude to you, and I certainly don't mean it that way."

"I understand," Hugo replied, raising the bottle of beer in a toast with a smile.

Dang, he was good-looking.

Another song came on, one that Emory didn't know

but Hugo seemed to like as he tapped time along the back to the Naugahyde booth.

"What does the Ace High remind you of?" Emory asked.

"1970," he deadpanned.

Together they laughed, finding his comment perhaps less deserving than their reaction indicated.

Falling silent, each pretended to listen to the music. Amid pretending, Emory caught the thread of a conversation from the booth behind her. She flicked her head in their direction.

Hugo leaned ever so slightly to the left, stretching. His blue eyes traveled over to the group of men.

Strangers with eastern accents and wearing down coats.

But at the moment, what she could catch of their conversation didn't amount to much.

"Remind me that maybe we should stop and get gas on the way back to the ranch. I want to see if Josie is working. She has a very good idea of all that's going on in town. Everyone stops in for gas or supplies."

"Sure, if you want. But don't you have pay at the pump out here?"

"Sure do, but lottery tickets, cigarettes, and milk are hot ticket items."

The tone of the conversation behind her shifted. She stuck up one finger to silence Hugo.

She pointed through her chest indicating the table behind.

Again, he glanced in their direction and offered a slight shrug as if to say that he didn't understand all the fuss.

"...tried to run me off. We'll see how long they can hold out."

Casual as she could make it, Emory turned around to pretend to check the door. One of the easterners caught her at it, so she offered what she hoped he would interpret as a friendly, vacant, smile.

Five people seated at the table, three middle-aged men and two...girls.

Girls wearing thick makeup whose skimpy clothes should have attracted notice considering the temperatures outside. Instinctively, people gave that table a wide berth as if they could sense something not quite right.

Emory pretended to adjust her boots, still glancing behind her.

Two of the men at the booth behind her wore tennis shoes.

22

IN LININGS, LEAD CAN
SOMETIMES PASS AS SILVER

AT THAT VERY SAME MOMENT AS THAT REALIZATION HIT, the front door flung open. Cade and whatever temporary buddies he trailed around with, burst in.

Cade.

The errant ranch hand didn't see her at all, as he and his pack of hangers-on muscled up to the bar and all but formed a wall, crowding others to the sides and forcing them to give way or to risk saying something about it.

Most sensible people wouldn't.

Obviously, Cade and his pack felt and acted as if they had the run of the place.

In no time flat, a line of tequila shots were poured, and bottles of beer chasers set up for the pack. Anyone with two eyes in their head and a lick of common sense could see that the evening stood poised to take a rougher turn.

Recognition must have rippled across her face.

"You know them?" Hugo asked, glancing around without trying to be obvious.

"The one. He used to work for us a while back. I'll tell you about that later."

"He looks like a gunslinger," Hugo muttered, derisive.

"He does tonight," she admitted, struck again by the cut of him that drew women like magnets.

But for once, he wasn't eyeing the women on the prowl, and that wasn't a good sign from what she knew. Cade was a ladies' man through and through unless something he considered more important loomed.

Something about the way that he held his shoulders said a fight was in the offing.

"You know those guys he's got with him?"

"No," Emory replied. "Never seen them before, but that's nothing new. I'm going to run to the ladies' room. I'll be right back."

Before he could formulate a response, Emory slipped out of the booth and headed to the back of the bar. Scanning the crowd as she cut through, she thought she saw one of the Holstead sons and some local hands seated near the pool table.

Those would be the people she wanted to talk to.

Inside of the bathroom, she stood gazing into the mirror for a moment to gather her thoughts. Sure as hell, she could feel the undercurrent pull.

Leaving the washroom, Emory headed straight for the group of locals. Two of them marked her approach.

"I'm Emory Cross," she said. "From the Lost Daughter."

One half stood and tipped his cap in her direction —*Rimrock Feeds* blazoned across the crown.

"Care to sit down? We can get you a chair," another offered.

With a slight apologetic smile, she shook her head *no*.

"Did you meet your new horse yet?" Ah. The third guy proved to be a Holstead.

"I sure did, and I've been working with him. Haven't saddled him up yet to see how he takes to that, but he seems smart and alert."

"That he is," said the Holstead. "Listen, Dad is real grateful to you guys."

"Not to pull you away from your night out, but I sure would like to talk to you for a few minutes. I've left a friend sitting at a table alone…"

"Shoot, if you want to talk up there, I can follow. These guys won't miss me at all."

"You got that straight," one cracked.

Holstead in tow, Emory headed back to the front of the bar. She paused at the halfway point to Hugo.

"Say, there are some people in the booth ahead of us that aren't from around here. Maybe we'll talk there if we won't be overheard, or maybe we'll have to turn around and come back here. Don't know, but I'll introduce you to Hugo. He's another brand inspector.

"Sorry that took so long," Emory said slipping into the booth, and moving over so the Holstead could sit.

"This is…gosh. I don't think I have your first name."

"John Holstead," he replied, holding out a hand toward Hugo with a nod.

The volume from that booth rose, voices loud as the liquor took its toll unleashing tongues and caution.

Cade remained hunched over the bar with his new buddies, but not one of them came across as out for a good time that night. Her presence didn't even register with him.

But then again, he never proved all that good at tracking.

Emory hunched forward and spoke in a low voice to

Hugo, offering an explanation. "Iver Holstead is the man who got shot on our place."

John adjusted his cap before crossing his arms over his chest. "He got run off the road last week."

"My dad mentioned that. Did he see who drove?"

The young man shook his head, angered. "Red fleet plates. Rental car."

"Here's what I think I know. I think your father sold off a piece of land for a cash payment and got cold feet."

John Holstead nodded for her to continue.

"He wanted the land back or wanted to assure himself about the sale, and perhaps he started asking questions a bit late in the day for those people's tastes."

Again, John nodded. Hugo listened but kept a close eye on the easterners.

"The way I think it is unfolding is that whoever 'they' are, buy up more and more properties and pay cash on the barrelhead. We all know something isn't right."

The young man's eyes darted behind Emory to the people seated at the table, then locked into hers. "It's going a bit deeper than that, from what we can tell. You should come out and talk to Mom, but I'd say they're using locals to get some of their dirty work done. There's people out here doing their bidding alright. It ain't just us against them, it's us against ourselves."

One hell of an accusation, it likely held a fair amount of truth.

Although she wasn't certain that she wanted to know the answer, she had to ask. "You know who the people doing the bidding are?"

"Sure do," he said, determined. He jerked his head over in the direction of Cade and his buddies as he stood.

"Before you go," Emory smiled like nothing in the

world could be wrong, just as Cade turned around and tracked her sitting with Hugo of all fortunate occurrences, "where's the law in all of this?"

"Ain't that the burning question. Seriously, Sheriff Preston's been out to the house, but nothing much came of it." The young man shrugged. "Well, nice talking to you, Emory, and nice meeting you. I've got to go back to join my buddies. Don't know that I would stay in here too late tonight. Just sayin'."

IT COULDN'T HAVE BEEN MORE than fifteen minutes later, voices flowed in an angry torrent, rising in the back of the bar.

This time, Emory didn't bother to mask her movements, but pointedly looked back at the easterner's table.

One of the men stared daggers at Cade and his pack. At that moment, Cade's eyes again registered Emory, but he left his place at the bar and passed by without a word or a glance.

His buddies pushed away from the bar, and all western in attitude like a replay of the fight at the OK Corral. With brawn and menace, they strode back to where the commotion gathered steam, tensions flaring and burning.

A fight brewed, and the volume rose over the music.

Face calm and body still, Hugo's eyes pinpointed the source of the trouble in no time flat.

One thing stabbed through Emory's mind and cut clean—neither of them carried a gun.

Then again, Emory reminded herself that she wasn't the law enforcement in Stampede and had precious little reason to act the part.

She couldn't see an obvious reason to go wading into another fight where she didn't understand the point.

"Maybe we ought to call the sheriff. You know him, don't you?" Hugo asked.

"I do, and I don't know if that's a good idea. It might be better if someone else made that call. Would you like another beer?"

Amazed at the question, he didn't utter a word.

"Sure you would," she told him.

Clearly, he found her behavior bizarre, but his Texas manners demanded that he offer. "I can get it," he said, rising.

"No, you stay here and keep watch. I'll go talk to the bartender to see what he says. He wouldn't tell you much. No offense." Emory leaped up to her feet in one swift, fluid motion.

"None taken," he replied.

She made a beeline to the bar, pretending not to hear the commotion in back. Acting for all the world like nothing could be wrong.

The bartender acted plenty uneasy, and rightfully so.

"Two Coors, please." The view down the bar's surface provided a clear shot of actions unfolding at the far end of the room.

"Bottle?"

"Yes," she replied, still staring down the expanse.

As the man set the beer in front of her, she leaned in low. "Who's causing the problem?"

He leaned in as well. "Tourists likely hassling the locals, but then the remnants from the Kittleson place are in the sway of those people sitting at the table ahead of you. That balding man is the one pulling the strings."

"Do you think someone should call the sheriff?"

Just as her words finished, a big crash came from the back.

The fight erupted in full force.

Emory grabbed the beers on the bar, and rushed back to Hugo, who, like many others, stood craning to see the commotion.

Sure enough, grappling bodies came clawing, scrambling, and swinging up the aisle. There weren't any catcalls or egging on whoops as the struggles headed toward the street.

To make matters worse, this wasn't just two guys fighting. At least eight people threw punches and squared off. This was no *friendly* fight.

Two of the local ranch hands pinned a guy Emory had never seen before. Locked in combat, they knocked a few spectators off their barstools who hadn't leaped out of the way at the sound of trouble. Their bodies, sprawled on the floor, added to the tangle and general commotion.

The fighters passed by their table in a blur of Levi's, legs, cowboy boots, and locked arms with punches thrown at intervals.

Hugo, still at the table, pulled out his cell and punched in three digits. "This is Brand Inspector Hugo Werner. Send enforcement to the Ace High."

Emory turned her attention to the bartender and leaned over the counter. "Do you have a gun back there?"

The man pulled up a rifle.

As she went to grab it, the fighting men blocked her off and threw the unknown fellow through the Ace High's plate glass window in short order with a crash.

The shower of shattering glass stunned the front half of the bar into silence. The fight still roared in the back of the establishment and never even skipped a beat.

Call finished, Hugo entered into the fray, grabbing one local by the scruff of the neck.

Making it through the bodies, Emory grabbed the rifle and shot into the ceiling without hesitation.

The crack of the rifle shot stopped everyone midthrow, midscramble, midanything. Everyone except Hugo who still spoke into his cell, finger pressed against one ear to hear the voice at the other end.

"Next one to move takes the next bullet," she called in a loud, clear voice. "Now, nice and easy, everyone sit back down."

Indeed, there she stood, rifle pointed upwards. Attuned to the movement of the people—preparing for the next false step.

The easterners hunkered at the booth, turtling down into their jackets, not as nervous and taken aback as they ought to have been. One thing she had to give them credit for—they proved smart enough to keep their heads lowered.

Searching around for Cade, Emory couldn't locate him. Nevertheless, she tried to figure out where he stood in all the mess.

"Aw, she ain't gonna shoot no one," a male voice claimed with swagger.

The clear sound of a gut punch and another chair clattering to the floor followed as activity lurched back into motion.

In a split-second decision, Emory lunged toward the sounds of the fight, rifle in hand.

"KNOCK IT OFF! Don't make me use this—because I will."

One of the men who earlier stood with Cade drinking, snickered with a local in his grasp. "Hell, she ain't gonna do nothin.'"

In one quick stride, Hugo leaped in his direction and belted him under the chin, lifting his feet off the floor. The blow sent him flying back like in a movie.

She caught Cade waiting and watching from the corner. Curiously detached from the proceedings. Odd.

"Emory!" Hugo shouted.

Crouching and slipping from their table with girls in tow, the easterners made it about three steps toward the front door.

"Stop right there," Emory commanded. "You lot, get your asses back here, I WILL shoot if I see movement. No one is leaving here until the sheriff arrives."

She returned to the middle of the bar, as sirens approached. The big guy with thinning hair acted used to giving orders. Judging by his expression, he had no intention of obeying any commands—least of all commands issued by a woman.

Emory aimed her rifle point straight at him. "SIT down."

He slithered back into place, as did the others.

Emory, half keeping an eye on them, edged over to the broken window and considered the body still prone on the sidewalk, surrounded by broken glass.

The sirens grew louder, pulling up in front of the Ace.

The back exit's push bar thudded right before the door slammed shut.

She lost one bystander or participant—maybe more.

Another siren approached from a different direction, the different pattern identifying it as an ambulance. The bar remained silent, until the back door opened and again closed with a thud. Directions came over his loud-speaker.

"Hands up, everyone! This is the Rimrock County sheriff."

If that wasn't enough to wake up the town and cause talk for the next twenty years, nothing ever would.

"Emory Cross? Identify yourself."

"I'm here," she shouted. "Someone went out the back!"

The screeching tires of a car slamming into reverse, then peeling out carried.

Everyone listened to the drama beyond as the ambulance pulled up.

A voice came from behind the Ace. "Deputy! Stop running, hands up!"

Another officer in front of the building ran around to the back of the building as Sheriff Preston entered the front door.

The sound of a single rifle shot reverberated.

Gun drawn, Sheriff Preston ran to the back of the building and out the door, Hugo hustling on his heels.

"Send the ambulance back here," Preston shouted once outside.

"What about the guy out front?" one of the deputies shouted.

"Can he wait?"

"I guess," came the uncertain reply.

"You can't hold us in here," one of the easterners challenged.

His hand also moved toward the inside of his parka.

She caught the movement. "Hold it or I *will* shoot you."

The back door of the bar burst open again. Sheriff Preston and Hugo drug in Cade between them, who still struggled.

"Everyone sit down where you are, even if that means

the floor," the sheriff commanded, taking charge of the scene.

Standing people lowered into their places.

"What happened in here?" He nodded at Emory. "You go first."

"She threatened to shoot me," the balding man piped up.

The sheriff glared at him. "You'll have your turn. Emory?"

"I don't know what started it. Check that man for a gun."

The sheriff signaled to one of the deputies to pat the man down. Sure enough, a handgun.

"You have a license for concealed carry?" the sheriff asked.

"I want a lawyer," the man replied with an accent that flattened out the *r*'s at the end of words.

"Handcuff him and take him down to the station," the sheriff said, sounding more tired than anything else.

No doubt a nasty legal battle would ensue on that front.

"Emory?"

"I asked for the bartender's rifle as Hugo called to report the trouble breaking out. You saw the guy that got thrown out the window. You'd have to ask the people that were fighting. I shot into the ceiling to get their attention. Now there's another bullet hole to join the others."

What she really wanted at that moment was to know what had happened out back with the single shot that required an ambulance. She knew better than to ask.

The sheriff didn't look that upset as he considered the passel surrounding Cade, both arms still grasped by

Hugo and a deputy. "OK, Timmons, what's your part in all of this?"

Cade did not look at the easterners, on purpose. "Nothing," he replied. "I just felt like fighting."

"Book him," the sheriff replied. "Now, who else?"

"The guy Hugo laid out." That man raised himself to his hands and knees but still couldn't stand.

The sheriff eyed him. "He'll live."

Everyone else remained silent. The sheriff walked through the crowd. "Fine. Show me the backs of your hands. Everyone hold them out now. That goes for the women, too."

People held out the back of their hands. The sheriff separated the ones with bruised knuckles, moving them over to Hugo and Emory's booth.

"Who threw the first punch?" Although he aimed the question at anyone, he meant it for the locals.

But no one would say anything further.

The code of the Old West silence held strong and firm, the assumption prevailing that the easterners would crack first.

But, oddly enough, they didn't. Not even when the balding guy got hauled off in handcuffs.

23

GOSSIP—THE LIFEBLOOD OF THE COMMUNITY AND OFTEN MORE TRUE THAN NOT

HUGO DIDN'T HAVE MUCH TO SAY FOR HIMSELF AFTER THE bar cleared out, people were lectured, hauled off, or wished a pleasant night—which came across as ridiculous even at the time.

Welcome to Stampede, Colorado, where the Wild West remained.

The carnage of fragmented glass lay on the sidewalk, shards glittering in the moonlight and the stray remnants crunching underfoot.

Blood on the ground again. A different day and a different location—yet the telltale dark pool colored the snow bright red, morphing into a darker wine color on the sidewalk. Still, all that spilled blood would provide another piece of the overall equation.

The one that demanded they fight. The one that demanded they bleed.

Drained, Emory and Hugo climbed into her grandfather's truck. This time those famous manners slipped, and Hugo didn't help her with her door. He sat there, silent. His reticence struck her as odd as she stuck the key into the ignition, turned the engine over, and shifted into reverse.

She long eyed him, but he stared straight ahead.

Stopping in the middle of the road, she put the truck into gear, and drove down out of town, leaving the gleam of the rare streetlights behind.

"Every night doesn't go that way," Emory offered, but Hugo didn't look like he believed her.

Yet, he answered. "Uh-huh. It's kind of rough. Still want to stop at the gas station?"

"No, not really," she replied as the bright light over the island pumps came into view. "Oh, what the hell." She pulled into a parking spot. "You want to come in or wait here?"

"I'll wait," he said, processing.

She eyed him with a question, but he refused to respond.

Peering through the windshield and through the store windows, sure enough Josie stood at her post behind the cash register.

Emory swung the door open wide, and the electronic bell rang.

"Hey there, Josie. I'm coming back from the Ace."

"And you're two trucks late," Josie chuckled. "Girl, you just can't help yourself, can you?"

Josie peered beyond her to Hugo sitting in the truck. "Who's that?"

"Hugo Werner. Another brand inspector."

"Well, bring him on in here so I can get a look!"

Emory glanced over and waved. Thankfully, he gave her a half-hearted wave back. "He's not too happy right now, and he won't come in. Say, even before the fight happened, I wanted to stop by and talk to you."

Josie's eyes twinkled. "Did you now."

"It's true. I want to know what you're hearing about these easterners buying up ranch land."

For once, she swallowed whatever words threatened to burst forth, and looked like she thought about it hard. "It's not safe here anymore."

"It's feeling that way," Emory replied, leaning against the counter. "Partially, at least. We're trying to figure out the best plan to deal with it. Who are they?"

"People you don't want to mess with."

"Well, it looks like we're going to have to. You heard about Iver Holstead getting shot at our place."

"I did."

"Have you met them?"

"Do their cars need gas? But they ain't friendly, and they keep to themselves. Do you ever watch those organized crime shows? You know, those true account ones."

"No—" Emory replied.

She stared into Josie's eyes. Josie stared into hers. "I see," Emory said. Whatever you tell me, I didn't hear that from you. Where do they stay when they're here?"

Silence.

"Come on, Josie. It's for the good of everyone."

"Up Highway 169 at the upper reaches of the Blue River Ranch. You know, that big log mansion up there. The one the movie mogul built back about five years ago. From what I hear, they squeezed him out, too. And he was from California."

Emory nodded. "Thanks, Josie. And I mean it."

"You best take care, Em. One other thing. You know, I get the feeling they think we're all dumber than dirt out here."

"Why do you say that?"

"Heard 'em talkin', I did. They huddled over by the beer case, saying something about a shipment of what sounded like drugs for some big party. Guess they're flying people in by plane." The clerk sniffed. "Takes too long to drive in from Denver, don't you know?"

"You're a star, Josie."

"Yeah, well, don't tell anyone. It'd ruin my damned reputation that I've worked so hard to build."

Emory swung back into the truck, eyeing Hugo as she started the engine.

"Are you going to wake up your father to tell him what happened?"

She shifted in the seat before backing up and pulling out onto the highway. "No, I don't think so. It'll keep until morning."

A long hesitation and finally a *very* controlled voice. "Were you truly going to shoot that man?"

His question came as a stab...and a challenge to her judgment. "I wouldn't have wanted to, but he was *pulling a gun*, Hugo."

A vein throbbed in his cheek, visible in the dim interior. "Well, everyone knows you can shoot. What about your old boyfriend?"

"My old boyfriend?"

A mirthless chuckle. "The one that got hauled off to jail."

"Cade?" She couldn't believe that he picked up on anything between them. But obviously, he had. "He was never my boyfriend, just another ranch hand. We worked together for a while. Nothing more."

"I ain't that green, sweetheart."

Emory pulled over and stopped the truck alongside the road. "I'm telling you the truth, Hugo. One thing I don't do is lie."

A coyote loped across the road, lit by the headlight's beams. Coyotes were tricksters according to some of the tribes, and she figured they had that part pegged. She only saw them along that stretch when matters of the heart figured. Maybe she was in for another heartache.

"Sure about that?"

She looked at him straight on. "Of course, I'm sure."

Something in her tone or expression broke the ice of his reserve. His smile reflected in his eyes that shone from the moonlight overhead. He leaned forward and kissed her.

A very real kiss.

And she didn't pull away but leaned in for more.

She smiled back at the Texan and kissed him again, forgetting all about the coyote that ran across the road and hunted through the sage and the brush.

THE NEXT MORNING found everyone rising early and gathered in the kitchen around the coffeepot. Hugo was up as well, dressed and pressed, and leaning against the counter as he spoke with her father, scruffy in his faded work shirt and stubbled chin.

As she stepped inside the room, Hugo gave her a look that made her heart miss a beat.

Grabbing a cup of coffee, she might have just made it in time, judging by the fact that outside of the window, Monty headed square for the side door off the kitchen.

"Does he eat breakfast with you?" Emory asked as Monty clanked his single-spur way over, and straight into the house without knocking.

They still didn't go for locked doors, apparently.

"I locked that door last night," Emory groused.

"And I opened it up this morning," her father said.

"Think maybe we should start locking the doors? It

was open when we got in last night as well."

"I heard you two giggling. It wasn't like anyone could just sneak in here."

Monty poured himself a cup of coffee, dumping four teaspoons of sugar into it.

Emory tore her eyes away from his actions.

"Let us tell you about last night," Emory sought out Hugo as she spoke. "It got downright western, and Cade's landed in jail."

"Another man got shot in the leg," Hugo offered.

Emory realized that she never even asked about that. "Do you know who that was?"

"Some drunk out taking a piss, I believe. Wrong place, wrong time."

"Still, that might be a problem," she offered. "That all came as the result of a BIG fight that broke out at the Ace High. I'm not sure exactly why Cade got arrested, but sure as hell, he got led away by one of the deputies."

"He did escape out the back door," Hugo corrected.

"Hugo helped to stop him," Em offered, still a bit conflicted on that count seeing as how she had lost one.

Her father stuck his meaty, gnarled hand out for the Texan. "Good job. Did you take a piece out of him?"

"Sir?" Hugo asked, taking the offered hand.

"Didn't Em tell you that I shot him in the foot? I'm still mad at myself. I should have aimed higher."

Clearly, that information added another piece of the Cross puzzle that Hugo didn't know how to interpret or to understand. "I fired a warning shot. He stopped."

"Huh," her father scoffed. "Maybe he's starting to wise up that people actually will shoot him." Another chuckle at the memory that only he found funny.

Emory sought to explain. "I told Hugo a bit about Cade. He didn't leave here in the best of terms."

Her father could have cared less. "Hell, he tried to run drugs through the property. I got no more time for Cade Timmons."

Hugo and Emory exchanged glances. Her father smashed any traces of doubt Hugo might have held as far as a romance with Cade was concerned.

"One of the Holsteads was there, John. He said I should go talk to his mother. But here's one thing. At the table in front of us, the people were from the East. One of the men turned out armed. Cade claimed he just felt like fighting. Maybe he started it all, but I would have said his actions came at that man's bidding. They both got hauled in, by the way. Cade and the stranger."

"How are you planning on working this?" Monty eyed the patriarch.

"I'm not finished yet," Emory said, interrupting the interruption.

Irritated, Monty switched his weight to the other foot and blinked behind those dang fool glasses.

Equally irritated, Emory resumed. "On the way home, we stopped at the Kum 'N Go. Not naming names, but it seems those people are holed up in that movie producer's place. He left. Apparently, they are going to have a party. They travel by plane and their guests travel by plane. *Private* plane."

Lance's mouth twitched as he formulated an opinion. He stared out of the kitchen on to the range beyond. "OK, here's the plan. First the livestock, then breakfast. Monty, you stay put out here and don't let your guard down. Em, you go talk to Mrs. Holstead and then try the sheriff and see what you can get outta him. I would, but he ain't going to tell me squat. I'll head into the Ace High to see if anyone's talking there, but that place don't open until noon. In the meantime, I think I'll head over to the airport and visit my old pal, Richard. Used to beat the shit out of him in high school. Let's hope that old charm factor still works. Hugo, who do you want to pair up with?"

He looked startled. "Emory, of course."

Her father nodded and bit back a smile. "Good choice," he replied, blowing into his coffee.

"Safe choice, seeing as how she ain't one for the *vida loca*," Monty griped.

Hugo just stared, and Emory couldn't blame him. Seldom was she referred to as a patently safe choice under any circumstance.

EMORY AND HUGO set out for the Holstead spread. The morning rose bright and clear, the sky a cloudless blue.

The trip to the Holstead place passed in near complete silence as Hugo admired the view. Or harbored unspoken second thoughts. Emory couldn't guess with any accuracy, considering his silence. In time, he spoke.

"What is the game plan here? The real one," he asked. "I mean, are you trying to solve who shot Mr. Holstead, or are you trying to run the strangers out of town?"

"Either, I guess."

"I think you'd better have a clear objective in mind since bullets have already started flying."

Emory turned the options over in her mind. "The main objective is to get whatever this mess is cleaned up once and for all. We've all got to live here, and there's cattle to be raised, meadows to be mowed, and all that comes with ranch life. Not just a bunch of high-priced homes and properties that shut the door on the rest of us. We claimed this valley first."

"The tribes might disagree with that assessment," Hugo drawled, "but go on."

"Fair enough. The Ute's hunted through here. But after the Ute, we came and fought to survive. Literally. Hank Cross fought to raise cattle and his family —to carve out an existence. Just like you said Texas wasn't settled by wimps, well, neither was Rimrock County. You know, maybe it was good that you stayed in the car last night, otherwise you might have knocked Josie off her game. But people are afraid of this group. She thinks they're organized crime."

"Yeah, but you knew that all along."

"Don't like to be throwing labels around." Emory gripped the steering wheel a bit tighter.

"Labels don't kill a person."

"Bullets do. And sometimes bullets fly because of those damned labels."

What she offered was another Cross type truth—and another lesson learned the hard way—firsthand.

Killing their speed, Emory drove up to the Holstead's house slower than she normally drove. If the family proved jumpy—and all indications held that they were— they had no reason to spark off a powder keg of panic. Nice and easy, they rolled on up, parked in the center of the ranch yard nice and visible, and both alighted from the truck with hands in plain sight.

"Mrs. Holstead? Mr. Holstead?" Emory called out. "It's me, Emory Cross. I've brought a friend along as well."

The front door opened, and Mrs. Holstead offered a wide smile, especially when she saw Hugo.

"Emory! How nice to see you." She came out into the yard and shook Hugo's hand.

"This is Hugo Werner. He's visiting us for a couple of days. He's a brand inspector, as well."

"Would you like some coffee? I can put some on and it will be ready in no time."

Emory shook her head. "Please don't go to any trouble. Speaking of trouble, did you hear about last night?"

"Are you here to see John?"

"He can surely be a part of this conversation if he's around. Anyone can...with the last name of Holstead."

"Hang on a minute. Let me get him." The woman jogged over to the barn.

She returned, followed by a son covered by dust and grime.

"We got rules against fighting in this family. My boys know that," she said by way of explanation.

Another interesting difference about how their two families went about things, right there.

"Hey, John," Emory said, feeling for him. Thinking how her dad would have been proud of the young man who stood before her, humbled and sheepish that morning. "We're out here for two reasons, but I have the feeling it's the same reason deeper in. From what I understand, Iver's shooters haven't been caught. Then there was the bar fight last night, and I swear that balding man meant to draw on me."

Mrs. Holstead's eyes grew wide. "Did he?"

"No, ma'am," Emory replied.

The young man offered a crooked grin. "We were sitting there with our beer, and Cade comes storming back for no reason and lays one on Travis, and that's when the fight broke out. Travis said he hasn't done nothing to no one." John shrugged.

That sounded about the size of it from what Emory could tell. "I'm forming the impression that that booth ahead of us were some of the people that are behind all this turmoil and problems. With all the money flowing around, it can't all be legal."

"When Iver started thinking about what he'd done, and how he sold for cash, he got in touch with them to try to back out of the deal. They told him to keep his mouth shut."

"Oh? How'd he get in touch with them?"

A funny look came over Mrs. Holstead. She clearly didn't know. Maybe it was another secret between the married couple. "Just a minute. I'm going to track down Iver."

She went back into the house, leaving the three of them standing there.

"You get chores for fighting, is that how it goes?" Hugo deadpanned.

"Always has. Today I get to clean out part of the barn."

"Are we asking your mom the right questions?" Emory searched his face.

"Yeah. They still haven't caught anyone."

"Did you get hauled in last night?"

He shook his head. "That would be Cade, that fat guy from the East, Mark Sherman, and a blowhard friend of Cade's who talks funny."

"Funny how?"

"His *r*'s ain't right."

Mrs. Holstead called from the porch as she made her way back to them. "He's coming back in. Had cell phone coverage that time."

"Does he carry a radio?"

"Not always, although he knows he should. Especially now."

"Mom, I told Emory that she should talk to you about what you know and think."

The rancher's eyes darted over to her son, flitted past Hugo, and landed on Emory. "I'll bet you can guess what I think. You're probably thinking the same thing yourself."

"I'm thinking we've got a serious problem. I want to know how to contact these people. And where to find them. And to get to them before they get to any more of us first."

The old "us vs. them" remained alive and well and living in Stampede, if not even further afield.

True enough, Mr. Holstead pulled up in an ATV.

"Hi, Mr. Holstead. Thank you for Outhouse, although I haven't had all that much time to work with him. He and Kai get along great, so maybe I'll be taking the pair of them back down to Greeley when I leave. He'll give me something to do."

A brief smile flitted across Iver's face. "Glad you like him."

His wife turned to face him. "Em's asking good questions. How did you meet those people that bought the upper land in the first place?"

He shifted his weight, uneasy and not wanting to say.

"Out with it," his wife said in a tone that left little room for argument.

"Well, you see, I should have known better. That's the part that gets me. I was talking to Curt Hooper in the feed store. You know, he used to sell real estate on the side, after he got his license twenty years back. I told him that I wanted to sell the upper pastures because we aren't using them anymore, and prices are way up. He said to list it with one of the agents in town. I asked him how much he thought I could get, and he said twenty thousand, which sounded about right."

The rancher searched Emory's face. "That sounds like

a fair price," she said in a gentle voice.

"One of Cade's sidekicks was in there."

"Cade has sidekicks?"

"Now he does. This one goes by the name of Blaze Redshirt, and that can't be real. Anyhow, this Redshirt guy comes over, says he couldn't help but overhear, and how he works for a Mr. Balzetti who bought the old Bar W after that movie producer person left. All that type of thing. He said they would offer top dollar cash, and that I could save the real estate commission if I dealt directly with this person that his employer knew. And that's how it started. The word *cash*."

"And…" Emory prompted.

"I arranged with that Redshirt person to meet at the back road into those pastures the next morning at 10:30 a.m. I agreed to write out the bill of sale, but they said that they didn't want it run through a title company, but a lawyer of theirs would do the paperwork, all nice and legal and notarize it. I've got the paper in the house. Do you want to see it?"

Hugo and Emory exchanged glances. "Sure do. Let's let Hugo look it over while you continue with the story."

The rancher turned to his son. "It's in the top desk drawer. Could you go get it?"

The young man jogged off.

"They handed me stacks of bills. One hundred thousand for something I figured was worth twenty. That's when greed won out over common sense. And then I started to think about it. Think about what I done—of course, that came later. Why would they want to overpay like that? And they ain't running cattle, and although the views are nice, it's a long way from anything at all."

"Please tell me the cash is in the bank."

"Yes," Iver nodded vigorously. "There's no reason to

have that kind of money lying around out here. Of course, it lifted the teller's eyebrows when I came in with it to deposit."

John jogged back and handed Hugo the bill of sale.

"Then what?"

"Then I decided something wasn't right, and I wanted to cancel the deal. I called up Cade—and it took some doing to get his number—and told him to get the word out that I changed my mind. Cade tried to convince me that *that* stance might cause problems, but I decided to take my chances. Bad idea."

Cade. Damn it.

"I asked him how to get hold of those fellows. I've never laid eyes on that Mr. Balzetti, but I seen the lawyer and that Blaze fellow. The queerest thing is that Blaze dresses the part, but I'd swear he didn't know what he was looking at. Otherwise, he would have asked about the water, wouldn't he? I mean, there's an old windmill up there, but it needs work. A lot of work, and that ain't cheap these days."

Hugo nodded and handed the paper over to Emory. "Looks legal to me. The lawyer's name looks to be something Anderson."

"That's right," the rancher nodded. "Joe Anderson. Kind of slimy if you ask me."

"Lawyers often are," Hugo agreed.

"How did you even get hold of these people to tell them that you wanted to cancel the deal?"

"Cade got hold of that Blaze Redshirt, who got hold of someone they referred to as The Boss...and it all fell apart from there."

"Did you tell Sheriff Preston any or all of this?"

"I left Cade out of it," he nodded, like that made all the difference.

"Then how did you explain how all of this transpired?"

"Well, I told him about that Blaze Redshirt. He knew who I meant, although he never said as much. You want Redshirt's phone number? He's just the middleman, and I don't think it'll get you anywhere unless you want to *pretend* that you're selling land, and then he'll still wonder where you got this number. Whatever you do, don't tell 'im that I gave it to you."

That offer brought an unexpected stroke of fortune. "Sure."

He showed her the number, and both Hugo and Emory put it into their phones. She grinned at Iver. "Maybe we can use it to spook him. Anyhow, who ran you off the road?"

"Two jackasses, but it could have been anyone. Maybe just two guys driving too fast after a couple of beers too many. They had those red plates. Probably came down from the ski area—just tourists out for a good time."

At that assessment, Mrs. Holstead started wagging her head. "That ain't it, and you know it," she turned toward Emory. "They told Iver they would be happy to cancel the transaction for $120,000. Twenty more than we got paid. Now, how could we do that? But now, you see, all that money has gone through the bank, and there is a bill of sale. No, those people who pushed him off the road did it as a warning to keep his mouth shut. Didn't they?"

She aimed her question straight at Iver.

Who shuffled a bit. "I like to give people the benefit of the doubt, Mother..."

His wife cut him off. "Not anymore, and not unless we know them, and Cade Timmons doesn't count."

24

LET'S RIDE

"Now," HUGO STARTED IN THAT SLOW WAY OF HIS. "WHY would your father keep someone on the payroll like Cade?"

"My former boyfriend, you mean? Just kidding. Cade has a past. My father thinks people with pasts are less likely to go around talking. But that didn't work in Cade's case. He'd go on down to the Ace High, starting drinking and flirting, and talk about working on the Lost Daughter. Maybe he didn't say anything of note, but as a rule, we don't like being talked about. His bragging mouth is what got him fired."

"Nothing so bad's going on that I can see…"

"You sure about Monty? 'Cause I'm not." Her words were only half in jest.

"I think so, but he's…eccentric. Definitely eccentric."

"And armed to the teeth." Emory made sure her tone made her words sound final.

To that detail, Hugo grunted—a grunt that could have meant darn near anything, but she got the feeling that Hugo really did like Monty.

"He gets along with Dad just fine in any case. Now, let's go into town and pay the sheriff a visit." She thought about that. "Say, maybe we'd better call first." Emory pulled the car over at the side of the road and took out her phone. The sheriff's number was stored in her contacts.

"Good morning, Sheriff Preston—this is Emory Cross. Hugo and I were headed in and hoping to talk to you. Is that OK? Great. We'll be there in about twenty minutes."

She clicked off the call and pulled back out onto the road.

"I'm getting the feeling that not everything out here is what it seems," Hugo said at length.

Emory shrugged. "No place is. I learned that out on the plains. Didn't you?"

"Hell, I learned that in Afghanistan. And I have a soft spot for Monty."

"It's how it's always been out here," she replied. "I guess I was foolish to hope it might settle down."

SHERIFF PRESTON SAT behind his desk going over reports when they entered his office.

"Who do you still have locked up?" Emory asked by way of a greeting.

He rose, held his hand out for Hugo while giving Emory an amused glance. "Glad you still don't mince words. Take a seat."

They each sat down in one of the heavy 1960s steel chairs with green-covered padding and a token back cushion. Those hummers would last another century or two. But she had far more important matters on her mind than aging office furniture.

"We just came from the Holstead place. John's cleaning up the barn as punishment for fighting."

The sheriff chuckled and shook his head. "I doubt John had much to do with anything, other than throwing a few punches."

"I know you can't tell us everything, or maybe you can BUT, where's the easterner that was about to draw on me?"

"Released." He said it as the forgone conclusion it was.

"Figures," Emory shrugged off the all-but-inevitable. "What did you find out about him?"

"Now, Em, I'd sure like to be able to tell you all of that. His name, and it checked out, is Michael Duggan. Doesn't look Irish to me, but whatever. You're right, he's from New Jersey."

Emory threw down what she considered to be a damning piece of evidence. "More than that, he wore tennis shoes."

"Yes, he did," the sheriff agreed, "and I know what you're driving at. But we need proof."

"Where's this Duggan staying?"

The sheriff stretched, stalling. Unsure how much he truly ought—or wanted—to divulge. "Up the valley at the old Kittleson spread. He didn't have a license to conceal carry, but hell, if I kept him in for that, I'd have to arrest a whole lot of other folks wandering around, and I sure don't have the time or inclination for all of that."

The logic behind that appeared undeniable.

"You heard tell of a guy going by the name of Blaze Redshirt?" Emory glanced at Hugo, who turned his cowboy hat in his hands—a clear sign of growing unease in the Texan.

Another low chuckle of disgust from the sheriff. "Hell, we hauled him in, too. He's one of Cade's pards."

This time, she intentionally did not look at the other brand inspector. "Cade still in?"

"Nope, got bailed out with the rest of them. And if that don't tell you something, nothing ever will."

Despite knowing better, she still glanced over at Hugo, who gave her a long side-eyed stare. Which, of course, the sheriff caught.

Not wanting to be the focus of attention, she charged on ahead. "Not to put too fine of a point on anything, but what *are* you doing about any or all of this? My father's digging in his heels, and I'll swear something is about to go off. Big time."

"Yep, I'll agree. It sure does have that feel."

Despite his words, Sheriff Preston did not appear inclined to rise further to the occasion.

Emory gave it another shot. "Did Iver tell you that when he tried to give the money for his land back, they were informed that they would have to pay $120,000 to make that happen?"

Preston nodded. "Yes, he did."

"And did he tell you that Blaze was the link?"

"A link. There may be others, and in fact, likely are."

Emory leaned forward in her chair, locking eyes with the sheriff. "You aren't exactly giving me much to go by here…Tell me straight. Are you any closer to figuring out who shot Iver?"

"Off the record?"

"Of course."

The sheriff put his hands flat on the desktop. "I'd say it's the Blue River lot, wouldn't you? But the fact of the matter is that I don't have enough proof to build a case that would ever stand."

"The motive is money laundering."

"Sure is. And to make that gain traction, I'd need one of the locals to start talking. And they sure don't seem to be getting ready to do that. Not until something else really bad kicks off."

And as far as the sheriff was concerned, that finished their conversation.

For that day.

He rose to his feet, signaling their meeting had ended. "Glad to see that things are going well for you, Em. Can't help but take a bit of credit for that myself."

Hugo, quick to take the hint, stood up immediately.

Emory, however, didn't. She took her time rising and offered a smile that said, as far as she was concerned, matters were far from over.

"WHAT DID he mean by that comment?" Hugo asked outside of the sheriff's office.

She had hoped he hadn't caught that part and inhaled, letting it all out in a rush. "Dad underreported cattle on the BLM, Cade shot his mouth off too much in town, and I ended up with a job as a brand inspector, largely due to bringing Terry Overholzer in to oversee the proceedings."

His mouth quirked, and his eyes lit with laughter that never made it to his lips. He started to say one thing, then thought better of it. "Do you want to stop for lunch somewhere?"

"Not really. I mean, there isn't anything we're going to learn at the Tastee Freez, or at least I don't think there will be. Besides, they're closed for the season." She paused. "There is, however, a restaurant that's up for sale. Let's see if they are serving today. It's been kind of hit-or-miss these last couple of years. But if they're open, let's see if anyone has approached them to buy."

Inside of the truck, she pulled out her cell—still charged. She caught Hugo eyeing it as well. Well, she'd come by that reputation honestly.

"I'm going to try Dad to tell him what we're doing."

The call dropped. "No service, or he's out of range. No matter. Let's go check the restaurant out."

THE WEATHER-WORN restaurant sagged a bit under the huge FOR SALE banner unfurled across the old false front. The sign blinked OPEN, so Emory and Hugo hopped out of the truck and ventured inside.

Glancing around the interior of the largely undeco-rated restaurant, seven or eight tables were occupied by unsuspicious people of no particular stripe.

"Take a seat anywhere," the waitress called out, carrying a tray filled with plates.

Emory claimed a spot over by the window, mindful of leaving Hugo the door-facing seat.

The waitress dropped off two menus along with two glasses of water.

"Is the owner around?" Emory asked, holding onto the menu. "My name is Emory, and we have a ranch down the road."

"New owner or old owner?"

That surprised her. "Old owner, I guess. Come to think of it, I've never known who owned this restaurant by name."

"Well, he doesn't come in because he's getting on in years, plus he'd get too many complaints about the food." The waitress laughed as if her witticism was the funniest thing in the world. "Seriously, he lives down in Denver now. You know Jake Hamilton? It's his dad."

Emory blinked and frowned, bewildered. "I know that name, but nothing more."

The woman settled down a notch to explain. "The restaurant actually sold last week, you see, and we're under new management. I haven't met the new owner yet, but I will."

"Then why is the sign still out?"

The woman shrugged. "I guess they just haven't gotten around to taking it down yet. But get this. They paid more than the asking price, can you believe that? Hell. This place has been on the market for at least five years that I know of. Now, what can I get the pair of you to eat?"

BACK AT THE LOST DAUGHTER, Lance Cross had already cracked open a couple of beers with Monty when Hugo and Emory walked in.

"Well?" he asked his daughter, taking a draw.

"Well, what?" Emory frowned at the six-pack on the table.

"Hugo, want one?" he offered, pulling out one of the bottles by the neck, and holding it out for the Texan.

"Might as well," the Texan said, taking a chair and making himself at home at the table.

"Sourpuss, you want one?"

Monty let out a terrific belch.

"Charming," Emory muttered, "and no thanks. While

you two yahoos are sitting around drinking and belching —which I thought you no longer did by the way—Hugo and I were making ourselves useful."

"Whoa, whoa, whoa. Who said we were sitting around belching and drinking beer?" Her father reacted in mock horror.

"I just did."

"This is our first one. Monty's been riding the fences all morning, and I've been working, too. One beer ain't going to do nothin'. What's got you so riled up?"

"Life," she snapped. "Now, that old restaurant in town has sold for over the asking price. We visited with Sheriff Preston, and he believes that the easterners holed up at the Blue River are the group behind Iver's shooting. Not to mention that Cade ain't exactly coming off clean either. John Holstead is stuck cleaning a barn on account of fighting in a brawl that Cade started for no reason. I don't know...did we learn anything else, Hugo?"

"We did," he answered. "You now know that one of the people hooking up these sales goes by the name of Blaze Redshirt, and that he's a friend of your former ranch hand."

"You sure got that former part right." Her father took another swallow, but not before raising the bottle in Emory's direction just to piss her off.

She ignored the taunt. "They've all been released from holding. Every single last one of them, and that includes Cade."

That missile across, none of the men reacted much. "Well?" she demanded.

"OK," Monty said, like it was of negligible consequence. He turned to Lance. "What does she want from us?"

"Hell, I never know." He frowned at his daughter as Hugo suppressed a laugh. "What *do* you want, Emory?"

Getting under her skin, she glared at them. "We know where they're holed up. At the Blue River Ranch —that movie producer's place, or whatever. Before that, it started out life as a high-altitude ranch. The original name escapes me at the moment. They must have staked us out, why don't we do the same for them?"

"Well now," Monty warbled. "She has her uses after all."

The men's beers rested, forgotten for the moment.

"That's another thing," she needled. "If we weren't going to drive, what's the shortest way to get there?"

"Damn it," her father swore. "Through the BLM land."

"I think we ought to backtrack that way first."

Lance Cross mulled that over, unwilling to make a commitment at that precise moment. "I made it over to the airstrip and asked about flight records. A record's kept, but that butt-munch at the airstrip ain't going to let me see it. He kept babbling on about FBI agents pounding on his door, or some such nonsense. He always acted scared of his own shadow—a flinchy little shit who liked airplanes."

Her father broke off, thinking.

"You know, maybe he wasn't making the door-pounding business up," Lance muttered.

Not a one of them felt the need to disagree. Whoever pounded on the man's door may not have been the FBI at all. That could be the easterners, or people in their pay. Odds were that the pounding accomplished what those men wanted. The man was scared.

Everyone seated at that table knew the code well. Intimidation usually guaranteed silence.

The Cross family—as a tribe and operation—had perfected that code over the years. As it suited them.

Hugo, as an outsider, was likely cut from a more refined cloth.

Hell. Everyone was.

ONE HOUR LATER, the three Crosses checked their cinches and the horses' tack, making sure their rifles were loaded and their scopes were clear. Hugo's mission was to drive the highway over to the Blue River Ranch to investigate how close he could get to the perimeter on public land, and what reaction he would receive.

"Think we need a snowmobile? Someone ought to have one we can borrow," Emory muttered, sticking her foot in the stirrup and swinging up into the saddle.

She got a growl in return. "Don't know yet. Let's see how deep the snow is," Lance replied, swinging up into his saddle as well.

No further words needed as the family rode over to the back gate—the men admiring their handiwork in the form of the new skull adornment that Emory found pretty near to abominable. The sound of the snow under the horses' hooves provided a reassuring familiarity, and Kai acted glad to leave the confines of the pasture and stable.

"You're gonna have to give that boyfriend of yours some riding lessons," Monty quipped. "Don't know how it can be that he don't ride."

"How it can be is that they didn't have a horse," Emory countered.

"Enough talking," Lance Cross said. "This ain't no family social. Now, come up with an excuse if you get caught or challenged. One that doesn't involve lead if it doesn't have to. Em?"

"I'll tell them we lost a steer and I'm looking for it."

He looked over at his cousin. "Monty?"

"Shit."

"That ain't good enough." Her father stopped Draco to wait for a better answer.

"I'll tell them I'm the Welcome Wagon."

Her father gave up.

"Now," Monty wheezed, "what would you be doing."

"Hell," her father growled. "I'd tell them that I don't answer to anyone. If they don't like it, they can get the hell out. Then, I'll ride."

"That's not the best plan," Emory countered.

"Like I give a shit," he replied.

In near silence, soundless beyond the birds overhead and the chattering black squirrels in the pines, the horses maintained their steady pace toward the fence line of the rechristened Blue River Ranch—a stupid name on account of how the Blue River ran its course miles away. They all stopped on the faint trace of an old road in the stand of barren aspen trees, ringed by a fringe of pine.

Lance Cross pointed for Monty to take the uphill cut. "That'll swing around behind the house. I never asked, how's your sense of direction?"

"Just fine," he said. "If you're worried I won't find my way home, there's no need on that count."

Lance nodded. "Em, you continue on straight, and I'll head down to the bottoms and the brush and will approach from the downhill slant. Questions, either of you?"

Each of them knew their objective. Gather information and see if their presence went undetected.

The wind picked up, blowing through the pine needles creating the sound of a sad, rushing stream.

At one point, through a clearing in the trees, Emory thought she saw Hugo's truck threading its way up the county road, but just as quick as that, it disappeared around a bend as the pines and ravines pressed in like a fortress, blocking much of the view. She pointed out the truck to the others in silence, their notice a mere nod or a flick of their chins.

Monty peeled off, as did her father. He nodded to her as he turned Draco and headed downward. Emory continued along, the snow deeper in the ravines and washes, with drifts reaching Kai's hocks and knees at times.

Each of the Crosses pressed forward on their assigned routes through the snow with only the occasional horse nicker for conversation, and even that caused a stab of concern.

Sounds carried and ricocheted in the quiet mountains, and that couldn't be helped. While snowmobiles would travel faster than horses in the snow-covered terrain, the whine of the motor would give away their locations in nothing flat.

Previously dead set against such modern and intrusive methods, the Crosses didn't own a snowmobile out of principle.

Maybe that principle needed to change with the times. Then again, maybe it didn't.

She and Kai headed straight for the mansion and the drive that led up to it. In a quarter of a mile, a full view of the pitch of a roof was blocked in part by a slope came into view, followed thereafter by the entire structure and its walls of glass as rider and horse neared. Large plate glass windows stretched from the ceiling down to the floor—specially tempered to withstand the wind.

A view that went two ways, both in and out.

The newest inhabitants probably never once considered that aspect of their fancy Colorado hideaway. They sat in a fishbowl for the entire world to see.

The house stood on a rise, and as such, required a long driveway to reach it. Plowed and sanded, the long driveway had a modern-day drawbridge barring or granting access—a gate shutting out the county road, fixed on perma-lock and controlled by a code and keypad.

Hugo again passed in front of the house, following the road and attracting no attention that she could see. He drove up a ways, turned, and came back down doing his damnedest to draw the inhabitants' attention.

The split rail fence along the road delineated their land, built more for show than anything else. The mansion boasted multiple wraparound decks and a four-car garage. Every vantage point provided a commanding view of the valley and the mountains beyond.

It stood completely exposed.

Raising the rifle scope up to her eye, she could make out furniture inside of the interior. Located five hundred yards away or so, she watched a person cross through a room, heading back further into the depths.

Hugo made yet another pass in front of the house. This time attracting enough attention that a man came outside to gauge the disturbance.

Heaven help them all, Hugo pulled up and got out of the truck.

The man came about halfway down the drive and pointed east along the road before indicating a left-hand turn.

Hugo got back into his truck and offered a wave as he drove off.

Damn Texas plates.

The man slipped as he returned up the driveway. Looking through the scope, Emory thought his footwear looked like running shoes, but she couldn't be certain.

And the gathering afternoon shadows deepened, with nothing much to see for the mansion's inhabitants to see.

25

AMBUSHES CAN GO IN EITHER DIRECTION

As planned, everyone made it back to the Lost Daughter.

Hugo waited in the kitchen. When he heard horse's hoofbeats, he came out to determine which rider had returned.

His smiled widened when he saw that those hoofbeats belonged to Emory and Kai.

She pulled up and laughed. "I watched you stop in front of that big fancy gate and ask for directions. That was pretty ballsy."

He laughed. "Texas plates and a lost tourist. What could be easier?"

"See or learn anything of note?"

"They don't seem to be a working outfit up at that huge palace. I guess that's for entertaining. If they're doing anything at all with ranching, I don't think it's coming from there."

"It seemed quiet from what I could tell at the distance."

Hugo eyed her. "Did you get a good look at the guy I

was talking to? His arm rested in a sling, so he might have been one of the folks you clipped the night Iver got shot out here. Beyond that, a service van waited behind the house, barely visible. Maybe they delivered catering or something—it felt like a party's in the making. You figure anything out?"

She dismounted and looped the reins over Kai's head. "I think we'd be smart to rent or borrow a snowmobile. Someone ought to trace over there at night, and the snow is pretty deep in places for a horse."

"If you can find one with a trailer, I can haul it."

She half shrugged. "Dad might know of someone—and speak of the devil, here he comes."

Lance Cross appeared in the distance, his black jacket and Draco's coat stood out black and solid against the snow background. Both she and Hugo watched Lance's slow canter in. He moved in perfect timing with his horse, an inherent rhythm that few people had. She'd forgotten just how admirable of a horseman her father remained.

"That sure looks nice," Hugo said. "Wish I could ride."

She eyed him and shook her head at the travesty. "We can teach you how, you know."

He smiled. "Maybe in the spring. Tomorrow I ought to get back to work, but I'm worried about leaving you lot out here. I can't help but wonder how this all's going to go."

Emory tilted her head. Not one of them had the answer for that question, but that old tingling sensation warned her that blood would be involved.

Lance rode up, Draco tossing his head, licking and chewing.

"He seems to have enjoyed himself," Emory said.

Her father patted and spoke to the horse. "Who is she talking about?"

"Either or both. I'm taking Kai in, want me to take Draco as well?"

He dismounted and handed her the reins. "I never turn down free help," he teased.

"Monty hasn't come back in yet. Did you see Hugo stop and ask for directions?"

Her father chuckled. "I did. Well?"

"The man wore a sling. He might be one of your intruders," Hugo offered for the second time. "I think food was being delivered in the back. The ranch operations aren't located there, I wouldn't think."

"That reminds me," Emory interrupted, turning the horses. "I need to try Terry again, after I get these guys untacked. I want to know where those bulls were delivered. If we can string holdings and purchases together, maybe that tells us something right there."

"See? I always said you was smart. Any party they'd have at that house would mean more planes coming in. Let me see if Richard feels like talking. Hell, maybe I'll even sympathize with him this time around."

"The snow was deep my way," Emory added. "I think someone should drive out there at night by snowmobile."

"You volunteering?"

"I am…if you find me a snowmobile."

"Call the sheriff," Lance instructed. "And try to be charming while you're asking, OK?"

That struck as plenty rich coming from him.

EMORY HEADED off to the hitching post outside of the barn, leading the two horses as Hugo came beside her.

"Can I help with this part?"

"Sure," she said with a smile. "You know, there is one whole school of thought that states if you can't handle a horse on the ground, you shouldn't be riding them. We can consider this some of your ground training. What do you think?"

He smiled and gave her a quick kiss as a reply.

"I take it that means yes," she said.

Hugo's eyes fixed beyond her. "Here comes Monty."

The eccentric cousin rode on in, displaying a fair seat as well. The tradition held that to a person, Crosses could ride. Her father watched him ride as well.

Monty dismounted in front of Lance and launched into a conversation that neither of them could hear.

Monty pointed off in the distance, nodded his head in violent agreement with something Lance said, then let loose with a brown stream of tobacco juice.

Emory drew her attention back to the horses, Hugo, and the task at hand. "We'll catch up with all that later. Let's get these boys done."

At the hitching post, Emory replaced Kai's halter and bit with a rope headstall, loosened the cinch to remove the saddle, with the plan of hanging up his saddle blanket to dry. She grabbed Kai's saddle with one hand.

"Here, let me," Hugo rushed around to her side.

"No need, I'm OK," she said. "You do Draco next, and I'll watch as you go along."

Holding the saddle through the tree opening, hanging the saddle up proved awkward due to its weight, but she still displayed practiced moves that came as second nature.

"This spot here is where Draco's saddle goes," she said to Hugo, patting it as she turned. "Pride of place, because he is the boss's horse. Isn't that right, boy?"

Em stood off to the side.

"Now, unbuckle the chin strap and ease the straps down from around his ears nice and gentle," she instructed. "Horses don't like their ears messed with as a rule."

Hugo did well, holding onto the reins while removing the headstall and bit with care.

"Now, uncinch the saddle and lift it and the blanket off him. They go where I showed you."

"Yes, ma'am," he grinned, and her heart expanded a few inches.

When he had finished stowing the saddle and blanket, she tossed him a brush. "Now start brushing him down, and keep away from his face, and watch out for your feet. Draco won't mean to hurt you, but he might by accident."

Emory picked out Kai's feet first, dislodging the clods of ice from the sole, frog, and shoe. First, she did the front feet, then the back feet. When she was done with Kai, she walked over to Draco and Hugo. "Want to give it a shot?"

Her father stuck his head into the barn. "When you two are done in here, come on into the house."

With that, he left.

"How about you can do this some other time?" Emory said, leaning into the side of the horse, lifting up first one front foot and then the other, then moving on to the back feet.

"What do you think he's going to say?"

"It's probably not 'how do you want your steak' this evening, but I guess that's still possible. Monty must have seen something we need to know about. Are you really leaving tomorrow?"

He hesitated. "Let's see what he has to say, but I'm

supposed to. Don't suppose you managed to call Terry yet."

"No. Let's see what Dad wants, then I'll call real quick. It's probably his dinnertime."

"He'll understand. He'll even be relieved to hear from you, I reckon."

With that, together they walked back to the house, and Emory surely could hear those warning bells clanging inside her mind.

———————

MONTY and her father were seated in the kitchen, cold and without food cooking. Each stared at an opened bottle of beer in front of him, but neither were drinking. A battered flask stood in the middle distance between the two beers.

"Problem? You two aren't drinking, and that can't be good."

She went over to the refrigerator and pulled out two more bottles and handed one to Hugo as he sat down at the table.

Then she turned around to lean against the counter, drinking her beer and eyeing the men seated underneath the old hanging kitchen light that was old enough to be coming back into fashion again.

No one said a damn thing.

Her father knuckled his beard stubble. "Got a call from the airstrip. A few planes have come in late this afternoon. The Blue River has been picking them up and driving off with them. Guess there's a party brewing, and we ain't invited. Fancy that."

"If we go the upper route and curve back around, you

can see into the backside of that monstrosity," Monty offered.

"What good does that do us?" Emory took a sip of her beer.

"I'm just saying it wouldn't be all that hard to pin them down. One armed person uphill can cover the back. The front can be handled by where you were, but that wouldn't be the most dangerous position, because likely they would shoot straight ahead. That's what people do when they panic. A downhill person could keep them contained. I'm just saying, if that is their center of operations, it's all doable."

"Legally speaking," Hugo began, trying to interject some measure of normalcy. "When whoever came on to the Lost Daughter, they committed a Class 5 felony. The problem is that you don't have proof who was trespassing. That's on top of the attempted murder. Any of us going onto their property will face the same charges if it is deemed a working ranch."

"You still have that receipt from New Jersey?" Emory asked, realizing that Hugo had a valid point, but it wasn't the type of point that slowed them down much.

"I do," her father replied.

The Cross blood flowing in their veins precluded any of them from speaking with complete candor in front of Hugo, no matter how much they liked him. He wasn't a Cross, and that distinction counted for everything at that precise moment.

Emory could read the thoughts in both her father's and Monty's eyes.

"Maybe we'd best turn it over. Sheriff Preston might be able to get it traced," she spoke careful in her phrasing.

Hugo appeared on the verge of asking—but sensibly thought better of it.

"I found it caught on some long grass in one of the old corrals." Emory's eyes challenged each one of them in turn.

"It could have blown in from anywhere," Monty frowned.

"Don't think so," Emory countered. "Besides, I already told Sheriff Preston that he was looking for people from New Jersey. This is a needed link to place them on the Lost Daughter."

"Money laundering is a federal crime," Hugo interjected. "Attempted murder for exposing the crime ups the stakes significantly."

"We're allowed to shoot on our own land," Lance Cross said. "If we want to inflict real damage, we would draw them over here. If we want to scare the hell out of them, we take the fight to the Blue River."

"I don't know about any of you, but I don't feel like going to jail for murder. Juries don't care much about the law of the West. They tend to concentrate on legalities," Emory chided. "Besides, I like my job. I'd be bound to lose it."

"We could take some lame-ass potshots at them to draw them over here, and then we could really let loose. That's what the AK-47 is for." Monty nodded acting like he'd come up with the best plan in the world.

Hugo, staring at the table in front of him a good portion of the time, rubbed his forehead and brushed back his hair, uneasy at the turn in direction the conversation veered.

"What we need is an FBI agent who is game," her father proclaimed.

"And what are the odds of that?" Emory spluttered.

"No idea," Lance admitted. "That's for you two to figure out. Now, who's hungry?"

———————

As her father pulled together a meal in the kitchen, Emory stepped out into the living room to call Terry Overholzer.

"Em?" He answered on the first ring.

"Hi, Terry. Yes, it's me. I figured I'd give you a call. Sorry if I caught you at dinner."

The senior brand inspector had food in his mouth but did his best to try to make sure that it didn't sound like it. "No problem, Em. Good to hear from you. How's everything going?"

"Hugo is up here, I guess you know."

A chuckle. "I do know that, as does Dave. It does his little ol' heart good. He thought you two might make a good pair."

"Dave," she laughed. "I'll bet he watches Hallmark movies when he gets the chance. Say, I think we've got a clearer understanding about what the trouble is up here —as far as we're going to. Do you know how we would get the FBI involved in a case if we needed to?"

"I'd say the first step is to report it—but local law doesn't like to see them coming ninety-nine times out of a hundred from what I can tell. And that's not firsthand knowledge, but from what I've gathered from those TV shows."

"They're money laundering, Terry. And they're intim-idating people who don't want to sell or play along. They're buying up whatever is coming on the market. Maybe they'll just buy up everything, and then will leave the area when the time rolls around for them to sell it again…"

"Do YOU believe that?"

"Not really. They brought in girls who bear a strong resemblance to the prostitute at the National Western. Some girl OD'd at a party they held a few weeks or so back. Nothing much happened as far as we can tell, other than the girl died and it got the town to talking."

"Well, that's just the thing, Em. When people like that move in, they bring their way of life along with them. If you're dealing with organized crime—and it sounds like you are—it needs to be rooted out. And I am NOT saying that you are the one that needs to do it. Call Bob Preston and talk to him."

"I was there earlier today."

"Alone?"

"No, with Hugo."

"Call him right now and talk to him, one on one. Chances are those elements are banking on the fact that Stampede is a small, out of the way place where nothing much ever happens."

"I found a receipt from New Jersey on the property dated three days before the shootout."

"Does Preston know that?"

"Not yet."

"Give it to him, Em. Then let the man do his job. Besides, I thought you two got along."

"We do. I have nothing but respect for Sheriff Preston. It's just that he doesn't always do things the way we go about them."

"Within the law?" Terry's voice might have teased, but he truly wasn't.

"Very funny." But yes, they both knew he spoke the truth. "I'll be back to work soon."

"Sounds great. It will be good to see you, Em. Dave will be glad to hear that you're OK."

As she hung up the phone, it hit her. The realization that the two brand inspectors honestly cared about her. Not about the ranch or her family's reputation. They cared about her, and whether or not she actually was fine.

That realization put a fair-sized lump in her throat.

But she was fine. She was always fine. Had to be, in fact. It was just another part of the Cross family code.

26

HORSES MAKE LARGER
TARGETS THAN SNOWMOBILES

"CALL PRESTON," HER FATHER SHOUTED FROM THE kitchen when she finished speaking with Terry.

She glared in the direction of the kitchen. "I was planning on it."

She stepped outside on the porch to make the call private, making the approximate location where Iver bled. The stain scrubbing must have happened while she worked the National Western—it stood to reason that Linda Paulson provided the motivation behind that cleanup.

She punched in the sheriff's number.

"Hi, it's Emory Cross. Say, a couple of things. First, I found a receipt from New Jersey by one of the old houses. Dated three days before the shooting."

She could feel the sheriff's attention shift and rise at the other end. "Next, do you or the department have a snowmobile that we could borrow for the night? Well, because the snow is kind of deep in places for a horse at night. I want to go see what the inhabitants of the Blue River spread are up to. Suppose you might have noticed that more private planes have been arriving today, haven't you?"

He had. He also agreed to deliver the snowmobile in exchange for the receipt.

"Sheriff? One other thing. I think, no matter how unpopular this idea may be, that you might want to consider getting the FBI involved. They're the ones who are supposed to deal with money laundering, correct?"

As feared, she almost lost the loan of the snowmobile over that one.

Nevertheless, in the end, he agreed to load up the machine and bring it out to the Lost Daughter in exchange for the receipt.

"Thanks, Sheriff," she said, hanging up and still wondering what their next step ought to be, beyond taking a picture and making a copy of the receipt. Just in case anything happened it was aways best to have a couple of fallback positions.

CALL FINISHED, Emory stepped back inside to three pairs of eyes trained on her.

"He's bringing out a snowmobile for us, and I'm giving him the original receipt. I'm taking a picture of the receipt. Hugo could you take a picture as well? Then we'll make a hard copy back in the office, providing the copying function on the printer works."

Her father, stirring a pot on the stove, grumbled. "It works."

"What's that?" she asked, coming over to his side to peer around his shoulder and into the pot.

"Chili," he growled. "Slow elk chili."

"Slow elk," Monty chanted, inhaling his spit wrong, and ending up in a choking, spluttering, coughing mess.

Hugo stared at him, bemused.

Emory didn't feel like rising to the bait, so she passed on back to the office and pushed the power button and waited for the machine to turn to life.

Retrieving the receipt placed in the desk safe for keeping—in the topmost drawer whose lock didn't work—she studied the address of the New Jersey restaurant and felt her tension rise. When the copier warmed up, she took a couple of copies, placing one in the file cabinet along with the livestock bills of sale.

Retracing her steps with the original receipt in her pocket, both she and Hugo snapped pictures of it with their phones.

Then each of them filed by the pot to ladle out a bowl of chili and settled into a silent meal.

Waiting for the sheriff to come.

THE SHERIFF ARRIVED JUST as everyone finished their meals. At the sound of his truck, Lance and Emory rose from their places at the table to greet him.

Her father flung open the door. "Would you like some chili? Hell, if we'd have known you were coming this soon, we would have waited for you."

Sheriff Preston shook his head. "Thanks for the offer, but I've got dinner waiting at home. Maybe you lot can help me unload the snowmobile. It's filled up and ready to go. It is the sheriff department's machine. I toyed with the idea of loaning you mine but figured it might be safer for all involved if you looked to be law enforcement."

Emory held out the New Jersey receipt. The sheriff

pulled out plastic gloves to handle the evidence, along with a sealable plastic bag to put it in.

"I've already touched it," Emory admitted. "At the time, I just thought it was trash."

He nodded. "Where did you say that you found it again?"

"By Idella's old house. It's the tallest one out there."

After placing the receipt in the back, he placed it in an inner jacket pocket. "Do I want to know what you're doing with the snowmobile?"

She eyed the sheriff. "Not sure how to answer that. Tell him, Dad."

"We all took a ride today to see what was happening at the Blue River," her father explained, providing the background. "They looked like they was setting up for a party or gathering. The plan's for Em to ride out tonight just to watch for a while, to see what they are up to."

Preston didn't appear to hold that idea in much favor. "Hell, Lance. They're gonna drink a lot, do drugs, and probably bring in some paid entertainment, if you get my drift. What more do you need?"

"Motive," Lance replied. "Why in the hell did they come out here shooting?"

"You know that as well as I do. Because of Iver. Now Emory, have you driven one of these before?"

"Yes," she said. "I'm not going to do anything wild like trying to jump it. Say, question for you about that Balzetti man. Does he have a record?"

"Sure does. But for that matter, so does Cade."

Yes, they all know that much, and her father spat. "Have you pieced anything together yet?"

"That's part of the reason why I'm out here. I asked Iver earlier today if he would press charges, and he said *no*."

Emory's heart clutched. "He said NO? But, why?"

"Shit," her father offered. "He was always chickenshit when push came to shove."

"That might not be all the way fair," Emory countered, although she didn't believe the protest she offered one hundred percent. At least, not in its entirety. "Everyone knew the Holsteads were scared. But Hugo and I were just out there. Something else must have happened."

"If it did," Sheriff Preston said, "he's not saying."

A nerve in Hugo's cheek throbbed. His eyes locked into Emory's, but as an outsider, he held his tongue.

The sheriff let that new information sink in. "If he ain't going to press charges—and it's looking might bleak on that front—I don't have much of a case."

"Money laundering for the FBI," Emory reminded him. "Call them in, and it will at least make things uncomfortable for the people buying up properties."

The sheriff stuck one of his hands into his back pocket, leaning into the notion. "None of the locals are coming forward on that count—not since they're making out like bandits when they sell off or sell out."

"For the time being," her father argued, eyes scanning the darkened ranch, assuring himself it still held firm. "Something tells me they'll pay in the end. Never let go of the land without one hell of a fight. Never."

"You could press charges for trespassing," Sheriff Preston suggested in a practiced, neutral tone.

Lance Cross's gray eyes snapped back onto the sheriff. "We don't know who they were."

"Well, now. We could draw 'em out." Monty's voice startled them, lounging against the door frame, they hadn't heard, or noticed, his approach.

Her father sniffed and put his hands in his back pockets. "Yeah. We could. Em?"

Emory felt the Cross family ghosts rise and heard that same creepy laughter as when she held the Lost Daughter's vented hide in her hands.

"Another gunfight?" Emory shrugged. "That's what it would amount to, isn't it?"

"Likely so." Her father's voice came out flat, but she could tell he warmed to the idea. As for Monty, well hell. This seemed what he lived for. As for Hugo...maybe it was for the best that he leave the Lost Daughter. He didn't need to get wrapped up any further in their fight.

The sheriff didn't flinch, just waited for their response—dead calm.

"Tonight? Is that what we're thinking?" Emory asked, jutting her chin at the snowmobile. "Before we go off half-cocked, how would this all work, legally?"

"It would certainly be best if they fired first," the sheriff replied.

"That's kind of, um, strange advice coming from the law." Emory glanced at Hugo who offered the slightest of nods that he agreed with her statement.

"Oh, I'll never admit to it," the sheriff claimed. "None of you have a recording device on, do you?"

"Shit," Monty replied, finding the question preposterous on behalf of all of them.

"No recording devices," Emory stated, just to be clear.

"I live here, too," Preston stated. "And I'm one of you, even if we don't always see eye to eye about how things are supposed to go, and how problems get handled. But in this instance, I'm saying likely your way will be more effective than the law. Now I'm no expert, but the land and ranches that are already sold, are now in essence gone even if the money was in the process of being laundered. I mean, those people SOLD, and I wouldn't think land titles would revert back to them, but maybe that's neither here nor there. The point is that a bad element has come in, the man who got shot won't press charges, and since his was the most serious case, he's setting an unfortunate precedent where the law is concerned. It's unlikely that any of the other ranchers will stand up to this group. Except for you lot."

"Hell, Monty there's got an arsenal," her father cracked.

"Not sure I wanted to hear that," Sheriff Preston countered, "but it proves my point."

Monty spat, delighted that his collection hadn't gone unnoticed. "I've got a gun for damned near any occasion—"

Lance cut him off. "I hear what you're saying—and what you're not. What's your part in all of this?"

"I'll arrest them, once you get them where you want them."

Lance Cross chewed on that. "That'll change how we go about things."

"I ain't never worked with the law before," Monty chortled. "Why—"

Emory cut him off. "I suppose I could drive the snowmobile up near their house and shoot out one of their lights or a window or something that would get their attention." Emory looked to her father.

Preston started back to the snowmobile trailer. "I'll leave the details up to you, and the less I know, the better. Call me when you want me out here, along with a few deputies."

"They'll see your cars," Emory pointed out.

He shrugged. "One of the deputies has got a twin cab. We'll bring the one vehicle out here, until more are needed after the arrests. Do you have anyplace we can park that is out of sight?"

"Maybe one of the hay shelters, and we can put a tarp over the truck." Her father wasn't overly concerned either way. "Well, you go get that dinner of yours, and we'll figure out what we are going to do. I guess we're doing it tonight."

"OK," the sheriff said. "I'm not sure I like using Emory as the lure."

"Em?" her father asked.

"It should be fine. Now, why don't you guys get that snowmobile off the trailer? No need to just stand out here jawin' when we've got planning to do."

THE CROSSES and Hugo sat down at the kitchen table after everyone helped themselves to a second bowl of chili. It never boded well to fight on an empty stomach, if it could be avoided. The clanking of silverware against the dishes grated against Emory's nerves. Everyone, she noted, looked straight down into their bowls as if the plan might come from the meat and beans.

"I've heard in Texas you don't put beans in your chili," Emory flung out across the table.

"That's right. We don't consider it chili then." Perplexed by her mundane questioning, Hugo's eyebrows lifted.

"What do you call this then," Monty asked.

"Good," Hugo replied.

Her father grunted. Another point scored.

The meal finished up in short order. Her father pushed his bowl away from him, further toward the center of the table and out of the way. "We all agree the plan is to draw the hired guns back here, correct?"

"Key-rect," Monty replied with a glint that bordered on glee.

Those ghostly warnings zinged up and down her spine, lodging at the base of her skull. Monty had claimed the role as the Cross family's modern-day gunslinger.

Hugo pulled his shirt collar away from his neck, his attention locking into Lance Cross.

Lance drew out a map with his finger on the table for the plan of attack.

"The way I see it, Em will drive the snowmobile out the back gate, and when the Blue River house comes in sight, I suggest that she shoot out a window, aiming high. Just shooting out a light is kind of chickenshit and might not even draw them into a response. Plus, it's a tiny target. Blow out a window to get their attention. And you're going to have to wait, to make sure it draws them."

"I might shoot out the lights after the window. That'll add to the confusion. Panic might drive them to react, instead of to plan their moves."

The elder Cross considered that option. "Maybe. Guess it don't much matter one way or another. Unless they've got a snowmobile handy, they'll probably come in by the road."

"How do we make certain that they'll know it's us?"

"I suppose we could cut down the entrance skull. You could drive it over on the snowmobile and stick in on that big, fancy gate of theirs. Kind of like an Old West calling card."

Hugo's eyes grew a shade wider.

"That ought to take the mystery out of it," Emory said

with a dark humor and turned to Hugo. "They're the ones that left us the present of the first skull. They stole two of our steers and returned one head. Or so we think."

"They thought it would scare us, so I hung it up for them," Lance crowed. "No fear here, but they may want to reconsider how they view us. Monty, what do you think?"

Calculations passed behind those crazy blue glasses. "A lot depends on which way they come. The cemetery's good if they come in through the back gate, the tall two-story house is good either way."

"The upper story isn't all that stable," Em cautioned, and received a disapproving scowl from her father who didn't approve of her traipsing around the unstable buildings.

"I went up there to see if that's where one of the shooters hid," she explained. "The stairs aren't that great, but if Monty watches his footing, he'll be fine. He can take a flashlight. That bedroom window has a fine view of the front porch and the ranch road. Another window overlooks the back gate."

She locked her eyes on the blue-glassed wonder. "Just try not to step through the floor if that's your position. Some of those planks are rotten."

Her father looked over at the Texan. "Hugo, it might be best if you make yourself scarce. It's not that you ain't welcome, but this ain't your fight."

"No," Hugo drawled, slower than usual. "But I can stay on to help."

"Guess that means you're planning on sticking around, is that it?"

"Dad!"

"Never mind," her father replied, holding up one hand. "It's none of my business."

"Too straight, it's not," Emory added. "What am I supposed to do once I shoot out a window or two, and maybe some lights? You know, all of that, and the skull, will be considered evidence against us."

"I suspect that Preston will prove highly ineffective in any investigation he might do. Besides. I want that skull back when everything is over. We'll just hang him right back up where he was, if we can."

"Where do you want me to position?" Hugo leaned forward, elbows on the table.

"Maybe in the cemetery, like Monty first thought. There's not much cover there, but I can't imagine that they'd go up that way for any reason. It's got a good view of everything but the house." Lance nodded, thinking aloud. "Or you can take the upper floor of the barn. Your choice. Think on it."

Emory shifted in her seat. "I want to take Idella's house. I also want to make sure that all of the horses are inside the barn before I head out."

"Monty's better suited for Idella's house," her father said.

"Yeah, but I was the last one in there, and know it better. Monty, if you are going to use that AK-47, where do you think you ought to be?"

"What, or how many, are we expecting they're going to send in?" Monty eyed around the table.

"There's a lot we don't know," Lance admitted. "We don't know if they have guards at that party, we don't know if they're all going to be drunk or drugged out, and while I'm assuming they'll drive on over, I could be flat wrong."

"Where are you going to be?" Monty asked him.

"I'm going to be down in the gully by the old wagon road. No need to let them get near headquarters, unless it can't be avoided."

"The snow might be deep in places," Emory cautioned.

"Sure might," her father replied. "That's why I'll go down there right now. Where are those damned snowshoes?"

"You never told me what I'm supposed to do after I shoot up the ranch."

"Why, you come back home," Lance said. "You get in the house and defend it, unless you're still insisting upon Idella's."

"I am," she said.

"I'm figuring to freelance it," Monty claimed. "I'll have to wait to see how the spirits move me."

"They'll move you, alright," her father replied.

Emory believed her father's words held more truth in them than even he likely believed.

The ghosts circled, chided, and warned. At least they always did, as far as the Lost Daughter spread was concerned.

Why does she want Idella's house?

27

NO SENSE ON PLAYING SHY OR TIMID—NOT WHERE GUNFIGHTS ARE CONCERNED

THE SPIRITS WERE CALLING, SURE ENOUGH. PENDING gunfire had a way of drawing them out.

Sheriff Preston would arrive as Emory drove out, or at least that was the plan as it currently stood.

Emory pulled on her snow boots and strapped on a rifle, ready to head out of the back gate. The half-moon hung in the sky, and considering her mission, she felt a shred of thanks that the moon didn't blaze bright and full.

The snowmobile's motor turned over. Her father waited, holding a garbage bag containing the skull in his right hand.

"Take your aim from the cover of the trees. No need to be standing out against the white of the snow. I've heard about them night vision goggles, and still don't know what they do, but it doesn't pay to take chances. Here's the skull."

She nodded and eyed him, lifting off the seat and placing the top of the bag where she would sit, and leaving the head to lay in the back behind her.

"First, I leave the calling card. Second, I go back into the pines, and start picking off targets. Third, I hightail it home and take up position in Idella's."

"I'd still feel better if you'd let Monty have that one."

"Nothing doing. I've got a strong feeling that I'll be safe in that house. Besides, Monty's itching to play Dirty Harry. I can just tell. Can't you?"

"Yeah, unless the spirits tell him otherwise, I guess. Here…" he handed her a radio. "Keep it handy in your vest pocket. Let me know when you make contact, and when you are headed back. I have no idea how long it takes to get to the mansion in a snowmobile. Assuming all goes as planned, in a truck, I reckon it will take them about twenty minutes to drive here—if they know where they were going. Which they won't, not right away. It will take them a few minutes to get their bearings and to start driving. Those few minutes might be important. Now, if you can't make it back to Idella's or the house, hunker down where you are, and don't draw them to you if you are out in the open. Monty and I can handle it from here. Don't give your position away without a clear shot. Got it?"

"Got it," she paused. "That's a pretty long speech for you. Say, Hugo served out in Afghanistan, but I don't know if they fight the same out there. He doesn't like his back to be toward that door."

"That makes good sense, I'll keep an eye on him, but there's precious little anyone can do when the fight is on."

"Those people may just stay home and call the sheriff."

"They might," her father shrugged. "Then we'll just have to come up with another plan, because this has to be resolved one way or another. Go give 'em hell."

With a nod, Emory drove off, raising her hand in Hugo's direction, who stood at the kitchen window, looking out at her.

THE WHINE of the snowmobile's motor bothered her, being far more used to the quiet plodding of a horse. Half of her wondered whether or not it would have been advisable to simply drive the truck on the road, but that would have presented the additional hazards of road traffic. At least this way she was out on her own and didn't have to worry about any stray and oncoming traffic.

Besides, she didn't think she'd be able to shoot and drive worth a damn.

She glided over the snow, down the cow path and headed straight back to the Blue River house, built to lord over the land below. It stood about halfway up a mountain slope, one of those fancy log mansions that were built to last, and cost plenty of money while they were building it.

It was the western ideal of a fabulous log cabin on steroids.

It took her about twenty minutes to reach the outer perimeter where the windows radiated light out of the house and onto the decks—acting as a beacon in the darkness.

"It see it," she said into her radio, voice low although there was no one likely to hear even if her voice carried.

Her father's reply came through. "Fine. That took you nineteen minutes, from what I can tell."

"I'm going in to drop off the skull."

"Radio me back when you've done that and have taken up position."

"OK. Over."

"Over," her father replied.

Emory headed nearer to those blazing windows, the outlines of people clear and unguarded. Hugo read it right, a party unfolded, full tilt. Aware of the need for caution—she skirted the perimeter first, cautious and careful not to meet an arriving guest.

Still closer she moved in, watching for approaching headlights on the road. But the road under the Rimrock County sky filled out dark and unlit. No cars or trucks approached. And she moved in closer still.

In an abundance of caution, she never changed gears. The snowmobile's whine remained the same at her slow approach.

She stopped within ten feet of the gate and dismounted, removed the skull from the confines of the garbage bag and stuck the spinal cavity atop one of the ornamental fence spikes.

Well, that fence spike wasn't ornamental any longer. A very real purpose was bestowed upon it. A purpose that suited the Lost Daughter Ranch very well.

The skull looked the part of a talisman or totem, a grinning cadaver upright on the spike, rough and rotten.

Emory took a second to admire her handiwork before returning to take up her shooting position.

She glanced over her shoulder at her handiwork and to the bright lights above wondering just how long it would take them to discover *their* intruder.

Guests traipsed out onto one of the balconies in time, laughter and indistinct conversation flowing.

Emory pressed down on the accelerator harder.

RETURNING TO HER POSITION, she watched and waited. Through her scope she saw balcony-stationed interlopers pointing at the apparition—three men skittering down the snowplowed drive and aiming for the skull. They had no idea what waited for them on the fence.

Too damned bad.

Spying them through her riflescope, she had them in her crosshairs.

Intending to scare the hell out of them, she took aim at one of the upper windows where the light shone through knowing that the glass would spray.

"Left the skull, people coming out to look, am shooting now. Over."

"Over," her father's voice returned.

Emory took aim, exhaled, and squeezed the trigger slowly, slowly. With accurate aim, she shot out the window.

The guests' screams and shouting carried, reaching her.

The men on the driveway crouched down before jerking around, trying to understand the cause of the shattering explosion. Next, she took aim at one of the lamps near them. A pair of lanterns stood—one on each side of the fancy gate.

Again, she pulled.

The bullet twanged off the metal in an Old West cinema sound. *Damn.*

She aimed again, and the light exploded. The second of the pair in her sights, she pulled the trigger and out it shattered.

Satisfied, she slung the rifle over her shoulder and headed back for the Lost Daughter. In her original plan, she had intended on shooting out one of the porchlights, but she'd already gotten everyone going enough.

Retracing her approximate path, and following the tracks where she could, Emory hunched over the handlebars just in case someone behind her had sniper skills.

She doubted that possibility, but one never knew.

And she let the motor go full throttle and whooped good and loud, hoping they caught the song of the snowmobile and the sound of their stolen empire's collapse. She broke loose with one ear-splitting whistle—the kind they used to communicate over long distances on the range.

Let those strangers come a-calling.

They'd be waiting.

EMORY TORE back through the back gate and into the Lost Daughter.

She left the back gate hanging open in an invitation, should they draw from that direction. Failing any certain idea where the Cross men were positioned, she pulled up near an old shed, far enough away from Idella's house to draw the intruders off track if they approached up through the back gate. All the while recognizing that her tracks to her firing position could—and would—give plenty away. If they were smart, they would read the tracks and figure out her position.

If they weren't smart, it wasn't her problem.

"I stashed the snowmobile behind an old snow fence. Over."

Her father's voice came through. "Take your location now. Don't dawdle."

Like she needed to be told.

"Moving. Over."

As she pulled out a flashlight inside of the old house, the hair on her arms rose. The cards felt stacked against them—she could feel the ghosts and their warning.

"Here they come, down the ranch road," her father's voice urged.

She ran up the stairs, not as carefully as she ought. Seventh step up, her foot broke through the rotten wood step.

She pulled up with all her might, but she couldn't get her foot free. A sharp gouging pain stuck into her leg. Adrenaline coursing, she set her rifle down, braced both hands onto the landing, and pressed up, ignoring the wood gouging into her leg.

"Shit," she cursed.

"I'm stuck," she said into the radio. "My foot went through a step."

"Dammit, Em—"

A shot rang out. Answering fire ensued.

"They're coming up the back, too," Emory said into the radio, still fighting to free her leg.

"I'm coming," Hugo said.

"Don't!" Emory whisper-screamed into the radio. "I can get it. Stay where you are! Dad?"

More gunfire.

Emory took her rifle butt and smashed the step imprisoning her leg. Blood flowed, but she didn't care.

No one came through that front door.

"Hugo?"

Another crack of bullets flying, this time whizzing off the outbuildings.

Emory crawled up the remaining stairs and over to one of the windows.

The staccato of the AK-47 let loose from the barn's hay door. Horses screamed from within, but there was no help for that now.

"Dad," she called through clenched teeth.

He didn't answer.

Where was Hugo?

A snowmobile pulled up beside Idella's house at an awkward angle for a shot.

Her jeans were bloody wet, running down her calf and pooling in her boot. Her injured leg wouldn't bend.

She dragged that leg as she approached the upper window, standing off to the side of the frame, viewing another snowmobile traveling up from the back gate. She watched the man dismount. Exhaling to slow down, she took aim and fired.

He crumpled down, but still held on to his handgun. He fired in her direction—a blind shot.

She took aim and shot him again—this time in the shoulder. That should end his firing...but there were no guarantees.

Emory drug herself over to the other window, leaving a trail of blood on the rough floorboards.

Out in the middle of the ranch yard, light still intact and shining, a body lay on the frozen ground, unmoving.

Hugo.

Sirens approached as the deputies hauled down the ranch road.

Hugo remained still.

Invisible and coming from behind her, Emory could have sworn she heard a woman cry. She took those sounds as the ghost of Idella.

"Save him," she whispered into the dark, empty house. Tears pricking and panic building.

But ghosts couldn't save the living.

Sheriff Preston emerged from one of the buildings, gun drawn and two other deputies crouching behind.

Her radio came back on. "Em?"

"Dad, Hugo's been shot. He's in the yard."

"I see that. Preston will see to him. I'm coming to get you now. The ambulance is on its way."

"See to Hugo. I can wait. Where's Monty?"

"Still at his location in the barn." She could tell from her father's voice that he moved out of the house.

"Shit," came Monty's voice. "Don't you worry about me none, girl. All I've got is a flesh wound. Now let's see to that Texan. He's down, alright."

"See to him first, guys. Promise me." Her words were a demand.

Emory thought she saw Hugo move, but maybe it was just her mind playing tricks on her.

"Stay where you are, Em."

But of course, she didn't.

28

SOMEONE WILL ALWAYS WANT
WHAT YOU HAVE

EMORY LIMPED OVER TO THE TOP OF THE STAIRS, THE DARK cover of night broken by the blue and red strobing of the sheriff's lights. She sat down on the top step and stuck her bloody leg in front of her. She lowered herself down one step at a time, sitting on each board as she descended.

Just as she approached the broken step, her father ran into the old house.

"Did you see Hugo?" Emory gasped.

Judging by what she could see of his expression and the way he held himself, the news wasn't good.

"Hang on there. Let me help you," was all that he said.

"Hugo?" she demanded.

"I won't lie to you, Em."

"He's dead, isn't he?" Her heart stuck to her stomach.

"The ambulance crew are working on him now."

"You have to get me to him," Emory said, putting her arm around her father's neck.

"We're going," he half lifted her as she hopped down the steps, bracing himself along the wall and the stair.

"Rotten wood. I *knew it*. Maybe we should just pull the whole damn thing down and to hell with it."

At that moment, she didn't care one whit.

Her father half carried, half dragged her out into the ranch yard. The ambulance people kneeled by Hugo's side but leaned back on their heels, defeated. They watched the Crosses' approach; hangdog looks until they saw her leg and the piece of wood stuck in her calf.

"Hugo!" she shouted, but the body did not move.

She broke away from her father and collapsed onto the ground. Emory clawed at the ground and pulled herself toward him.

He laid unmoving and lifeless. A single bullet hole gaped in his chest.

"Hugo," she whispered, and laid across his chest.

Her father came up behind her leaving her for a moment.

"Em," he cautioned. "We need to get you seen to."

He allowed her another moment, crouched down alongside her and Hugo's body.

"He shouldn't have died!" she shouted, full force. She repeated herself in a harsh whisper. "He shouldn't have died. It was never his fight."

"He made it his, Em." Lance Cross gently pulled Emory away from the lifeless body and kissed the side of her forehead—expression closed down except for the concern in his eyes and written across his face.

"Emory," Sheriff Preston came up to them, bothered but trying not to show it. "You need to let the EMTs look at that leg."

Emory turned on him, harsh and feral. "Did you get those bastards? Did any of THEM get killed?"

"Three arrested, one dead. A local. Blaze Redshirt."

"Who are the rest of them?" Her father's voice held firm and decisive.

"Don't know yet. I half expected to see Cade Timmons's hide, but he wasn't a part of this. I'd say the rest are hired guns from elsewhere. The FBI is coming in to help."

"Fair enough, given the circumstances. Here comes Monty," her father remarked. "He's looks worse for the wear, too."

Monty came up holding his side, single spur still jangling. Blood stained his shirt red. "Shit," he said standing at Hugo's side. "I liked that Texan."

All the men eyed Emory with concern. If she even noticed, she didn't care. "This wasn't his fight. He was coming to help me."

Monty dragged his one-spurred self over to her and squeezed her shoulder. An EMT came up to him, but Monty held the man off for the moment. "It's not your fault," he comforted, "but that probably don't help none."

One of the EMTs pulled up a stretcher over to her and helped her to sit. He scissored the leg of her jeans, cutting the denim and peeling it away. He frowned at the large wood fragment sticking in her leg like a fractured weapon. "When's the last time you had a tetanus shot?"

She shook her head, uncaring and absent.

The other medic lifted Monty's shirt to check his side wound. "We'll be taking both of them in. Both will need stitches and tetanus shots for starters." The medic looked to Lance. "Sir, are *you* alright?"

Her father nodded, decisive. "Fine. You two keep each other company in the ambulance," Lance Cross said to Em and Monty. "I'll follow behind you in the truck."

"Check on Kai, Outhouse, Drago, and the other horses first, will you?" Emory asked.

"Sure thing," he nodded. His blue eyes under his hat brim traveled over to the Texan's body.

NEITHER EMORY nor Monty had to spend the night in the hospital. As the EMTs predicted, both received tetanus shots and stitches after their wounds received attention and a thorough cleaning. Lance Cross waited in the reception room. Emory hobbled out on crutches.

"Where's Hugo's body?" Emory asked.

"Not sure, sweetheart. I'll call the sheriff and we'll figure all of that out once I get you both home and settled."

Monty limped out on his own accord about ten minutes later. Lance pulled the truck around, and Monty took the center seat so Emory could sit with her leg stretched out

The rest of the ride home passed in silence as they took the left-hand turn onto the ranch road and rumbled under the barren crossbeams.

"I'd kind of think you'd want that skull back," Monty half sang.

"It's already back home and stashed and on the porch," Lance replied. "But yeah, it sure looks naked now. I'll get it hung back up once I get you two settled."

Emory's eyes welled up and the notion that maybe she had placed more trust in those damn rotting skulls than she had ever let on. She'd never forget that shy grin Hugo gave when he removed the tarp on the skull he brought for the back gate—and how he'd won over the Cross men at the precise moment.

Both her father and Monty caught the turmoil behind the tears and fell silent. Her father focused his eyes straight ahead on the road with a singular determination, rubbing his knuckles across his beard stubbled chin to feel something other than his daughter's pain.

Emory squeezed her eyes shut but didn't let the matter slip away all together. "You'd think that skull we returned to them would be evidence," she muttered at length.

"You would," her father agreed. "But who's to say?"

"The easterners," she countered.

"Yeah," he said disgusted. "And then they can go ahead and explain a whole lot more besides."

He had a point.

WHEN THE TRUCK pulled up in front of the ranch house, her father came to a stop. "Monty, you're staying in the guest room for the night. I don't want you in the bunkhouse and having a problem and me not knowing about it."

"I ain't going to have no damn problem," Monty muttered.

"My ranch, my rules," Lance said, silencing any further debate.

Everyone settled around the kitchen table as was their custom. Lance pulled out his cell, scrolled through his contacts, and clicked.

"This is Lance Cross," he said, disposing of the preliminaries. "We'd like to know where Hugo Werner's body has been taken."

Her father listened, moving over to a pen and a piece of paper. "You explained it to them, did you?"

Her father tucked the phone against his ear as he looked over at his daughter with a nod. He met her eyes.

"Yeah. Give me that number. We'll call him, but it won't be easy."

Her father hung up. "Hugo's body is in the morgue at the hospital. Preston wants us to call his father to decide the next steps. Mr. Werner will want an explanation. Guess the mother is dead."

Her father seldom gave respect by using labels such as *mister*.

The three Crosses exchanged tired glances.

"I had no claim on him," Emory said, heart wrenching, "but we should offer to bury Hugo here on the ranch. He died defending us, this ranch, and our way of life. Any objections?"

"None at all," her father replied. "We can offer."

"No objections over here," Monty echoed.

A Lost Daughter burial conveyed the highest sign of regard the Cross family could bestow upon the fallen Texan.

The Crosses all locked eyes across the expanse of that damned kitchen table.

"Em, you'd best make the call. And be prepared that his father will likely refuse our offer. Hell, I'd refuse if someone wanted to bury you someplace else."

Emory crutched her way outside to be alone, to gather strength and solace from the cold mountains beyond. She gazed at the rimrocks and the mountains in the distance, darker blue against the deep blue of the night sky. Her grief made her selfish, or so it felt. She had no valid right to delay—not when Hugo's father's world lay shattered.

She returned into the house, took a drink from the open bottle of whiskey on the counter without benefit of a glass. *For courage*, she told herself.

She claimed her seat at the kitchen table, setting her

crutches to the side. Her father seated at her left hand, ready to step in if needed. Monty sat in his seat, waiting and watching.

Her father's scrawled handwriting screamed the phone number on the torn piece of cast-off paper resting on the battered oilskin tablecloth.

She picked up the phone and punched the number into her cell.

It rang. One ring, two, then three…

A man's voice answered.

"Mr. Werner?" her voice cracked. "You don't know me, but my name is Emory Cross—"

Hugo's body returned to the Lost Daughter in a plain pine box as the family favored. His father would come out in the spring to visit his son's final resting place, but for now, it was the Cross family who would stand in for him. They took that obligation seriously, believing in their hearts that deep down, he belonged with them.

Emory called the brand inspectors from Hugo's district along with Terry and Dave. The funeral was set two days after his death. It took those days to make arrangements. Hugo would claim the winter plot—a grave dug a long time back that always waited at the ready for a winter death.

They had one now.

Emory called the brand inspectors, Sheriff Preston, the Holsteads, and Linda Paulson.

"Do you want me to let Linda know?" her father asked.

"No, it's best coming from me," Emory replied. "She's probably already heard the news anyhow."

Her father nodded.

THE SNOW FELL with a gentle grace on that February day, the sky a leaden gray and the mood somber. Emory wore the same black dress she had worn on their first dinner together. She put it on first thing in the morning and waited upon a gray winter sky that had no hints of blue or clearing.

A gray sky felt fitting on that day, as the snow fell from the low-hanging clouds that shrouded the higher mountains and shut them all down on the Lost Daughter, as if to keep them there forever.

The old clock kept time on the wall, ticking as the minutes and hours drained away. Tick, tick, tick,

At nine thirty that silent, unspeaking morning groaned into life.

Cars and trucks threaded their way down the rutted ranch road. Terry and Dave, tasked with retrieving Hugo in his coffin at Stampede's morgue, arrived first.

Both alighted from the truck, hands outstretched to her father and Monty, both of whom had cobbled together some semblance of a suit for the sad occasion.

Emory, upon seeing them, came out of the house and did her best to remain strong, but she faltered, encountering the concern and deep, heartfelt sadness in both brand inspectors' eyes.

Dave had tears brimming in his eyes, and she gave them each a quick hug although no words came.

Linda Paulson drove her Jeep to the ranch yard and parked it. She pulled out crockpots of food and other items. She looked over at Emory and shook her head in sympathy.

Emory held up a hand in a tentative wave, which she dropped down by her side, defeated.

When the minister arrived from town, Terry and Dave climbed back into their truck, leading the procession up the old wagon track to deliver Hugo Werner to his grave.

The mourners followed Emory and Lance Cross, at the head of the procession. Emory looked around for Linda and indicated that she should be in the first row following them.

Looking the most concerned for her, woman to woman, Emory's gesture seemed to mean the world to the historic preservationist as she fell into place.

And her father nodded his thanks.

Together, followed by the others that morning when the sun didn't shine down upon the ranch, they all stood beside the grave. Watching as the coffin lowered down into that dark, gaping hole that waited for the man far too soon for his years.

Emory dropped the first handful of dirt upon Hugo's coffin lid. "I wish you had stayed away," she said, stricken.

As she turned from the grave, she passed near Linda Paulson, who opened her arms and Emory clung to her for a long minute. Before, in silence, she broke away.

When everyone but Linda dispersed, they all sat at the kitchen table. Linda kept offering food that none of them felt like eating, worry etched around her eyes as she did her best not to hover. As the evening shadows descended, Emory shuddered.

"I just can't seem to get warm," she murmured, "but the time has come."

She hobbled upstairs to change her clothes into jeans

and a winter coat. Anxious with the fact that Hugo's grave stood unmarked for the time being.

"The brand will be on his tombstone like everyone else, right?" she asked upon returning to the kitchen.

"It will," her father replied. "Want me to come with you?"

"No," she replied. "I'll go by myself."

She loaded some split logs, fire starters, and matches into a carrier, and limped her way out into the barn to retrieve an old Lost Daughter branding iron.

She carried her supplies on foot, crutches abandoned for the trip.

She struggled up the wagon tracks to reach the Lost Daughter graveyard. Once up at the comparatively level ground, she stared at her ancestors' markers.

"He wasn't a hired hand," she told them, "but he died for the Lost Daughter. His name is Hugo Werner. I feel he's earned the right to be here."

The breeze picked up, murmuring their assent.

She built a fire and heated the iron. One by one she seared the brands into the wooden boards.

When the ashes had cooled enough, she retraced the brands with the cooled ash, filling in the marble and granite Lost Daughter brand that they all carried in a type of rechristening that only they understood.

She waited to hear if the ghosts started speaking objections of the stranger lying around them, but they never did.

After about the hour it took to attend to traditions, she limped back down the sloping road, falling in the snow on the way down but picking herself back up. She couldn't have cared less if the stitches tore.

She knew that eyes were upon her, strained and watching from the kitchen window.

She entered the house without speaking—with nothing left to say.

Crutching through the kitchen and not meeting their eyes, she labored up the narrow stairs. Stopping at the dark window that overlooked the hillock where the cemetery was located, it didn't matter that the graves couldn't be seen from the house at all. It was the closest window to them.

Emory leaned against the casement, closed her eyes, and listened. Of course, the ghosts were restless.

A disembodied female voice threaded through her mind.

"There will be more to come," the voice whispered, and she believed the warning to be true.

A LOOK AT: ON THE FRINGES

**From Award Winning author Randi Samuelson-Brown, a
gritty tale about one woman's stark determination to create
her own destiny.**

Maude Montgomery, gifted with the second-sight, is trapped in
a bad marriage to a confidence man who doesn't inspire too
much confidence in her. Yearning for a better existence, she
gets more than she bargained for when her husband abandons
her in a remote outpost of Nebraska.

Alone for the first time in her life, Maude has a decision to
make—return back East to nothingness and mediocrity, or head
deeper into the West to find her fortune. She chooses to take
her chances in the west, and lands in Cripple Creek where she
learns gold is *not* scattered about in the streets.

Armed with little more than an untested belief she can sense
gold ore deposits, Maude becomes tangled up in the gold
camp's underworld and is instrumental in the makings of a
mining swindle. Uncertain where to turn, or who to trust, she's
about to learn first-hand that all that glitters might not be gold,
and freedom demands a hefty price.

AVAILABLE DECEMBER 2022

ABOUT THE AUTHOR

Randi Samuelson-Brown was born in Denver, Colorado, and grew up in Golden. She writes historical fiction and has always enjoyed uncovering strange and obscure historical facts and details. Randi's undergraduate degree is in history, and she continued on to postgraduate research at Trinity College, University of Dublin. Frontier fiction and the shadier aspects of the Wild West has always held a place close to her heart. *The Beaten Territory* was her debut novel (rereleased as *Market Street Madam* in paperback) and *The Bad Old Days of Colorado: Untold Stories of the Wild West* was her first nonfiction novel and was a finalist in the 2021 Colorado Book Awards - History. The first book in her Dark Range series, *Brand Chaser*, was released in June 2022. The forthcoming third book in the series will be *Branded Vengeance*.